FAIR HARVARD:

A STORY OF

AMERICAN COLLEGE LIFE.

"Quorum cognitio studiosis juvenibus si non magnam utilitatem afferet at certe, quod magis petimus, bonam voluntatem."

NEW YORK:
G. P. PUTNAM & SON.
LONDON: S. LOW, SON & MARSTON.
1869.

PREFACE.

THIS story, the product of hours wrested from severe professional labors, the author offers to the Public without diffidence.

The opinion of those friends whose criticism he most values, he has already taken.

"I should advise you," said one, "to commit what you have written," (the labor of some months,) "to the flames, or to the North River,"—'*sive flamma sive mari libet Hadriano*'—"and to throw off something more worthy of your powers."

"I should recommend you," added the other, "to append a tabular view of the college studies to your story, so as to give the book, at least, a certain value."

Thus urged, the author feels it to be a crime to keep his work longer from the Public.

CONTENTS.

FAIR HARVARD.

CHAPTER I.

" Ne pueri, ne tanta animis assuescite bella."

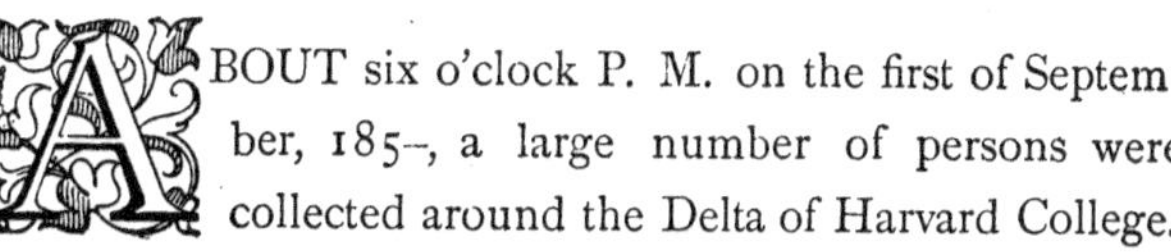

ABOUT six o'clock P. M. on the first of September, 185–, a large number of persons were collected around the Delta of Harvard College. The walks edging the green were thronged with men, and the streets blocked with carriages from Boston and the neighboring country.

These bore a fair freight of laughing girls, accompanied by a chaperon or an obliging father. Near the central point of the south side of the Delta a barouche was stationed, in which were seated two young ladies, surrounded by a group of gentlemen.

"Arn't those Sophomores ever coming, Mr. Morris? They are making us wait a long time," said one of the ladies to a gentleman, whose air of sedate superiority proclaimed him a Senior of the college.

"There they are, Miss Campbell. You can just see them coming down the middle walk of the college yard," replied Mr. Morris, carefully adjusting a scholarly eyeglass. As he spoke, a long line of young men became visible through the trees, rapidly winding towards the Green. Their raiment was limited to a shirt, trousers, and an inebriated stove-pipe hat, on which the name of their class, 185–, was cut in letters of appalling magnitude. They were marching two and two, and kept harmonious time to the chorus of "Left, left, left her far behind me," a strain heard not infrequently by the startled burghers of breezy Boston, and echoed yearly by the hills of Lake Quinsigamond.

"Isn't this splendid, Nell?" asked a handsome girl with a classical face who was seated beside Miss Campbell, and watching everything with great interest. And indeed the scene was not without beauty. On the right of the carriage, beyond the Green, rose the square, substantial houses of the gentry of Cambridge, half hidden among vines and shrubbery, and shaded with venerable trees. Towards the left could be seen the brick walls of Holworthy, one of the college dormitories, an angle of Hollis, or Massachusetts, with glimpses of the Library and old University Building. The sun was just setting, and the thick trees beyond the Green were sifting its golden sands. The men crowding the walks were all in high spirits, many of them chatting with the ladies in the carriages, and the rest debating with each other with eager gesture.

Among them, the Seniors and Juniors of the college were

easily distinguished, as they sauntered magnificent, ambrosial, some whom love of glory inspired, others gathered to witness the ensuing foot-ball game as a spectacle, and criticise the men of the year who were now to win their spurs.

"That fence is one of the goals," remarked Mr. Morris, pointing to the wooden bars which divide from Quincy Street the base of the triangle. "The other is that path which runs across the Delta near its apex,—where the Freshmen are standing. Which side do you favor, Miss Leigh?" he added, addressing the girl seated by Miss Campbell.

"How young the Freshmen are!" answered the girl, looking with a feeling of pity at the body of young fellows huddled confusedly together, who had begun to pull off their coats and waistcoats and to gird up their loins, "I do hope they will beat."

"Three cheers for the class of '5–!" shouts a sturdy Sophomore, the leader of that long column, which, filing past Holworthy, across Cambridge Street, through the gate of the Delta, has passed towards its eastern fence, and doubling and closing stands in crowded phalanx.

Three cheers and a tiger are given by the Sophs, who toss their hats high in air, while their ranks, impetuous, yet disciplined, sway, and distend, and gather.

"Three cheers for the class of '5–!" cries a fine looking fellow on the opposite side, and three rousing cheers burst from the Freshman lines, which effort of vocal power is chastened with clapping of hands and ironical laughter by the Sophs.

"Who is that Freshman?" asked Miss Campbell of Mr. Morris. The latter, albeit somwhat annoyed by such ill-directed curiosity, turned his eye-glass with difficult courtesy towards the body of children.

"I really can't tell you, Miss Campbell," he answered, "I'm not in the way of meeting these young fellows, and yet, now I look at him, I fancy I've seen him somewhere; why it must be young Saulsbury; I know his uncle very well. That Sophomore, the other champion, is Seaborn, a *Harvard* man, and I'm told a very good fighter. That big fellow near him is Ned Bilger; he is a rowing man too; and there's a man whom I think you know, Brandreth; he is every way their best man," and Mr. Morris pointed out on the edge of the Sophomore wave a youth of middle height, dark face, and agile as a cat.

"Have you ever been at one of these games before," he continued, turning to Miss Leigh.

"Look, they have begun," cries the girl in her excitement, not hearing Mr. Morris. The Sophomores have won the pitch, the kick-off is theirs;—a fierce yell: "Are you ready?"—"Yes," is shouted back, and the next moment Seaborn has struck the ball. It rises with a long graceful curve, and spans much of the vacant interval. Before the two armies join, we will pause a moment to compare their numbers and chances of success. About eighty men are ranged on each side. The larger portion of each body is chiefly useful in giving weight, but conspicuous in either van are a score or more of vigorous young fellows, emulous of fame, on whom the brunt of battle is to fall. The Sophomores have the advantage of being a year older than the Freshmen, and their martial uniform makes the match appear even more unequal. This causes the sympathies of most of the spectators to side somewhat unfairly with the latter, who, though less boisterous, are no contemptible opponents. The line of battle of the Sophomores is more extended than the Freshmen's; and their fighting men, confident of success, are scattered along the front. Their younger rivals are more compact, and in their centre stand five or six of their best men, a nucleus around which the rest cluster. Conspicuous in this group is Saulsbury, the boy whose name Miss Campbell had asked; a fine looking fellow, whose light hair, blue eyes, and clear skin prove him a New Englander, while his unconscious grace shows him an adept in athletic sports.

"Remember, Van Courtland and Rakeman; we must keep together," says Saulsbury, as the ball curves towards them, turning to two boys near him, the one a handsome fellow with regular features and a sharp New York accent, the other a boy whose dark eyes and quick words and gestures could belong only to a Southerner.

"Bravo, Bowyer!" shout the Freshmen, as a vigorous kick from a burly fellow with a thick neck and huge chest drives the ball nearly back to the Sophomore lines. At the blow the whole Freshman body, with loud huzzas shouting the name of their class, rush forward to meet the Sophomores, who are fiercely bearing down upon them, yelling wildly and brandishing a hundred fists in air. Swiftly each army spurs itself on. The ball rises but twice more. The two bodies crush madly together over it, and men are bowled over, trampled on, scramble up, thrust, push, kick, strike, fall and rise again with aching joints, battered noses, and darkened eyes. All along the lines burst shrieks of rage or shouts of triumph, which mingle with the voices of the spectators, as with cries of "Go in Freshmen," "Sophs," "185–" "bravo," and clapping of hands, they urge on the game.

A few moments more and nothing can be seen in the centre but a surging, swaying mass—though to the right and left, the skirts of the fight present frequent private encounters, where more skill is shown, exchanges are made, and men knocked down with method. Soon gaps are seen in the Freshman lines, as the Sophomore fighting men press through the yielding wings. In the centre of the fight, however, where the ball rests, the Freshmen still hold their own. Here Saulsbury, Bowyer, Van Courtland, and Rakeman are gathered with the best men of the class, striking fiercely, and taking blows sullenly, watching their opportunity. Suddenly Bowyer seizes the ball in his arms, and lowering his head like a battering ram breaks through the weak Sophomore centre, and makes towards the goal. With a loud shout Saulsbury and his friends press through the breach. Bowyer gains but a few yards when Seaborn grasps him by the shoulder. Bowyer hurls the ball towards the goal and grapples fiercely with his enemy. The Sophomore trips him upon the grass, and with his few supporters delays the Freshmen until the Sophomore wings can close around them. The plucky young fellows are then driven slowly back to their main body with many rewards of merit. The ball is again kicked between the two lines and the men fight fiercely around it. The Sophs now use more skill, and mass themselves against the sturdy knot of men in the Freshman centre. The battle hangs in even scale a few seconds. Then the Sophs force their way forward by sheer weight, and inch by inch drive the ball towards the goal.

"Well done, Saulsbury!" murmurs Morris, and "bravo!" shout the spectators, as suddenly, when the game seems lost, the ball rises once more, curling back to the centre of the field. Saulsbury has snatched up the ball at the very goal, and dodging a fierce blow from Bilger, gained a ringing kick over the heads of both sides.

The ball has fallen not far from the fence where Miss Campbell's carriage is standing, and down upon it sweeps the rushing, struggling mass.

"Isn't this horrible!" exclaims Miss Leigh, her face growing very pale and her heart beating quick, as she watches with greater earnestness every movement of the game. Saulsbury leads the van of Freshmen. His arms and face are stained with blood. His right cheek discovers a deep cut from which a slender stream is trickling. The boy's eyes are on fire with excitement. He has ceased to feel the blows that rattle round his face and chest. Through his veins pours the fierce delight which hope of victory lends to souls avaricious of honor. The swiftest runners on both sides arrive first at the ball, and engage each other, until in a few seconds both armies in full force are struggling, pushing, and striking as before. The men as they again crush together bear numerous marks of their former encounters. Their hats have been exchanged or have forever vanished. Their shirts are torn and checkered with blood and dirt. Their noses, mouths, and eyes are swollen and painted red or black with the grim pencil of war. Their shouts and noise have ceased, and all fight with a sullen rage and fierceness they did not at first display.

The battle redoubles along the lines. The Freshmen are now driven back a few yards, now with desperate rallies force back their enemies. The blows echo heavily from heads and bodies, and a low fierce growl creeps from the seething mass. In the front Saulsbury and his friends are fighting in unison, hoping again for a favorable chance. But Janus occasion presents first his Roman nose, and afterwards his *nez retroussé*, which is hard to grasp. The Sophomores, however, are again fighting without plan. On their left wing Bilger makes a lane through the Freshmen, striking right and left. In the middle, Brandreth, bestriding the ball, engages man after man, dealing graceful and vigorous blows on nose, chin, chest, and ribs, opening mouths and closing eyes in a most scientific fashion. On the right Seaborn, careless of the ball, has made a ring around him, and challenges any Freshman to meet him. Already four have been placed *hors de combat* by the stalwart boating man. Van Courtland, unable longer to endure the sight, leaves the ball and his friends and enters the lists against his stronger but less agile enemy. It is soon obvious that the Freshmen are being worsted. Yet they fight bravely on, and close their thinned ranks, like the Scots around their king at Flodden. Bowyer, Saulsbury, and Rakeman keep together though sorely pressed. The Southerner is at length led by his eagerness away from his friends and engages two men near the fence. One of them he strikes from him, and turning upon the other with a sharp shrill yell deals a blow with his clinched hand as with a hammer, cutting his own thumb to the bone against a row of startled teeth. Before he can reach his friends he is himself struck down by Bilger, the heaviest hitter in his class, and led from the field. "Poor fellow!" exclaims Miss Leigh, who has watched the fate of the gallant Southerner with deep interest, "I hope he is not much hurt." The plucky fellow catches the remark and touches his hat to the fair speaker with a smile of gratitude. The larger number of the Freshmen have now been knocked down and exhausted or disabled, and the rest are again forced back, and this time with fatal steadiness, towards the goal. The Sophomores no longer look after the ball, which is soon thrust out a few paces to one side of the *mêlée.* Saulsbury spies it, and is speeding to repeat his former exploit, when he hears a savage yell behind him, and glancing back sees Brandreth running towards him.

Suddenly from the Freshman lines a slender young fellow springs forward, his face burning, with blood about his mouth and neck, and his collar and scarf streaming behind by a single button. "Stop Hamilton," cries Saulsbury, recognizing a friend to whom he had been introduced the day before. The boy, however, aims two fierce blows at his unequal opponent. The blows spend themselves upon the air, but not so the clean straight return by which the Freshman is struck far to the rear.

"Go down, go down," shouts Brandreth to Saulsbury, who has now reached him, and with this command he delivers his left straight at the other's face. Saulsbury, however, proves himself no novice. Guarding the blow with his right he counters with great effect, sealing up the right eye of the Soph for many a day. Brandreth falls back a few feet and the Freshman hears a clapping of hands from the men and ladies near. Yet his time is short for the enjoyment of such sweet music. Another second and Brandreth, the most graceful, finished, and plucky sparrer of his class is again before him, and very ugly and unpromising is the glare of his surviving eye. Again Brandreth levels his left, flinging himself lightly forwards. Saulsbury guards his head with his right and counters as before. This is the last act of which he is conscious for some minutes. Brandreth has himself cross-countered, throwing his head to the left and bringing in his right with the whole weight of his body. Saulsbury's head forthwith reposes upon the lap of earth, his heels twinkle in the setting sun, his nose assumes colossal proportions, and the world grows black before his face. Presently a bystander sets him upon his legs and he gazes stupidly around him. The game is over. The ball has been driven home by the Sophs, and the men are separating for the next encounter.

During the respite that follows the first game you may distinguish among a group of Freshmen a wild-visaged, rough-hewn man in a state of fierce excitement. This gentleman is Mr. Timothy Gowan, who was born, and as he terms it, "raised," in what was then the beautiful village of Galena. He had supposed that he had in his youth seen something of rough life. Scenes in Western bar-rooms, where the knife and pistol played conspicuous roles, were not unfamiliar to his boyish years. On more than one occasion he had beheld eyes gouged out or noses slit at cheerful social gatherings over the convivial punch. He had imagined, however, that when he came among the more polished denizens of the East, he should find the manners of society assume a gentler tone. He had, indeed, been informed by his friends on the previous evening, that his class was about to engage in a little game familiarly known as foot-ball.

This consisted, as they kindly explained to him, in tracking, following, kicking, or otherwise impelling an inflated globe of rubber cloth towards a fixed mark or goal. Custom, they added, had made it incumbent upon him as a classmate to take part in the sport. Mr. Gowan had cheerfully consented, and had flung himself among the foremost in the rush after the ball. Now boxing is an art, but little practised upon the prairies, and the surprise of Mr. Gowan was therefore great, while plunging with obliging ardor into the spirit of the game, to find some twenty yelling monsters leaping upon him, still greater to find himself instantaneously knocked down, and, as he is now expressing it to some comrades in misery, "run over, trampled on, and made a door-mat of by a hundred hogs." "I'd give," he mutters hoarsely to his friends, rolling fiercely his empurpled eyes, "I'd give ten years of my life to feel a bowie knife in my fist."

The two following games were similar, but shorter, as the Freshmen had been seriously weakened by the previous struggle. Their leader, Saulsbury, could now do little more than walk through the game. The Southerner Rakeman, though he had insisted on returning to the field, was almost disabled. Van Courtland was exhausted by his long encounter with Seaborn, on whom he had left many marks, but who had taken terrible revenge on the slighter frame of the young New Yorker. Others of their best fighting men had suffered equally, and though the class upon the whole did well, they were speedily beaten.

The Sophomore and Freshman classes alone took part in the first three games, but now the latter were recruited from the Juniors, while the Seniors reinforced the Sophs. The two sides were thus very evenly matched, and the last three games were sharply contested. It was not considered a point of honor for the two upper classes to engage in the fight, yet the men who had earned a reputation for pluck and skill, commonly put in an appearance on the field. Thrice the combat was renewed with varying fortune, whereof it chiefly concerns us to know that our young friend Saulsbury had sufficiently recovered himself to be twice knocked down by Seniors of mark.—By the end of the last game it had grown dark. The spectators dispersed, the carriages drove away, and among them Miss Campbell's barouche whirled off to town, where it unloaded its precious freight. Meanwhile each class had formed in a ring and was singing, "Auld Lang Syne." The men then broke up in groups and went off in various moods, exultant, lugubrious, hilarious, or philosophic. The Seniors to play billiards, to their club rooms, or to the pleasures of Boston; the Sophomores to break windows and to wanton through the town; some to their rooms; others to the wine-shop of Lyons; all to talk over the fortunes and wounds of the six games.

We would now beg the reader to transport himself for a few seconds to a pleasant house in Walnut Street, Salem. Let him enter a genial dining-room, where he will find an elderly gentleman, his wife, and a young girl.

A servant has just brought tea, and a gentle domestic tinge, adapted to the place and hour, pervades the conversation of the family. "Henry," muses the lady, "I wonder what Wentworth is doing now! He must be studying those mathematics he used to find so hard. Are you sure he got that parcel and those blankets I sent him? His room must be very damp." "Yes, my dear," replies Mr. Saulsbury, "I have no doubt of it. The expressman was told to be particularly careful." "I am sure he will study himself to death," continues Mrs. Saulsbury. "I hope you write to him not to overwork himself." "What a goosey you are, mamma," says Miss Saulsbury a lady of fifteen, with a laugh. "I am sure Mr. Morris, whom we met last summer at Newport, did not look as if he injured himself by hard study." "I will write if I apprehend any danger, my dear," says Mr. Saulsbury, a merry twinkle in his eye.

While his family were thus debating his condition, Wentworth Saulsbury had joined his friend Hamilton, an acquaintance of yesterday, indeed, but regarded already with something very like attachment, and was reposing his battered frame, stretched at length in a long easy-chair in the latter's room. Hamilton had taken up his quarters—and very comfortable ones they were—in the third story of Harvard Block. In the middle of the room stood a broad oaken study table—near the fireplace a Yankee rocking-chair, and a lounge—on the mantel a couple of stone jars for tobacco, and half a dozen briar-wood pipes. A pair of dumb-bells, and a formidable Indian club lurked in one corner. On the table lay Felton's Selections, a volume of Livy, Whately's Evidences, Mr. Cuthbert Bede's celebrated history of Verdant Green, divers numbers of the Harvard Magazine, and the Atlantic Monthly for September.

Saulsbury, after resting a few moments, jumped up and looked in the glass.

"One might play Banquo's ghost with great success to-night, Hamilton," he remarked after surveying his wounds.

"Your nose has become a burning and a shining light within the last few hours," returned his friend. "Here's some water."

"I wonder who that man was, who keeled me over so

neatly! I never dropt so quickly in my life," continued Saulsbury, washing his face, and bathing his bumps, with lively pleasure.

"I heard some one say his name was Brandreth, and that he was the best boxer of his class."

"He used me up very effectually," said Saulsbury. "I know so much about him."

"Come in," shouted Hamilton, in answer to a tumultuous knocking, at which the door was flung open, and half a dozen Freshmen entered.

"How are you, fellows!" cried Hamilton. "Sit down, and have a pipe!"

The boys seated themselves after the manner of contortionists and college youth, all but one named Sweatrame, who, being a little overcome by the libations with which he had crowned his efforts in the field, delivered a short but impressive speech to his host. Among the Freshmen was Bowyer, of whom we had a glimpse on the Deita, Rakeman, and a boy with red cheeks, named Robin Ayres, whose birthplace the city of Nashua boasted itself to be.

"We have just come from Holworthy," said Bowyer, "some Sophs tried to haze one of our men; and we had a little scrimmage; but sneaky Brown came up and dispersed us, and told us to go to our rooms."

"By Jove!" exclaimed Hamilton, "I wish I had been there. Was any one hit?"

"No," answered Bowyer, "and it's no use to go now, All the Faculty are out. The yard swarms with Tutors and Proctors."

"They've caught two or three Sophs breaking windows," piped Ayres. "Hollo, Saulsbury!" said Rakeman, interrupting him, "what a crack you've got on your nose. You are cut up worse than Van Courtland. Did you see what a mouse he caught under his left eye? By the way, where was your friend Dummer to-night?" he added, turning to Bowyer.

"He was taken suddenly sick at the five o'clock recitation," answered Bowyer, who was in his division, at which reply all the students laughed.

"Men say there hasn't been so good fighting for a long time," said Rakeman.

"I don't believe there will be many men at prayers to-morrow," remarked Ayres after a pause. "I havn't looked at my geometry, and I reçite at eight."

"Fellows," said Bowyer, "we ought to get up a boat club this term. There are two or three months we ought not to lose. Suppose we have a meeting here, to-night. Hamilton, you call the meeting to order." "Pooh, pooh, old salt," objected Rakeman, "wait a few days. We can't row to-night."

"Order!" at the same time interjected Sweatrame, whose imagination had been rendered more discursive by a bottle of ale. "Gentlemen, what is order? ''Tis a way we have at old Harvard. 'Tis a way we have at old Harvard.' Gentlemen, I'm going home. I'm not—oh no—nothing of the kind—I assure you. But I'm going home. 'Rolling home, rolling home, rolling home' "—and with this Sweatrame emerged from the room propped by his led captain Ayres, who, as a tug-boat convoys through devious channels some richly freighted galleon, guided him to his room.

"Come, fellows, let's pud along!" urged Rakeman, after a long chat in his friend's room.

"Oh, 'tis up the river and down the creek."

Singing this stirring strain of the South, as they sprang down the stairs, the party lingered a few moments on the sidewalk.

"I say, fellows," cried Rakeman, "come to Lyons'. He's open—there's a light in his old den," and thither, impelled by sympathetic thirst, his friends followed him.

The "Lyon's den" combined in a long, low, smoky room the varied attractions of wine-shop, lunch-counter, oyster-cellar and coffee-house. A bar ran along the side opposite the entrance, surmounted on its left flank by a glass covered case sacred to cakes and tarts of price. By the side of this a humble trencher offered doughnuts, sausages, and hard boiled eggs to the cravings of car drivers who in five minutes must appease the hunger of a day. On the right of the bar as you enter stood six boxes a yard or more square, closed against the vulgar eye by a dingy curtain. On its left a door opened into a billiard room, which was still filled with men of the various classes.

"Who is that?" whispered Hamilton to Saulsbury, pointing to our acquaintance Morris, who was leaning against the side of the doorway nearer the bar, and who nodded kindly to our hero.

"That is Morris," replied Saulsbury, "a Senior."

"That is one of the men who knocked me down in the last game," said Hamilton, with a natural feeling of pride.

"What'll ye have, fellows?" asked Rakeman, who, with his friends, had crowded into one of the boxes. "Hollo, there are some Freshmen," cried a voice from the billiard room, which sent a thrill of recognition through Saulsbury's nose. "Suppose we make them treat us," and out from the room poured half a dozen men, headed by Brandreth.

"How are you Brandreth?" said Rakeman, nodding to the Sophomores. "What'll ye have, fellows?" he added, to the increased astonishment of Hamilton, who, thinking deeds of valor were called for, had instinctively doubled up his arm. Hamilton's arm, when extended, measured eleven inches, and when doubled was increased in size by a full half inch. But behind his arm ruled a soul athirst for glory, which in the late fights had made him covet and win the honor of being thrice knocked down by the ablest sparrers. His ambition still unsatisfied, he now again doubled his arm to achieve greater fame; and lowered it reluctantly at the lack of occasion.

The Sophs soon returned to their billiards, and the Freshmen laughed and told stories together an hour or more.

"Suppose we go back to my room," Hamilton at length said to Saulsbury. "I am all used-up."

"So am I," replied Saulsbury, and taking Hamilton's arm, he bade his friends good-night and issued into Harvard Square. It had now grown late, and the old square was lying fast asleep under the shadow of the huge elm which rises from its centre.

Early on the morrow, however, when the town here first awakes to life's fitful fever, the square will wear a different aspect. The two druggists will then brandish their rival pestles ; the milliner ply her pretty care ; the cars roll along the street. Soon the courtly barber, manhood's midwife, will draw his obstetric razor; inquiring students will throng the University Bookstore ; bespattered drivers will urge their lumbering oxen, squealing pigs, or tangential sheep with blows and ejaculatory prayers towards fragrant Brighton. Now everything is buried in slumber, and the town pump is nodding over its trough, like a parson asleep in his pulpit.

"Suppose we take a walk, instead of going to your rooms," suggested Saulsbury. "That cellar was very close," and at this the two boys strolled along the path running around the college yard.

The sight of the classical grounds, rich with the memories of the past and the hopes of the future, touched the minds of the young fellows with a pleasant melancholy.

"What a beautiful place this is!" mused Saulsbury, turning to his friend, as, leaning on the old fence, they surveyed the Green and the shadows thrown by the graceful elms.

"What a pleasant time we shall have here the next four years," remarked Hamilton ; "I don't wonder men speak of their college days with such fervor."

"What a fine class we have," said Saulsbury, as they

walked on. "I heard a Junior say that next to his class, it was the finest class in college."

"I hope, Saulsbury, that we shall have the right sort of class feeling, and that we shan't be split up into cliques. We haven't many Boston men. I heard a man say that they always made a division in a class, that they were good fellows, but cliquey. I remember when I was a sub-Freshman how I used to look forward to class feeling. I thought how pleasant it must be to know a hundred men, with all of whom you could thoroughly sympathize."

"What strange ideas we have of college life, when we are at school," said Saulsbury. "If we had only kept a diary of our thoughts then, how absurd it would seem now, and yet we are the same persons now as then."

"I am going to make it a point myself," continued Hamilton, "to call on every man in the class, and to know them all well."

"I heard Morris say last summer, Hamilton, that the knowledge of character you acquire in college, is worth more than all you learn out of books."

"I wonder who will be our first scholar! You, Saulsbury, stood first at Salem. The men from Exeter and the Boston Latin School seem to be the best fitted. When I left school, my teacher told me to make a system for studying. He said that you could never learn anything without a system. I am going to set apart certain hours for work and to 'sport my oak.'"

"If you stand high the first few months, Hamilton, I've heard that it is easy enough to keep a good rank the rest of the course. They get used to marking you high. I'm going to throw myself into boating and sparring and that sort of thing as much as possible. I heard a Senior say that he would rather be stroke of the Harvard boat, than the first scholar of his class."

"I don't quite agree with that," objected Hamilton, after due deliberation, and somewhat startled by his own boldness; "it seems to me that the first object of a man at college should be to be a good scholar. I should like to be stroke of the Harvard, but of the two I should prefer to stand at the head of the class, I think."

"Well, perhaps you are right, old man," rejoined his friend, "I am going to study hard too, but I am not going to be a dig."

As the young men walked on, their conversation grew more confidential. They talked of their school-days—distant theme! They alluded to their families with careless anecdote. They hinted at the tender passion from whose sweet slavery, they owned, they had not been altogether free. Now of course they had outgrown such pleasures, and their minds were filled with sterner thoughts.

Growing more open, they discovered the ambitions and generous aims that, under the *blasé* manner which one loves to see a college boy affect, lurk hidden but none the less strong. There is, indeed, something intoxicating in the first draughts of college life. Then suddenly a boy sees within his reach, all the pleasures of freedom with none of its responsibilities. The memories of his home are fresh and beautiful around him, and life is what sweet remembrance and proud hope paint it. Every college boy, in his heart, believes in himself and in the world, and thinks that a noble career lies open before him, if he will but fairly struggle for it. Such beliefs and feelings are the source of whatever is great and worthy in the world, and he who sneers at them, is but a shallow cynic. Golden dreams and bright ideals of youth! who could have the heart to dispel them? Fools! who with a touch of the world's wand would change the rainbow into a few drops of water. These dreams are the realities of life. "The truths we live to learn," the mean passions of the market, of the pulpit, of the court, these are spectral far more than the illusions whose place they usurp.

The pleasure of boyhood, says some one, is home; of youth, friendship; and of manhood, love. Perhaps the purest and most generous of these pleasures is friendship. This, under the genial influence of a college atmosphere, grows with a swiftness and strength elsewhere unknown, and the two boys, after a short hour's stroll, feel that they are already familiar friends.

"Good night, old man," said Saulsbury, as, returning they reached the door of Harvard Block. "I'm going with your permission to call you by your first name after this," he added, and taking leave of his friend walked to Linden Street, and was soon in his room in the second story of Danforth's. Saulsbury lighted the gas, and proceeded to take another look at his nose, which he surveyed with great satisfaction for some moments. He then threw himself upon the sofa and strove to rearrange the universe which the events of the day had thrown into confusion.

"I think I will write a letter to mother," he said after a vain attempt, pleased with the humor of making his mother a party to the dissipation of sitting up until one o'clock.

"Dear mother," he then wrote, "I have now been here five days, but I have been too busy to write to any one. I like college immensely, and have got a very pleasant room. Your box came safely with the comforters and blankets. As the thermometer now stands at 80° in the shade, I shall not need any more blankets at present. In fact if you have a spare refrigerator I wish you would send it down to me. I am working hard and making a great many friends. I am going to make it one of my objects in college to study character. We had several foot-ball games to day between the different classes, and our class, I am sorry to say, was beaten. Please give my love to father and Mary, and believe me your devoted son,

WENTWORTH SAULSBURY."

His letter finished, Saulsbury slowly undressed himself and found that he had already grown stiff about the neck and shoulders. As his head touched the pillow there passed before his eyes a picture of his home, his father, mother, and pretty sister. Then came a feeling as of a multitude of men rushing over him, followed by a herd of bisons. Then all things seemed mixed confusedly, save his nose, which remained fixed and increased in magnitude until it reached the size of a mountain beneath which our hero was soon buried in slumber.

CHAPTER II.

"Di, quibus inperium est animarum, Umbræque silentes,
Et Chaos, et Phlegethon, loca nocte tacentia late,
Sit mihi fas audita loqui; sit numine vestro
Pandere res alta terra et caligine mersas."

AFTER the severe intellectual labors of the day it is a not infrequent custom of the ingenuous youth of Harvard to refresh the weary mind with convivial ale, the social oyster, jolly songs, and conversation upon topics of less profundity than those that usually occupy the thoughts of young truth-seekers. The day before Junior Exhibition Saulsbury found Ayres' card upon his table, inviting him to meet a few fellows at his room that evening at eight o'clock. Thinking that it would be a pleasant party, our hero decided to go, and after supper, to pass away the intermediate time, sauntered towards the Post-office, as the custom is, and thence into "Lyon's" to have a game of billiards. Morris, whom he found there, with great condescension invited him to play. Wentworth succeeded in beating his venerable friend, who allowed him but fifty points, in two games in succession. In capital spirits he then walked to Harvard Block, hollooed to Hamilton, who ran down stairs to meet him, and the two thence strolled towards No. 1 Holworthy, where Ayres, who occupied the position of Tutor's Freshman, lived and sang.

"By the way, Lewis," asked Saulsbury, as they neared the room, "have you been up to get your marks for last month? What were they?"

"I got eight in everything except Greek."

"What did you get in that? I thought Greek was your strong point."

"Two fifths of one," replied Hamilton with a sickly smile, "and I only made two mistakes during the whole month. One day the tutor asked me, 'What is the point in that sentence?' I told him what I thought was the point. 'That is incorrect,' said he; 'the next;' and he 'deaded' half a dozen men. At length Hayward said he didn't see any point. 'That is correct,' said the tutor, 'there is no point!'"

"What was the other?" asked Saulsbury with a laugh.

"The tutor asked me why fig-trees grew in Lesbos. I told him I supposed they were imported from Asia Minor. 'That is incorrect,' said he; 'the next,' and he 'deaded' half the division until he came to Gowan, who said he did not know. 'That is correct,' said the tutor, 'they are indigenous to the soil.' Gowan got eight that month, and I got two fifths of one."

"I can sympathize with you, old man," said Saulsbury; "what mark do you think I got in Latin—four—the same mark as Sweatrame, who does not know the difference between subject and predicate. I used to learn every lesson almost by heart, and to write out a translation of it. 'Sneaky' must have thought that I used a 'pony,' and marked me down. He is just the kind of man to mark you from what he supposes your moral character to be. There s some romance in your mark. I'm not going to look at my Latin again this term, and then I think I shall get good marks."

"Come fellows," cried Ayres, whose room they had now reached, "don't talk 'shop,'" and, as his friends entered, he threw his geometry carelessly into a corner of the room. Like many boys, the warbler, though a fair scholar, tried to avoid a reputation for studying hard, and wished to be thought to recite from inspiration. "Tell me, Wentworth," continued Ayres, "is it true that Sweatrame was again blackballed at the last meeting of the Huron Boat Club. I wasn't there myself. I heard some one say that you blackballed him, Lewis. Don't you like him?"

"No," replied Hamilton. "I don't like him, though no one has a right to say how I voted. I think he has a bad influence on the class, which we ought to counteract."

"It is a hard punishment," said Ayres; "I had myself rather stand at the foot of the rank list, than be blackballed at our boat club."

"Hush! Talk of the Devil," said Saulsbury, as some one knocked at the door, which opened and let in Bowyer and Sweatrame engaged in earnest debate.

"I think he is a scrub," urged Sweatrame, "he dresses like a scrub, and seems to be as poor as a rat."

"He seems to me to be a very good fellow," objected Bowyer. "He fought well at the foot-ball games. I think you might call him a 'dig,' perhaps, but not a scrub. He talks and acts like a gentleman."

"About whom are you talking?" asked Ayres, who caught with eagerness anything affecting the social position of a classmate.

"Hayward," answered Bowyer. "Sweatrame says he is a scrub." The conversation was here interrupted by the stirring ballad of "The Bold Gallantee," which gave notice of the expected presence of Rakeman the haughty Southron.

"Sweatrame," cried Rakeman, as he opened the door, "have you heard my new conundrum?"

"No," replied the former.

"Which of the Grecian heroes do you most resemble?"

"I give it up."

"Ajax, sold!"

"Sweatrame says Hayward is a scrub," said Hamilton, to the new comer. "He seems to me to be one of the best men in the class."

"Scrub!" returned Rakeman warmly, "I reckon he doesn't know anything about him. He is a capital fellow. He rooms in my entry, and translates my Felton for me every evening. That Dummer whom I saw you with this morning, Sweatrame, seems to me to be a scrub. He wears a diamond ring, and asks you how much you think it costs and that sort of thing."

"Dummer is one of the richest men in the class," said Sweatrame, reddening; "he 'cuts' half the men in it."

"He must be very sharp," responded Rakeman; "if he didn't cut them, they'd 'cut' him."

"I dont believe in calling a classmate a scrub," broke in Saulsbury; "some of you fellows call half the class scrubs—many of them as good fellows every way as any men in it."

"I saw Van Courtland, Robin, as I was coming here," remarked Bowyer to his host after a short silence, "and told him you were going to have some fellows in your room. I dare say he'll drop in." A smile of pleasure lit up the face of the warbler at the thought of so great a swell as Van Courtland dropping into his room familiarly. Rising he then opened a bed-room door and out marched a dozen bottles of ale, and with them a Dutch cheese made its phlegmatic appearance.

"Come, fellows. Have a smoke," said Ayres, after they had well eaten, and passed round some briarwood pipes. Cigars Freshmen rarely smoke, both on account of economy, and because, shrewd fellows, they wish life to hold some pleasures in reserve.

"I'm afraid some Soph will throw a brickbat through the window. Dummer had one thrown into his room the other night," remarked the host a few moments later, and jumping up, he bolted his heavy wooden shutters with great care. While thus fortifying himself a light step was heard in the entry, and a graceful young fellow dressed with taste entered the room.

"How are you Van?" cried Rakeman and the rest of the boys, and a dish of oysters and a glass of ale were offered to the new comer, who was no less a person than our old acquaintance Mr. Schuyier Van Courtland of New York. Van, as his friends now called him, was born at Albany, in the old manor house, the home of colonial traditions. He had passed a year at Vevay, and a year or more at Paris, and had seen something of New York society, in which his mother had been a belle. His exclusiveness made him disliked by many of his classmates, but his engaging manners and vast knowledge of the world gave him great prestige. Among college boys, indeed, a knowledge of the world is more prized than a large arm, and after that nothing can be said.

"Van," remarked Rakeman when the former had finished eating his oysters, "you're a plucky fellow to wear a beaver. Didn't you hear how they treated Dummer the other day? He wore a beaver to recitation; and in the evening six men with masks came into his room: first they placed a chair on the table: then on the chair they placed his new hat; and at the words one, two, three, they made him mount the table and sit on his hat. 'Smile, now,' said one of the men, whom Dummer thinks was Brandreth, 'and say that you like it,' and Dummer was obliged to smile and thank the men for their kindness."

"There are Freshmen and Freshmen," said Van

"and this one, prefers that his hat should sit on him, rather than the reverse."

"Will you not have a cigar, Van," asked Sweatrame, pulling out half a dozen from his pocket, and offering him one.

"Thank you," replied Van, blowing a ring from his pipe. "I assure you I never smoke." Two or three of the men, however, accepted Sweatrame's proferred cigars to the injury of their host's *amour propre.*

"They are 'hazing' our men very badly," said Saulsbury shortly. "They have begun at the first letter, I hear, and are going through us alphabetically. After they had made Dummer sit on his hat, they ordered him to bring up a pail of water, and put his head in it."

"Yes," added Ayres, "and a Soph found one of Dummer's old razors and made him shave off half his moustache, and told him that if he shaved off the other half, the Med. Fac. would make a note of it."

"It's rough to be 'hazed' by such a 'scrubby' class," muttered Rakeman. "There arn't more than a dozen 'white' men in it. Come fellows, let's liquor up, Bowyer, let me fill your glass. Here's to ye."

"I have been training," remarked the latter, draining his glass, "and have drunk nothing but ale, and eaten nothing but raw beef for three days."

"You must be as strong as a moose. How much does your arm measure now, old man?" asked Ayres, who was a great admirer of his aquatic friend.

"Thirteen inches and a half. I hope to get it up to fourteen, in a month, by working hard."

"Bravo, Ned!" cried Rakeman, we shall have you in the *Harvard* next year. Suppose we make each man sing a song in turn. Ayres, you begin." The warbler offered much coy denial, but at length started the melody of "Fair Harvard."

"No heel-taps!" then cried Rakeman, rapping on the table with a poker, and all the glasses were drained, when Rakeman himself began the song with the original chorus.

"'Tis a way we have at old Harvard."

This song, the tune of which is the same as that of the favorite Oxford song with the chorus,

"'Tis a way we have in the 'Versity,"

Is learnt by each Freshman the day after he arrives at Harvard, and sung with startling energy every day, during his first term. This, more than any one thing, enables a Freshman to make real the illusion that he is an old member of the college, and versed in all its devious ways.

"Ned," asked Rakeman, turning to Bowyer after the circle of singers had been completed, "why do you look so solemn? What are you winking at with your left eye? You're thinking of something wrong."

"A terrible thing happened to-day," responded the child of Neptune, an expression of horror creeping over his face. "As we were coming into the Huron Boat House, this morning, I flung a boat-hook carelessly into a beam, as I thought, when snap—I heard a slight crack, and looking up, saw a hole as large as your little finger in the bottom of the Harvard Boat." A shudder passed over the faces of all the men present, at the news of the catastrophe.

"I don't wonder you look grave," said Wentworth, at length, "what did you do?"

"I went up at once to see Bilger and Seaborn, and offered of course to buy a new boat or do anything they wished. They were very kind, and said they thought that the boat could be mended, without doubt."

"Come fellows, fill up," exclaimed Rakeman, whose spirits could not long endure a curb; "to-morrow's Exhibition day, and there are no recitations, you know."

"What a jolly time we had last night, did we not, Rake?" remarked Sweatrame, filling his glass; "we wentas 'supes' behind the scenes at the theatre. You don't know, Hamilton, what a charming danseuse there was there. She had a foot that would drive you crazy."

Sweatrame loved to make parade of his dissipation. He had lived all his life in New York, and was considered a great connoisseur in wine and women. This excited great respect for him among the fast men of the class, but caused him to be hated with equal fervor by Hamilton and his friends. Hamilton, indeed, used often to discuss the question with Saulsbury, how so dissipated a man as Sweatrame could keep alive, and express his belief that some fine morning he would suffer the fate of spontaneous combustion.

"Suppose we go round to Dummer's to-night," suggested Van, turning to Hamilton, who, he saw, was annoyed by Sweatrame's topic of conversation. "The Sophs have threatened to 'haze' him again."

"They will be sure to do so if they hear of men collecting to defend him," interposed Ayres.

"So Dummer thinks, Ayres, and that's the humor of the thing. He hates to have us in his room, but can't help trying to appear grateful to men who are risking their eyes and noses for him. The night after he was 'hazed,' a small party of us sat up in his room with him until two o'clock. One of the guard got 'sprung,' and insisted on sleeping in Dummer's bed all night, so that Dummer had to sleep on the floor."

"I don't see what the Sophs could do worse," pondered Ayres.

"Brother Saulsbury's up in a pear tree,"

began Rakeman, beating time with his poker, when a stealthy step was heard in the entry, followed by a low knock. Rakeman at once grasped his poker and placed himself *en garde* before the door.

"It may be 'sneaky' Brown," the owner of the room whispered, at which each man seized a bottle and held it behind his back, while Wentworth turned down the gas. Again the knock was heard, and the door then slowly began to open.

"You don't catch this 'possum asleep!" yelled the knight of the poker, slamming the door to with a violent lunge. "We're ready for you. '5- forever!" A sound expressing unmitigated disgust followed outside the door, which issued from a mouth evidently underneath a banged nose.

"I'm Mr. Brown," growled out a voice, at which Rakeman opened the door, and the unhealthy face of the tutor peered through it. "I beg your pardon, sir," said Rakeman bowing to his instructor. "I thought you were the class of '5–. They have been 'hazing' us very badly of late."

"I thought," meanly insinuated the tutor, whose satisfaction at the above apology was by no means intense—"I thought I heard the sound of glasses in your room."

"I think it was some Sophs breaking windows in Stoughton," kindly suggested Rakeman; "I heard the same noise myself. We have ourselves got together to prevent their 'hazing' Mr. Ayres."

"You must make less noise, gentlemen," the tutor concluded with saying, and walked away, wondering why each man carried his right hand in so strained a posture.

"I did not at first recognize 'sneaky' in his disguise," said Rakeman, after the tutor had gone. "He has on a new hat. He must have bought that with the fine he levied on me yesterday, for cutting my name on the settee."

"Come, fellows, we must be off," urged Van. "We shall get Ayres into trouble, if we stay any longer."

The men at this all took their leave, except Saulsbury and Hamilton, who remained a few minutes; and then bidding their host good-night walked together towards the latter's room.

"I don't much like this sort of thing," said Lewis,

thoughtfully, after a silence of some minutes. "I know fellows call you 'spooney' for saying so; but the men drink, and swear, and talk in such a vulgar way often. If a man would not only not do any of these things, but would set himself strongly against them, he would have a great influence for good on the class."

"I hate to think how unpopular he would become, Lewis, though he would exert a fine influence, I don't doubt. It is cowardly, too, to be deterred from anything by a fear of unpopularity."

"Will you not agree with me, Wentworth," said Lewis, stopping and looking earnestly at his friend, "whenever men speak of low and vulgar subjects, either to leave them, or to make them talk of something else. I am going to do so myself."

"I don't know of anything so difficult, Lewis, but I'll do my best. Good-night. I shall see you in the morning." Wentworth left his companion at Harvard Block and walked towards his room, thinking of what Lewis had said, and revolving many virtuous resolutions in his mind.

"That man," he said to himself, "is the only man I have ever known who unites the purity of a woman with perfect manliness and pluck."

"That's the fellow," whispered some one as Wentworth turned into Linden Street, and at the words, four men in masks sprang out upon him, from the doorway of the corner house. Saulsbury was no coward, but the darkness and the surprise for a moment unnerved him. He, however, struck one fair blow at the man just in front of him.

The man stooped, the blow passed over his head, and the next moment Wentworth was seized around the waist, and thrown; two hands grasped his throat; his own were tied behind his back, his eyes bandaged, and his mouth gagged. Our hero exerted all his strength in a desperate struggle to gain his feet.

"How the child wriggles," muttered one of the masks, and gave Wentworth a blow with the flat of his hand, which made him writhe in a frenzy of rage.

"Lift him," now whispered one of the men, and Wentworth was placed in a vehicle which drove rapidly off.

He lay still, though burning with anger. "I'd give my life," he thought, "for one blow at that coward who struck me." They drove rapidly for several minutes, until at length the carriage stopped, and Wentworth was taken out, turned round half a dozen times, and led up a flight of stairs into a room.

"Mr. President, we have brought you the culprit," said one of the men who held Saulsbury.

"Remove the band," commanded a voice resembling the angry mew of a cat. The band was removed and our hero glanced around him not without a feeling of terror. The walls of the room in which he found himself were painted with revolting figures, representing the growth of Disease. In the rear a table was placed, on the centre of which rested a large Bible presented to Harvard by the pious youth of Yale College in expectation of a similar gift in return. Behind the Bible stood a box of medical instruments with a letter from the Emperor Nicholas. The front of the table discovered bunches of skeleton keys; a few delicate Freshman moustaches, with the names of their former possessors; rich folds of hairs marked, "the wig of Tutor Jones, captured Oct. 3rd, 185–;" and a billet with cords twisted around its handle.

The Bible itself sustained a punch bowl of singular shape, adorned with the motto, "Satano duce, nil desperandum," and two huge clubs, rough with letters and figures. The words "Hell Fire Club" on the larger of these would have recalled to the antiquary the deeds of iniquity by which that society had justified its name. Carved upon this sole memorial of a famous brotherhood were the initials of men distinguished in the law and ministry, who in their youth had furnished employment to the professions which in their advanced years had supported them. On the smaller club was the mysterious name, "Thundering Bolus." This weapon, in former times swung by the arm of the bravest Senior in the College, for many years struck dismay into the hearts of hostile villagers, trusting in their numbers.

Little desire, however, had our hero to examine these or the other objects of interest which the chamber held. His eyes were fastened on the scene before him. Directly in front of him sat a hideous monster, with horns projecting from his forehead, and his dress ablaze with flames. Next the Devil to the right, was a creature whose features were nearly eaten off by a cancer, while on the left leered a withered hag. Flanking these three stood a dozen wretches, each incarnating some malady.

Between Wentworth and the "Leeches and Doctors," for such was the title these horrors wore on their breasts, was a table covered with a sheet, on one end of which stood a small brasier with scalpels, pincers, and other instruments around it. Above, at the centre of the wall, before Wentworth, was hung a strip of black cloth, on which were written in scarlet six letters. The sight of these at once riveted our hero's eyes, drove a cold iron rod down his spine, and made him tremble with fear. These six letters were M E D. F A C.

"Remove the gag," ordered the Devil, and Wentworth's tongue was set free.

"Where's that d—— coward who struck me?" he exclaimed. "I dare——"

"Burn the profane fellow! dissolve him, flay him, dissect him," and other suggestions interrupted his words.

"Gag the rebel!" screeched the Devil. "'Delilah!" he added, "chasten the lawlessness of this young Samson."

At this, Wentworth was forced upon the table and the hag shuffled up to him, and slowly pulled from his head twenty-seven hairs and burnt them in the brasier.

"Remember," the Devil warned him, as the gag was again removed and Wentworth set on his feet, "that you are in the august presence of the Medical Faculty of Harvard University. You are charged," he continued solemnly, "with having spoken lightly of the godly society of the 'Med. Fac.' Is the accusation true?"

"I think you have done a great many mean acts," muttered Wentworth, losing all prudence in his anger.

"He blasphemes against the Med. Fac.!" shrieked a dozen voices, mingled with groans.

"Brother Plummer," commenced the Devil, "read the punishment decreed against one who offends against the majesty of the Med. Fac."

"Whoever," began a deep voice behind our hero, "shall speak evil against the Medical Faculty of Harvard University shall receive the punishment of air, fire, water, and earth, and the purification of assafœtida and brimstone." "Such are the words of holy writ," added the Devil. "Your own good compels us to punish you, with whatever pain to ourselves. Let the law be executed," he concluded, and waved his sceptre, at which sign each monster removed a leg or arm and brandished it over his head.

Wentworth was then blindfolded, led into the open air and placed in a blanket. Were we writing a romance, we should not allow our hero to be tossed in a blanket, but the spirit of truth, which rules all histories, compels us to set down the evil with the good.

"Are you ready?" cried one of the men, holding the blanket. "Now all together—one, two, three, toss!" and at the word our hero winged his way heavenward with such aid as ten stalwart devils could lend him.

Wentworth was now nearly exhausted with excitement and fatigue, yet he nerved himself to endure without flinching. Suddenly a device occurred to him. As he was descending from his third flight, feeling like Vulcan landing upon Lemnos he extended both his feet to the utmost. "Heavens!" cried one of his tormentors, "my head's broken," and Wentworth had the pleasure of feeling his heel strike a hard skull; this was, however, lessened at the same moment, by his falling heavily upon the ground.

"Let the punishment of fire be now inflicted," commanded the Devil, after Wentworth had been led back to his room. At this two bands, the ends of which were attached to hooks in the ceiling, were placed one round Wentworth's feet and the other round his chest. Again the boy broke out in execrations.

"Hush," whispered in his ear the voice of some one half relenting, "or they'll gag you," and with a sullen look of rage, Wentworth repressed his words.

The 'Leeches and Doctors' then placed the brasier beneath him; some fluid was poured into it and lighted, and our hero swung to and fro over it several times, and then taken down.

"Let the punishment of water be inflicted," commanded the Devil. At this, Wentworth was placed in a coffin, and borne from the room. Soon he heard a noise as of the turning of a windlass, and felt himself sinking lower and lower. "What if the rope should break!" he thought, and derived little pleasure from the reflection. Suddenly the bottom of the coffin struck water, and Wentworth heard the men talk ing above him. "Pull him up!" "pull him up!" No, bless him; give him a dowse; he nearly broke my head!" and the coffin sunk still lower. The water pours through the cracks: it covers the boy's ankle: it rises to his knee: the air grows dense : the water has reached his waist : his head seems bursting : his eyes start from their sockets ; and with a cry of despair, he loses all remembrance.

"You oughtn't to have let him down so far." "Confound the fellow ! Why does'n't he come to?" are the first words Wentworth hears on returning to consciousness, and at the same moment water is dashed in his face, and he feels some one chafing his hands.

The boy opens his eyes and looks languidly around him. "Where am I?" he asks, and shudders at the masks and figures.

"We've punished him enough." "There's game in the fellow." "We'll drive him home." Wentworth heard the men whisper to each other. A glass of brandy was then given him, his eyes were again bandaged, and he was placed in a carriage. After a drive of some minutes he was taken from the carriage and set upon the ground. He pulled off his bandage, and found himself by the familiar gate of Danforth's. Through this he passed, and groped his way to his room, where he was soon buried in sleep, not without strange dreams.

CHAPTER III.

"Ubi quid datur oti,
Illudo chartis."

NEITHER time nor the patience of our readers would permit our chronicling the daily events of our hero's course, as minutely as we have thus far done. It is also difficult to catch salient points of interest in college life, as day after day glides placidly along. Perhaps an extract from Saulsbury's diary will give our readers a better knowledge of the common current of his life than anything which we could write.

"185-. *Thursday, Dec. 5th.*—To-day I have determined to keep a diary of my thoughts and acts. This I shall write for my own pleasure in the future, and shall show to no one, not even my mother, or my sister. I rose this morning at half past six, and sprang 'uno saltu' from my bed into my hat." [Our hero here probably refers not to that hat of silk, which was wont both to protect his head from the sun and rain, and to fill his heart with the proud consciousness of manhood, but to a utensil employed for the purpose of taking a bath or 'tumby.' This we have inferred from a laborious comparison of similar passages.] "I dressed myself hurriedly in boots, pantaloons, and coat, and ran to the chapel. I have already 'cut' eighteen prayers, and have but one more to 'cut' this term without a 'Private.'

"I learnt at breakfast that I had gained nothing by going to prayers, as the monitor had been 'screwed up' by Van and Rake. After breakfast I walked to my room, read over my Odyssey, and at eight went to recitation, but was not called up. I was at first startled at finding Sweatrame know the meaning of a Greek word. While he was reciting, however, a page of a 'pony' was blown from his book upon the floor, which solved the riddle, and gave us great amusement. The men here do not recite nearly as well as we used to at Salem. Many of them seem scarcely to have looked at their lessons.

"After recitation, I walked into town to call on my aunt, at the Tremont House, but did not find her in. Before calling I stopped at the barber's shop under the hotel to get shaved. The barber was a low fellow, and said as this was plainly my first shave, he would charge me half price. I reproved his insolence, and reported him to his employer, who said that he would have him discharged. I have, however, withdrawn my patronage from the hotel.

"I took a car at the bridge, and reached Cambridge just in time for my twelve o'clock recitation in Latin. Brown called me up the first man, and I made quite a 'squirt.' Since I have given up studying Latin, I get very good marks. After dinner I dropped into Ayres' room, where I found Ned Bowyer, and enjoyed a profitable conversation for half an hour. We discussed the question whether George Washington or Napoleon Buonaparte were the greater general. Ayres took the side of the former, and argued that no man could be a great man in anything who was not also a good man. Bowyer thought that if Washington had had Napoleon's advantages, he would have been the greater general, but I cannot think so.

"Ayres, after Bowyer had gone, read 'the Woman in White,' and I looked over the Atlantic Monthly for December. I am ashamed to say that I had not before seen it, though it has been out two entire weeks. The articles were admirable, as they always are, and the 'Autocrat' surpassed himself. I walked to my room on leaving Ayres, stopping a moment at Bartlett's, where I bought a very pretty edition of Sir 'Thomas Browne's Religio Medici. This I mean to give Hamilton for a birthday present. Reaching my room, I read fifty pages of Irving's 'Life of Washington,' which I think a profound work. I then 'dug' on my Peirce's Geometry, and at five went to recitation. It would try the soul of an abolitionist to stand a weary hour, gazing at the black face of a long board as I did, without solving my problem. However, I worked out Van's for him correctly, which was something. Van is a man of great talents, though lazy. He knows the world thoroughly, without being spoiled by it, though whom of us indeed has it not somewhat injured? Some day I think Van will become a very distinguished man.

"After tea I called round at Hamilton's room to get my

Liddell's Rome, which I carelessly left there two days ago. Yesterday, rather a funny thing happened in recitation. The tutor said 'we will will now drop Liddell,' at which Van let fall his book with great noise upon the floor, much to the tutor's horror. After talking a few minutes with Hamilton, he suggested our calling to see Bowyer about getting up our club-table for next term. Bowyer told us that Van had already got up a table, but that he thought ours would be a better one. We agreed to ask Rakeman, Ayres, and three other men to join us, and to engage Mrs. Green of Winthrop Square for our cook. Bowyer and I were chosen by Hamilton as a committee to secure that worthy widow. I then returned to my room, and read over an article in the Harvard Magazine, written I hear by Morris, which really shows genius. I wonder whether I shall ever be able to write with such wit and power. I have just finished reading the last part of Christie Johnston—a charming story. It is now only ten o'clock, but I feel very tired, and am going to bed like a little boy of twelve.

"*Dec. 6th.*—I rose this morning at six. It was very cold and quite dark. The water in my hat I found frozen, and I had to break the ice with a dumb-bell. I took my bath, however, but did not feel the usual glow afterwards. I then swung the Indian club fifty times, and went to prayers, and thence to breakfast. After breakfast I went to recitation, but was delighted to find that Tutor Robinson had given us a 'cut.' We waited five minutes for him, and walked off just as he was running round the corner. Van and I then started off on a good long walk. Van said a few days since he had received a Public Admonition for 'cutting' recitations. He had at once sent word to one of his servants at New York, to send him any letter addressed to his father marked Cambridge, and had himself just received the letter containing the notice sent by the Faculty. 'thus saving my father,' he said, 'much unnecessary pain.' Van is a very good-hearted fellow, but quære, was it wholly justifiable? We walked about eight miles, and then went to Van's room. Van smoked two or three pipes, and tried to induce me to do the same, but I have 'sworn off' for the rest of the term. I went to recitation at twelve, but was not called up. After dinner I made a call on Gowan, whom I am getting to like very well. He is a man of vast ability. When he first came to Cambridge, he said he did not think 'pig tracks,' of it, every one was so 'stuck up,' but now he thinks everything 'high pie.' These Western metaphors are very expressive. I thence went to the Post-office, which I had neglected to do this morning. There I found a letter from mother, with a photograph of Mary, which was very pretty, but did not do her justice. Studied on my 'Roman Antiquities' till four, and after recitation, went to the gymnasium with Van. To-day, for the first time, I succeeded in going up a rope by my hands alone.

"Van told me that Sweatrame had raised money lately by ordering suits of clothes of his tailor, and receiving fifty per cent. of the cost, allowing the tailor to keep the clothes. I said this seemed to me to be a very low way of getting money. Van replied that Sweatrame doubtless thought that to get money was the first object; that the means or moral part of it was an after consideration, and, like every moral, should come at the end of the story. Van also told me a very wicked, but also very good story of a lady who ran off with a man, and left a letter for her husband, saying that though she could no longer love him as a husband, she should always regard him as a brother. After supper I left an order at Sawin's the expressman's, to call at Bowyer's room, to take a forty inch chest to town, and then dropped into Harvard Block to see Hamilton. We discussed the question whether a lawyer should defend a man whom he knows to be guilty. I went to my room at about half past seven, and have ever since been reading Raleigh's 'History of the World,' a work of grand scope.

"*Dec. 7th.*—This morning I rose at six, took a cold bath, and went to prayers. About a foot of snow had fallen in the night, and it was still snowing.

"Prayers are the things that try men's souls in college.

"To-day is Saturday, when there is but one recitation. At eight I handed in my Greek exercise, and returning to my room looked over 'Vanity Fair' for an hour or two. It seems to be an unhealthy book, and I think I will not read it. At the end of that time, Van called for me and we rode together into town. Van was measured for two suits of clothes, and bought a cartload of collars, scarfs, and such things. Van is an extravagant dog. After this we strolled into the Athenæum to see the Exhibition, and to while away the time, until the hour for dinner at Destre's, to which I had invited Van. This found us both very hungry, and we did it ample justice. Morris was there with two other Seniors, all of whom were very pleasant. They talked about their class elections most of the time. They said they felt sure that their club—the Mush-and-Milk—would carry all the offices, which I hope will be the result. After dinner Van and I went to the theatre to see Booth. We stayed through two acts only, and then went to Parker's to play billiards and enjoy ourselves generally. We found Rakeman and Sweatrame there, and staid until half-past eleven, when we all walked together to the Revere House, and took the last car to Cambridge. I was told by Sweatrame that two men were hazed yesterday in the most outrageous manner, and I heard a week ago, that the Med. Fac. had threatened to haze me again. Every night, therefore, I fortify myself against surprise. In front of the door I plant an abattis by tipping up three or four chairs with their legs towards the door. I then dig a ditch by filling my hat with water, and placing it behind the chairs. I then lay me down to sleep."

Thus, as the first Freshman term wore away, our hero grew in mind and body.

The last day of the term soon arrived, and Wentworth took leave of his classmates for a six short weeks, and drove to the station. As the cars rolled along it was not without a just feeling of pride that he looked back over the five months just past, and compared the present man of the world, with the then unsophisticated boy.

His thoughts first naturally turned to the change his body had undergone. His upper arm now measured a full inch more than before, and had reached the appalling size of thirteen and a quarter inches, while his chest was developed in not less dangerous proportions.

The shell that covered this manly form, had also changed its appearance. The semi-rustic garments of Salem, to the great grief of its fashionable tailor, our hero had long since discarded, and was now arrayed with the dazzling beauty which marks the proud gentry of Boston.

Wentworth's mind had also kept equal step with the growth of his body. He had read a great number of the works of the best authors, and could criticise them all with sententious brevity. As a matter, of minor importance, he had studied faithfully on the text-books of the college course, and in spite of several deductions, stood third on the rank list.

The knowledge of the world, however, which he had gained during the past six months, was what chiefly separated him from his former self. The society, the fashion, the great affairs in which he had taken part, though they had made him somewhat *blasé*, had given him a confidence and repose of manner in pleasing contrast to his former effervescence. He had learnt to attend a dinner without embarrassment, and in wines was a great connoisseur, distinguishing sherry and madeira with ease, and often Bordeaux from Burgundy. He had become, also, a good cue at billiards, and often made runs of five or six points. He had seen many men and known their manners, and the knowledge of character he had thus acquired was so great, that he could discourse by hours together on the different qualities of mind and body which marked his classmates.

Our hero had thus gained no slight acquaintance with the worlds of men and books. This, though it did not place him upon a level with the members of the older classes, one can readily see separated him by an impassable gulf from his former associates and the great mass of mankind.

Wentworth's manner, therefore, on returning to his native city, assumed something of that "hauteur," which makes the young 'collegy,' an object of great repugnance to the envious vulgar.

Wentworth's mother and sister, however, received him with increased admiration, and listened to his anecdotes with that interest which one finds, alas! nowhere, save with his female relatives of the nearest degree. Much they marvelled that one small head could carry such store of knowledge, or pass unscathed through so many perils.

"If I had known what sort of a place college was," Wentworth's mother would often exclaim, as she shuddered over the dangers a college boy encounters in the pursuit of truth, "I should never have let you leave home."

CHAPTER IV.

Ridete, quidquid est domi cachinnorum."

"I HAVE found a capital dodge for Barney Gumm," remarked Rakeman, two weeks after the beginning of his second term, to his friends who were seated round him at supper, at their club-table. "You know what a bore he is. So yesterday when he called to see me—'Barney,' said I, 'you know how delighted I always am to see you, but you remember how I was bored by Nutkins last term, and I am afraid to let any one in for fear it should be Nutkins. Now, Barnacle, when you call, if you will give three knocks, I shall know it is you, and will at once unlock the door."

"Isn't that a grand dodge? I'm going to tell Nutkins the same story of Barnacle."

"You are a great genius, Rakeman," said Wentworth, "to make the number of your enemies a cause of weakness. Our class is fortunate in having more than one bore. How astonished Gumm and Nutkins will be to find that now they know the countersign it is harder to get into your room, than before you let them into the secret."

"What a picayune 'runt' Lumpy Nutkins is!" the Southron added, as the men pushed back their chairs and tipped them against the walls near the windows. Ayres alone—with the terror of whose name boarding-house keepers are wont to still their children's cries—remained at the table unsatisfied.

The club-table room, where the young fellows were seated, was on the lower floor of one of the corner houses of Winthrop Square. The walls were hung with portraits of the ancestors of the landlady, Mrs. Green, all taken while confined in the stocks, by their country tailors. A large Bible, on which stood an empty card-case, rested on an ancient étagère in a corner.

The claims of art and religion thus satisfied, the rest of the furniture of the room was devoted to utility, and consisted of a large table, and a dozen chairs. Winthrop Square, on which the room fronted, is connected by Brighton Street to Harvard Square, from which it is only a few rods distant. Between the two squares once stood Porter's Tavern, famous in song, and still green in the memory of our dissipated fathers. There in their wild youth they devoured glorious suppers, and drank their good old madeira, singing jolly choruses to the music in the balcony above them. Now, alas! the tavern has passed away, and Irish women screech where students sang. There also now dwells the venerable James, high above the gaping crowd, an ancient merchant, who watches succeeding generations of students, and panders to their passion for peanuts.

Seated here by a window of the club-table room on a summer's noon, one sees playing on the Green a few ragged children from a Hibernian hive near the river. One, mounted on a post, is watching his comrades at leap-frog. Another, with a handful of pebbles, creeps after a courtly cock, who is catering to his cackling crowd of concubines. Hard by, a little Miss Yellowlegs is making pies with her autochthonous sisters, and embellishes the dust with her bright colored rags.

Later one beholds the conscious 'towney' on his evening promenade, with imitative repose and ambitious neck-tie. Him passes with graceful step a resplendent swell, one of Harvard's 'own'—"Elysian beauty, melancholy grace," on his way to the wharves to see the boats go out. If the day favors, the gardens opposite discover pretty misses with coquettish hats, playing croquet, a game of delight to all small-footed, fair-ankled daughters of Eve, but frowned upon by the modest feet and more moral ankles of less favored fair.

Still later, perhaps one hears limping by the groaning hack, filled with Irish ladies returning from a decent burial. As they pass, they wave their handkerchiefs, and address you words of sudden affection.

"Ned, you sly rascal! Stop that winking with your left eye at that girl. Ain't you ashamed of yourself!" cried Rakeman, who had himself been rapping at the window to a pretty serving-maid just coming from the variety shop opposite, with a pound of butter, and a toss of her outraged head. The 'oar' blushed, and Rakeman remained silent a few minutes watching Ayres, who continued to absorb toast with a heartless disregard of the rights of widows.

"Robin," at length inquired Rakeman, "if you were to be allowed to eat only ten pounds of food in one day, how many pounds would you eat in ten days?"

"A hundred of course. Don't ask me such silly questions."

"No Robin. Thirty is the correct answer. You would die of starvation the third day."

"You get off a great many asinine gibes," rejoined the warbler."

"Robin," returned the Southron, "you remind me, by your remark, that had you lived in the days of the Roman Republic, you might have been put to some good use, whereas now you do nothing but confound the calculations of political economists."

"What use do you mean?" asked Ayres, enraged at the interruption.

"You might then, Robin," replied Rakeman, "have served as a medium of exchange." Hamilton and Saulsbury laughed at Rakey's jest, and after a few moments Bowyer. Robin himself did not see the point until a month afterwards, when he came across the name of the Roman coin in recitation. He at once burst into a loud laugh, for which he received a "Private" from his Latin tutor.

"What a capital club-table we have, fellows," remarked Hamilton shortly. "I think we shall have a good influence on the class."

The theme pricked up Ayres' ears, and he paused a moment in his desolating career. "I have heard older men say"—he said hastily—"that if a man belong to a good club-table, he is sure of getting elected into all the Societies." The warbler paid dear for his negligence. Turning back to the table he cast a look of horror at the last plate of toast, escaping under cover of Hebe Bridget.

"My cousin once told me," said Bowyer, "that a man in his class, by controlling his club-table, though that controlled the societies and entire class."

"You, Robin, in that case," said Rakeman, "can easily make yourself autocrat of the class. The societies rule the class. Our club-table will rule the societies, and you with your appetite can easily bring us all to terms. Eh, Ned?"

"Rake," returned the 'oar'—"you're a droll dog. How I should like to see you sweating behind Seaborn in the Harvard: that would take it out of you."

"How I should like to see you on a plantation picking cotton, that would take it out of you, you old left eye winker. But I'm off. Who's going to Sweatrame's private theatricals to-night? They begin at eight."

"And a cruising we will go."

Singing this genial chorus, the jolly son of the South took Bowyer's arm, and the two sauntered off together, followed by the rest of the table.

"Lewis," said Saulsbury to his friend as they were walking toward Harvard Block, "I wish to make a proposition to you, that we learn ten odes of Horace by heart every week, and recite them to each other, keeping an account of our mistakes."

"Bravo, Wentworth, that is the very thing I want to do.

Tutor Rebus told me that no one ought to be considered a Latin scholar, until he at least knew the odes of Horace by heart. I heard of your reciting Horace the other day without a book. That was a very 'swelly' thing to do."

"These recitations cut up a man's time so, that it is hard to study to any purpose. I have a plan that saves the time from being wholly lost. I read over my lesson with a 'pony' before going in, and try to learn the Latin and Greek by heart during recitation."

"Why, Wentworth, do you use a 'pony." '*Equo ne credite Teucri*"—"A pony never does one any good."

"A translation," replied Saulsbury, "is only a condensed dictionary. There is a way some men have of asking the men who recited in earlier divisions, what questions the tutor asked, and looking up the answers to them. That seems to me to be unfair, but I don't see why one should not use means open to all. What right has the Faculty to waste four hours a day of time making me hear the ignorance of my classmates?"

"Well, Wentworth, perhaps you are right, but I should not like to do so myself."

"I am going to develop myself harmoniously this term, Lewis," said Saulsbury. "I remember reading in some book this summer, an idea that struck me as very true. That the harmonious development of body, mind and soul, was the only worthy aim of an intelligent being."

"To be stroke of the Harvard, President of the Christian Brethren, and first scholar, is the practical way of putting it, I suppose," returned Hamilton, laughing. "Have you read much this vacation? I have been reading Browning, Ruskin and Hawthorne. What a wonderful style Hawthorne has. I never read him before."

"I read Macaulay's Essays, and some volumes of Carlyle," replied Saulsbury. "How absurd Carlyle's views seem to an American! He seems to think that the greatness of one man is the degradation of all the rest. By the way, Lewis, are you going to Sweatrame's to-night?"

"No, I was not invited. We are not on very good terms. I should go by all means, if I were you. They will be very good, I have no doubt."

"Well, good bye, old man. If I'm going it's time to go."

Wentworth, with this, took leave of Hamilton, and calling for Rakeman, with him walked to the 'Bakery' where Sweatrame had his rooms.

"We'll all drink stone blind."

This pious song, which the Southron was singing, announced the approach of our hero and his friend, who were at once welcomed by their host. The room into which they entered was filled with chairs, seated in which were several of Wentworth's friends, laughing and talking about men and things. Across one end of the room a curtain was drawn, in front of which was a row of candles to serve as footlights.

"Excuse me, fellows, I must see to something behind the scenes. There's Van beckoning to me," said Sweatrame after seating his guests.

"What are you talking about, Ned, so earnestly?" asked Wentworth of his friend the 'oar.'

"We were talking about the 'Institute,"' Bowyer replied. "I wonder who will be elected among the first ten. They always elect the first scholar, so you're safe old, man."

"Not for that reason I'm afraid, Ned; I wish I were."

"It gives a man a great position in his class, to be chosen among the first ten," added Bowyer. "He becomes a sort of censor. It ruins a man not to be elected into the 'Institute,' and the first ten elect all the rest."

"I remember," said Wentworth, "Ayres told me he had heard it was a bad thing to resist hazing, or to do anything to provoke the upper classes, because it injured one's chances of getting into Societies. I told him I thought it of very trifling importance, compared with keeping one's self respect."

"One doesn't know much about college life, Wentworth, I suppose," said Bowyer, "until he gets into the Societies. Senior and Junior years are much pleasanter on that account."

"I don't know much about college Societies, Ned; I never talked much with the older men about them."

"My cousin tells me, Wentworth, that it is best never to speak about them. It injures a man very much."

"Oh, I'm the rambling rake of poverty."

The Southron stopped singing his ditty. "Are you talking about Societies, Ned?" he said. "I remember when I first came to college, seeing the sign of the Mush-and-

Milk Club—you know what it is: a man's name in white letters on a black strip of cloth—'By Jove!' thinks I, "that's a good idea! I'll paste up my own name in the same way! A Senior told me I had better not do it. That it was the sign of a Society, and it would get me into trouble."

"It would have ruined you, Rakeman, if you had done so."

And a shudder passed over the 'oar,' as he thought of the danger his friend had escaped. "Hallo, the performances are commencing," he added, as the whistle sounded and the curtain rose. The first scene represented the Faculty room, with the President seated alone at the head of a long table. A side door opened, and a student entered, trembling violently.

"Mr. Pidcock Poplett," said the President, naming the most bashful and effeminate boy in the class, whose sex had often been a matter of serious inquiry among his classmates. "Mr. Pidcock Poplett, the Faculty have been informed that your language and conduct toward the college goody who has charge of your rooms, has been grossly improper, and wish me to inform you that for this offence you are suspended from college for one year. If the offence is repeated while you remain in college, the penalty will be expulsion."

Poplett took out a handkerchief, and pressed it to his eyes.

"Cannot—cannot you intercede for me!" he cried in broken accents. "By the beard of St. Anthony, I did not make the first advances."

"I will state what you say," said the President; "but I assure you, I have no influence with the Faculty."

"Oh, it will kill my poor mother!" cried the boy, groping his way out, weeping at every pore.

"I don't think," mused the President, slowly rubbing his shrewd spectacles, "I don't think I have committed myself."

The door again opened, and a student with a leathery countenance entered, and bowed to the President.

"Mr. Norman Lovelock Buggs," said the President. "You have a room in College House."

"Yes sir."

"Mr. Buggs, complaints have been made by several students living in that building, that you have in your room a round tin article of great size, vulgarly known under the name of a hip or hat bath. That you have twice filled this utensil with water, once during the last, and once again during this present term, for the purpose of bathing, to the great annoyance of your fellow students, who have been kept from their studies by the disturbance. The Faculty have therefore voted you a public admonition. If the offence is repeated while you remain in college, the penalty will be suspension."

Buggs' face at first expressed astonishment, which, as the President continued, gave place to deep indignation.

"I never did such a thing," he cried, as the President finished. "I never have done, and I never would do such a thing. Oh, cannot you intercede for me? On the honor of a gentleman"——

"I will state what you say," said the President; "but you know I have no influence with the Faculty."

"Oh, it will kill my poor mother!" cried the boy in agony, and he pressed his handkerchief to his eyes, and went out of the room weeping hysterically.

"I don't think," mused the President, slowly rubbing his shrewd spectacles, "I don't think I have committed myself."

The door again opened, and a student, whose face wore a look of remorse, entered the room.

"Mr. Rumun Venus Weed," said the President, fastening upon the boy a look of the severest displeasure. "Mr. Rumun Venus Weed, the Faculty have received information, which they are forced to believe authentic, that you have on one several occasion liquidated, paid or satisfied a small fraction of a claim purporting to be held against you by one Hill, stable-keeper, in open violation of the laws of the Commonwealth, and the customs of the University."

"I confess," broke in the boy, remorse deepening on his face, "to have once yielded to this criminal weakness. But can I not plead my inexperience—my bitter, bitter repentance? I swear to you"——

"And the Faculty have accordingly voted you a public admonition," continued the relentless President.

"Pity, oh pity my youth!" besought the boy, clasping his hands in supplication.

"Young man," said the President, softening a little,

"the offence though new is rank. The Faculty think an example should be made of you, lest this custom,

> ——'like a new disease, unknown to men,
> Creep, no precaution used, among the crowd.'

I will, however, state what you say, but I regret to say I have no influence with the Faculty."

"Oh it will kill my poor mother!" said the youth, and groped his way from the room, as one stunned by a grief too deep for tears.

"I don't think," mused the President, slowly rubbing his shrewd spectacles, "I don't think I have committed myself."

The next scene represented a college recitation-room, and the personal habits of the different tutors were taken off. The mode in which recalcitrant Prodger lifted his leg, or sneaky Brown glared at the students, and delivered his sentences of death. The last scene discovered the Plummer Professor, reading a paper from the pulpit, in scriptural style, in which the Faculty were seen coming out of the Ark, and each member likened to some animal not of the highest dignity.

Thunders of applause in each case followed the falling of the curtain, and Van, Sweatrame, Ayres, and the other actors were called out, and obliged to make speeches of thanks to their audience. The Faculty song was next sung by Ayres, and a pleasant supper then made its appearance, and the men were soon devouring their oysters, and smoking and chatting in great spirits.

"The Seniors, this term," said Boywer, "had a great fight over their orator. The Mush-and-Milk was very hard pushed by the Anti-Mushes, but they got their orator by one vote."

"Doesn't a class elect its best men to the class offices, without regard to Societies?" asked Wentworth.

"Of course not," said Sweatrame, laughing at the innocence of his guest. "The Mush-and-Milk Club has its candidates, and the scrubs their candidates, and each party tries to elect its own men."

"Last night," Rakeman interrupted the conversation with remarking, "Brandreth came into my room to get me to file off some screws on one side, so that they could not be unscrewed, and about one o'clock called for me to go with him, and hold a candle, while he and Seaborn screwed up Tutor Jones. They had to open Jones' door with an axe this morning, and Brandreth gained a recitation."

"I wonder," remarked Ayres, joining in the conversation, "how Jones can stay in a place where he is so hated. I should think he would leave the college."

"I've heard," said Bowyer, "that one reason why Tutor Rebus is so popular, is that he always says 'you know' so and so, when telling a man anything. Jones always says 'of course' a thing is so and so. Rebus too always calls a man Mr. He is a perfect gentleman, and the most popular teacher in college."

"It seems strange to me," said Van, "that men should be praised so much here for being gentlemen, as if it were such a great thing. I remember father used to say that being a gentleman was like having a pair of legs—nothing to boast of having, though it would be a misfortune to be without them."

"I had almost rather be a law student than a tutor," said Sweatrame.

"There is a strong movement on foot to induce you to become a tutor, Sweatrame," which sally of Wentworth's was received with a laugh by his hearers, since Sweatrame was well known to be engaged in a desperate rivalry with Nutkins for the foot of the class. The competition was terrible, but the odds were in favor of Sweatrame. "Singularly enough," continued Wentworth, "some Sophs had some theatricals night before last in my building, and Seaborn invited me into his room to see them."

"I should think some fellows in that class would act very well," remarked Rakey. "Tell us about them."

"That Brandreth, is a capital actor. In one scene he represented Professor Alchemist. He had a table before him covered with retorts, blow-pipes, and all that sort of thing, and with two bottles of ink on it. Brandreth stood up dressed in black. 'Gentlemen,' he began, 'in my last lecture, I showed you some of the peculiar characteristics of solids. In my present lecture I propose to illustrate some of the singular propensities of liquids. You will observe that I hold in my right hand a piece of white letter paper. If now I dip this paper which I hold in my right hand, into a colorless substance like water, as I now do, you observe that no change takes place in the color of the paper. If, however, I take this bottle of black ink in my left hand, as I now do, and grasping the letter paper firmly in my right hand, dip the paper into the black compound, which I hold in my left hand, the paper becomes immediately of a deep black color. If on the other hand I take this bottle of red ink in my left hand, as I now do, and still grasping the letter paper firmly in my right hand, dip the paper into the red compound which I hold in my left hand, the paper becomes immediately of a deep red color. These experiments afford the most delicate test of the quality of these liquids, and prove that the first compound is an alkali or base, and that the second compound is an acid. The discovery of the wonderful properties of this paper was made in a singular manner.

"'Chemistry was just emerging from its empirical state, and the united aim of chemists of genius was to discover some test for liquids to introduce the element of certainty into chemistry, and raise it to its just position as a science.

"'In the year 1814, in an alabaster room lined with red and blue litmus paper, sat a thin spare man. Who was that thin spare man? That thin spare man was Sir Humphrey Davy! Sir Humphrey Davy, like all great chemists of that period, was endeavoring to discover a test for liquids.

"'Taking a piece of white letter paper in his right hand, he first dipt it into the compound of oxygen and hydrogen, vulgarly known as water. The experiment did not succeed, and no change took place in the color of the paper. Any other man would have despaired. Not so Sir Humphrey Davy. Drinking off a glass of sulphuric acid, Sir Humphrey Davy lit his oxy-hydrogen blow-pipe, which emits a lambent-colored flame, and heated a vessel full of alcohol until it entirely evaporated. Sir Humphrey Davy then dips the letter paper into the residuum of that compound. The experiment does not succeed, and no change takes place in the color of the paper.

"'Any other man would have despaired. Not so Sir Humphrey Davy. Drinking off a glass of nitric acid, Sir Humphrey Davy grasps the paper firmly in his right hand, and taking a bottle of black ink in his left hand, dips the paper into that compound. The experiment succeeds. The paper becomes immediately of a deep black color. Chemistry becomes a science. Imagine the joy of Davy. Sir Humphrey mixes a tumbler of sulphuric, nitric, and muriatic acids, and crying "Eureka!" drains off that compound. Excitement and pleasure combined, throw that great and good man for the first and last time in his life, into a state of beastly intoxication.'"

"Bravo, Wentworth!" cried Rakey, "what a memory you've got! You're a brick made of Richmond clay."

"You Southern and Western men have very humorous expressions," said Wentworth. "Yesterday I called on Gowan—you know him, Van, that bright fellow from Illinois."

"You call on the queerest men, Wentworth. I don't know him."

"Well, *tant pis pour vous*—you ought to know him. He's one of the most talented men in the class. We were talking about his life out West. He said he once 'wrestled' for six months, until one day he struck a rich uncle between wind and water, who fitted him for college.'

"What did he mean by 'wrestling?'" inquired Rakeman.

"He said 'wrestling' was not to be fixed." All society, he explained to me, was divided into three classes: the 'well fixed,' the 'fixed,' and the 'wrestling.' Every one, he said, belongs to one of these three classes. If a man sees a year of a house, food, clothing and coin before him, he is 'well fixed.' If he sees two or three weeks, he is 'fixed.' But if he is not certain of a night's lodging or a day's meals, then he is 'wrestling.' Isn't that humorous?"

"I confess I don't see anything funny in it," said Ayres. "I don't see how you can know such a scrub."

"You will probably see the point, Robin, in the course of a year. I assure you, it may well be the aim of any one of us to be just such a scrub."

"Come, Wentworth, don't be quarrelsome. Ayres, give us a song.

"Ubi sunt oh pocula,"

hummed the tuneful Southron. "Sing us one of those Scotch songs of yours." Ayres returned to his former state of good nature, and sang for half an hour.

"Come round to my room, Wentworth, won't you?" said Van, as the party broke up, and taking Wentworth's arm, he walked with him to Browne's, where he buried him in a luxurious arm-chair. "I wish you had been here night before last, Wentworth," he said. "I had a boxing soirée in my room. You'd have seen a 'set-to' between Ayres, the Canary or Stallion, and Barney Gumm, the Cambridgeport Chicken, who happened to drop in. Rakeman and I got up the match after much persuasion. Each of the men swung his arms around for some minutes like windmills, when by some chance the Canary's bunch of fives lit on the Chicken's peeper. The Chicken's soul was up in arms. Retreating a few yards, he levels his left arm at full length, like a spear in rest, and aiming it well, rides full tilt at the Canary's nob, striking it fair and square and spilling much good claret. By the way, Wentworth, you are getting to be such a 'dig,' that it is injuring my reputation as a 'bird,' to know you; you must reform, old man."

"It seems to be rather against a man here not to be a dunce," said Wentworth, good humoredly.

"Well, Wentworth, you know that except yourself there aren't any good fellows in the first half. Now don't deny it for the sake of seeing what you can say for a bad cause. I feel very 'seedy,' to-night. I went to a 'bat' in Sweatrame's room yesterday, and we smoked and drank till three. It was very slow. Nutkins was there and Sweatrame got him very well 'soaked.' That Nutkins is the most fortunate man in the class. He can get roaring drunk on the best liquor for twelve cents. Such a constitution is a saving of hundreds of dollars a year to a fast man."

"I heard," said Wentworth, "that Sweatrame tumbled out of the window about fifteen feet. I wonder he didn't break his neck."

"You'll find in your Bible somewhere, Wentworth, that God softens the ground for the falling inebriate, or tempers the wind to the shorn lamb, or something of that kind."

"Van, I wish to propose to you," Wentworth shortly remarked, "to carry out with me a plan for physical development. You're one of the best boxers and athletes in the class, and I want you to assist me."

"Well, Wentworth, I suppose I'm fool enough to do what you ask for a little while. I was afraid you wanted me to learn the Iliad by heart."

"You must agree, Van, every other week, to box twice a week, and to take a run or a row or a ride every day. You will soon be in splendid condition."

"You will soon be in heaven or elsewhere, Wentworth. Why, you are making a prize-fighter of me."

"Well, Van, it is better to be a prize-fighter, than such a *blasé* fellow as you are. I've been reading up about training. I'm going to begin myself next Monday and practice it every other week. You get up early in the morning, take a short walk before breakfast, eat a raw beefsteak, and cracked wheat or hominy, then you run or row for a couple of hours, and after resting, drink a glass of sherry with an egg in it."

"Stop, Wentworth!" cried Van; "repeat that about the sherry. You touch me there."

"You dine on beef or mutton, and one potato. In the afternoon you exercise for an hour, take a light tea, and in the evening refresh the mind by reading something not too profound, like the 'Wilkes' Spirit.'"

"You then, Wentworth, I suppose, place a volume of Bancroft's History under your head, and sleep like Rip Van Winkle. There's too much pleasure in the life you describe for a moral man like myself. Can't you have something for a foil at least? You might introduce a treadmill for the time not occupied."

"You'll soon be in splendid form, Van. You know if you take care of yourself you'll be in the Harvard in a year or two."

"Well, Wentworth, madness is catching. I'll try it with you a few weeks. What an odd devil you are. This week you are a 'dig' of 'digs.' Next week you will be sweating like Hercules. I suppose you'll take up a fast line soon, and trifle with the affections of goodies, or have prayer meetings in your room every night. Don't hurry off, old man, it's early yet. Well, '*au revoir.*' I'll see you to-morrow." And Van nodded to Wentworth, who bade his friend good-night, and returned to his room to work on his Horace.

CHAPTER V.

"Largior hic campos æther et lumine vestit
Purpureo."

"VAN, are you going to Mrs. Morris's to-night?" Wentworth asked his friend, a few weeks after their pleasant evening at Sweatrame's room.

"No, I don't know them," replied Van. "Come round to my room when it's over, and I'll have a punch ready for you."

As this was the first large party at which Wentworth had ever been, he thought it well to be punctual. At the hour of eight, therefore, he presented himself at Mrs. Morris's door. Finding no one in the dressing-room, and fearing that he was too late, he pulled on his gloves, and hastened to the drawing-room. His invitation had stated that there were only going to be a few friends. Wentworth had not, however, imagined that these few would be limited to himself alone. Yet, as he entered the drawing-room, this seemed to be the case. Wentworth gazed at the mirrors, the baskets of flowers, and the white cloth stretched across the empty floors, and the shudder which passes over the bravest captain at the sight of the thirsty saw-dust sprinkling over the cleared deck, crept over him. The thought then flashed upon him, that he had come too early. "What!" he exclaimed, "if any one from the upper classes should know that I came before the family were dressed? For heaven's sake let me get out of this place." Wentworth turned and was making for the door, when he was aware of three ladies entering the room, two of them young, and the third about forty, evidently his hostess, Mrs. Morris.

"This is Mr. Saulsbury, is it not?" said the eldest of the ladies, coming forward. "I'm delighted to see you. You have neglected us shamefully this winter. Miss Leigh, let me introduce Mr. Saulsbury to you."

"Will you not take me to a seat, Mr. Saulsbury?" said Miss Leigh, as Wentworth bowed to her. "One gets so tired standing before dancing!" and at this request Wentworth led the girl to the window, as Morris senior, and two or three of his classmates, entered the room. "I have seen you somewhere before, I am sure, Mr. Saulsbury," said Miss Leigh, seating herself on a lounge in a bow window, which looked into the trees and shrubbery which encircled the house. "Oh, I remember, it was at the foot-ball game last autumn."

"I saw a great many stars then," said Wentworth, laughing, as he thought of his personal appearance at that combat.

"You ought not to talk to ladies in that way, Mr. Saulsbury. How horrible those foot-ball games are!

They're almost like prize-fights. I would not have gone to them, if I had known what they were."

"Though persons talk against prize-fighting, they always read the accounts of them with great interest," said Wentworth.

"I confess I do like to hear about such things," said Miss Leigh, "though it is very wicked to say so." It is so pleasant to see persons in earnest about anything now-a-days. The men one meets in society are so frivolous. They do nothing but dance, and talk small talk. Don't you like all physical exercises? I used to row at Newport last summer. I enjoyed it ever so much. I wish girls could go to college, and call round on each other in their rooms, and talk and read. A lady's time is all taken up in making and receiving formal calls. Do you like the Seniors' class song? I heard Mr. Morris singing it at tea. A classmate of yours, a Mr. Sweatrame, was introduced to me the other evening. What a horrible story was told about him! it can't be true—that he was seen at the theatre intoxicated. I don't think society ought to 'cut' a man for being once intoxicated. It might make him desperate. Though I don't see how any woman could ever marry him. Perhaps, after years of repentance"——

"I thought ladies preferred fast men, Miss Leigh. There is so much joy over finding the lost sheep. Rakeman often quotes the saying, 'Reformed rakes make the best husbands.'"

"Your friend must be a very wicked fellow, Mr. Saulsbury. Is he as handsome and clever as you say? I should like to see him very much, though I know I should not like him. What a night this would be for a walk on the beach at Newport. How clearly the stars shine through the trees."

"Do you remember the most beautiful lines in Shakespeare, Miss Leigh?

——'Look how the floor of Heaven
Is thick inlaid with patines of bright gold;
There's not the smalldst"——

"Miss Leigh, may I have the pleasure of the next waltz with you?" broke in an odious voice, and to Wentworth's rage, he saw Seaborn about to carry off his prey.

"Excuse me a moment, Mr. Seaborn. Mr. Saulsbury, I am going to present you to Miss Campbell. I'm a sort of hostess, you know. You'll like her very much. She's very bright. Some persons call her a flirt, but it isn't true."

"I think Mrs. Morris told me that you were a Junior, Mr. Saulsbury," was the first remark Miss Campbell made to Wentworth, which flattered our hero immensely, and at once set him at his ease. "I'm so glad to find that you're not going to dance. My foot was nearly crushed by the gentleman with whom I waltzed last. He scarcely seemed to touch the floor."

"He must be a very graceful dancer, Miss Campbell."

"Graceful is but a faint term to express his skill, I assure you. You have no right to laugh at me. You have no sympathy for suffering, I see."

"Not when it is the cause of so much pleasure to me."

"Men are always so selfish. I shan't be able to dance

before the German. I have often heard Mrs. Morris speak of you. Why didn't you go out this winter? Men who can talk ought to make it a principle to go into society. There are so few men who can do anything but dance. Isn't Miss Leigh charming? She is so full of life. She is a great favorite with both men and women, which is very rare; don't you think so?"

Thus Miss Campbell talked on, and Wentworth listened to her with admiration, careless of the dancers whirling madly past him. Miss Campbell had that power of sympathizing with her hearer, which is so dangerous to the peace of mankind. She asked Wentworth about his favorite authors and pursuits, and flattered his vanity by praising what he himself admired. And soon our hero found himself talking with an earnestness which surprised the reticent New England boy. Miss Campbell had also a bewitching way of raising her eyelids as she spoke, and darting a clear glance from her almond-shaped eyes which impressed the meaning of her words, and the brilliant yet soft beauty of her eyes, with equal force upon her hearer.

The words of a beautiful woman! With what an ecstatic charm do they touch the soul of a boy! Had Mr. A or Mr. B said the same things, their remarks would appear little better than commonplace. But spoken by a beautiful woman, each word as it issues from her lips clothes itself with the beauty of its source. The last illusion to leave the mind of youth, is that a beautiful woman can ever be stupid. I have known college boys even distrust their own talents, sooner than admit this saddest of truths. If such is the power of beautiful stupidity, the effect of Miss Campbell, who was beautiful and by no means stupid, upon the susceptible mind of our Freshman, can be readily imagined. A few of Miss Campbell's sentences seemed more precious to him than all the homilies he remembered to have heard. "I had rather," he thought as he watched the strings of pearls dropping from the kiss-worthy lips of the arch beauty before him—"I had rather hear Miss Campbell for half an hour, than listen to the Reverend Doctor Eider Down week together." And yet the clergyman under whom Wentworth had sat from his youth up, was one of the main pillows of the Church. So insidious is the influence of woman!

The time passed rapidly, and Wentworth was greatly surprised when Miss Campbell's partner for the German came to take her to supper—for which ceremony he had also engaged her—and to end our hero's pleasure for the evening. After supper the chairs were arranged for the dance, and Wentworth took his station among the unwholesome cluster of damp wall-weeds near the door, and addressed now and then a few words to an ancient duenna, who held her seat near him. It is a much greater pleasure to the writer of this history, and doubtless to its readers (if any) to see the enjoyment of others than to engage in it himself. Wentworth, however, had not yet attained to this state of Christian perfection. As he stood among the uneasy throng by the door, though his face still preserved the polite and vacuous expression which society enjoins, beneath the surface were raging the fiercest passions of envy and jealousy.

Much our hero wondered at the audacity of Brandreth or Seaborn as they whirled the fragile compounds of muslin and flesh on their reckless course, now scouring the fender, now shaving with flying skirt some frightened father stranded on the shore. As Miss Leigh, who danced with a grace only girls born at Papantis' can attain, floated swiftly by him, or Miss Campbell's silver feet wove a magic web for the entanglement of the hearts of youth, Wentworth's body hugged the wall, to avoid being swept away by the curling waves of the tempestuous petticoat, but his soul swelled high with rage.

The social position of a Freshman is indeed not enviable. The fair sex, whose opinions are mostly the shadows of the foul, look on a Freshman with that worst of sentiments, pity. They regard him with a sort of motherly affection which, though the holiest of feelings, excites, '*horresco referens*,' nothing but the bitterest ingratitude in the breasts of its objects.

Wentworth had also this evening suffered as he fancied the Olympian superiority of the Senior, which disdains expression, the sedate pride of the Junior, and, hardest to bear, the parvenu conceit of the Sophomore. All these our hero had endured, and enduring, plumed his philosophic pride, trusting in the change revolving time would bring. Suddenly he beheld a sight which caused the room to swim in darkness around him.

There dwelt in the aristocratic village of Longwood, rich

son of a richer father, a youth named Gully Bustin. Twice had the mounting ambition of this young man tempted him to try to enter Harvard College. Twice had he been rejected and relegated to his former ignominious status. Mr. Bustin had rather a good face and figure; but he wore a black lace neck-tie; nor was his family of very ancient origin. All his sins, however, which were many, were forgiven him by the fair, for he danced much and well. As Wentworth surveyed the black cares attached to their brilliant pleasures flitting past him, he caught sight of Master Gully Bustin, of whom he had heard mention, dancing with Miss Campbell, and as much at his ease as a Senior or a prince.

"A sub-Fresh!" he muttered, and the thought that he, Wentworth Saulsbury, member of the University, was idly taking root upon the shore, while a nameless being—a sub-Freshman—was braving it upon the open sea, proved too much for his philosophy. Wentworth swore a terrible oath, which shook all the barbers' poles in the country, that never should razor mow the bristling forest of his chin until he had learnt to dance with grace and ease. "I will make myself the best dancer in college," he resolved, "and waltz once with Miss Campbell. Then I will stand by the door and let all the girls languish for me." Thus resolving, he bowed to the ancient duenna and walked to the supper room.

"How are you, Saulsbury? I'm glad to see that you have brains enough not to dance. Take a glass of wine with me," said Morris, pouring out a glass of Burgundy for our hero, and filling the glasses for the Seniors who were standing round him.

"'Hands to hands, boys, hearts to hearts, boys.'

"We shan't have many more suppers together," he added with a sigh.

"I wish I could exchange places with you, Saulsbury. You have the pleasantest part of your life before you."

Wentworth remained in the supper-room a few minutes, and then, begging Morris to excuse him to his mother, whom he would not disturb, he took his hat and coat, and stole quietly into the free air. Remembering his engagement with Van Courtland, he walked gloomily towards his room at Brown's.

"Oh, the little black bull came down from the mountain!"

sang the well known voice of Rakeman, as Wentworth entered.

"How are you, Wentworth!" cried Van. "I order it up. Make yourself at home, old man. We shall finish our game directly."

Wentworth seated himself and watched Van and Rakeman at play.

"Order up a right bower, Van?" said Rakeman; "you're mad. See, I've euchred you. Come, take your revenge; I'm ten dollars in."

"No more to-night," answered Van. "You know we agreed to stop at half past twelve. I always make it a rule to stop at the time fixed, if I'm a loser. The man who wins can't propose to stop, you know."

"Well, Van, you're a martinet. Mix up the punch, old

man, and be temperate in the use of water. What sort of a time did you have, Wentworth? You look like a poor man who has just become the father of three healthy children. Van says you've been at Mrs. Morris's! Did you see any pretty girls there?"

"There was a Miss Campbell there, Rake, who is a fearfully handsome girl. She has a figure like one of Guido's Hours, and her eyes—do you remember that description in the Arabian Nights? 'God said of her eyes, 'let them be,' and they were, affecting men's hearts with the potency of wine.' "

"Stop," cried Rakeman. "You make me uneasy; you remind me of what has made my life a curse;" and a shadow flitted over the jolly face of the Southerner, for like all men at his time of life, Rakeman had suffered from the fatal effects of the tender passion. "Money won at play," Rakeman continued, surveying his earnings with pride, "I consider consecrated. It should be spent only for sacred objects. The oyster is, I think on the whole, the noblest work of God, and I propose to invite the two club-tables to an oyster supper at my room next Wednesday. Here's to you, fellows! Van, this punch is worthy of your guest;" and Rakeman drained a tumbler of Van's brave punch with a generous relish.

"Van," said Wentworth, "I want to go on a lark. The sight of a sub-Freshman at Mrs. Morris' filled me with disgust. I must have a change of scene. Suppose we go to New York, Friday night. We can get back Monday morning, and only cut one recitation. There are no good tailors in Boston, you know."

"Are you going to take up the line of a swell?" said Van, laughing. "I told you you would come to that soon."

"Another line!" cried Rakeman. "I'll go with you, though. It will be good fun."

"I used to meet a Miss Amy Saulsbury, last winter," said Van; "she was a charming girl, and a great belle."

"She's a cousin of mine. I haven't seen her for three years. We'll make her give us a certificate that we have attended church while we're there. But I must be off, old man. It's nearly two o'clock."

"So must I," said Rakeman. "Good night, fellows;" and Wentworth and Rakeman took a last glass of punch, and made their way to their rooms, leaving Van to retire to his peaceful couch.

CHAPTER VI.

"Hermes omnia solus, et ter unus."

"I WONDER what makes me feel so fearfully blue," remarked our hero late one Summer's night, throwing himself back in his easy-chair, and looking at the pleasant stretch of country on either side the azure Charles. It was the last day of Wentworth's second term in college, and he had just returned from a supper, given by him to his club-table, at Parker's. The windows were open, and he listened a few minutes to the delicate noises that tickled the ear of Night—the voice of the frog the organist, the cricket with his merry fiddle, and the love-sick tree-toad, without experiencing great relief. "I can't think what makes me so out of spirits," he repeated, with an effort to shake off his despondency. "What a good song Rakeman sang to-night.

'Ye brothers, when I'm no more drinking,'

"Let me think of something pleasant. What a jolly time we had in New York, and what a pretty girl Cousin Amy has grown to be!" and Wentworth's mind recurred to a scene he well remembered. A bright graceful girl, with inviting lips, was standing opposite him. "Don't you know, Wentworth, it is improper to hold a lady's hand so long? See, you have bruised it, you're so strong," and the girl leant nearer our hero, to show him the mischief already done. "Why, Wentworth," she exclaimed, darting back,—"How dare you! We are too old for such ceremonies. You Bostonians are all barbarians. Be sure and come to see me to-morrow, and I'll try and reform you, though I've little hope!"—and the girl blushed, and shook her head reprovingly at her cousin, as he took his leave. This reminiscence lessened Wentworth's gloom, and he looked around his room in better spirits.

"How attached you become to your room, after living in it a year," he mused, gazing at his books and pictures with the kindly eye of possession.

The room justified some degree of pleasure. Its original furniture had long since disappeared, and had given place to heavy oaken tables, lounges, and easy-chairs. A large carved book-case stood against the wall, on each side of the entrance, filled with rare editions of books, richly bound. The side of the room opposite the door, was nearly covered with a huge photograph of the Roman Forum, flanked by a bronze statue of the Venus de Milo, and a dying gladiator of the same metal. Engravings of no little value, were hung thickly around the walls, with two or three landscape paintings by American artists. Among these as foils shone opposite the mantel, a proof copy of Müller's Madonna di San Sisto.

Wentworth surveyed his treasures a few minutes with relief, but could not keep his mind from recurring to his life during the past term, the thought of which, though he would not confess it, weighed upon his conscience. During the first two months of the term, indeed, our hero had carried out his plans of study, and exercise, with great regularity, one week reciting his Horace with Hamilton, and studying far into the night, and the next rowing, sparring, and running with Van and Bowyer.

Toward the end of the second month, however, Wentworth had taken up a third line—that of a swell. This character required him to give, and attend pleasant dinners and suppers, at his own or his friends' rooms, at hotels in breezy Boston, at Point Shirley, or whatever place promised good cheer. It also made him intimate with a great many fashionable tailors in town, upon whom he levied for all varieties of cloth—and color to hit the changing hour and season.

Our hero's literary tastes made him also a great connoisseur in large paper copies, white vellum, and the secrets of the book trade, and in the selection of fine engravings, and the like, the results of which soon enlivened the stern simplicity of his room.

This third line, moreover, obliged him to attend the different places of amusement, the theatres or operas, which the capital offered, and to learn to distinguish between the stars that shone, or the voices that warbled from time to time upon their stages. In fact all the pleasures which it becomes a man of the world to seek and enjoy, Wentworth had plunged into with the hearty recklessness of youth.

"*Dum vivimus, vivamus,*" was a quotation at that time often upon his lips. His erudition had discovered this saying, and the knowledge of Latin one gains at college enabled him to quote it with great accuracy. It soon, however, proved so much pleasanter to ride than to run, to dine than to fast, and to dress like a bird of paradise, than in the shirt and pantaloons of a training man, and to do any of these things than to learn Latin odes by heart, that Wentworth's third line soon swallowed up the other two.

These various pursuits, though developing doubtless the harmonious man, took away greatly from Wentworth's rank, which fell from near the head of the class, towards the foot of the first half. They also, as a shrewd observer might readily guess, cost a great deal of coin or credit. Wentworth's allowance was a thousand dollars a term, which was large for a college-boy in America. His father was known, moreover, to be one of the wealthiest men in the State, and Wentworth found little difficulty in obtaining credit. His name adorned many pages of the books of the confiding stable-keepers of Cambridge and Boston. It might also have been discovered by the curious in numerous tailors' interesting unpublished MSS., and was well known to hotel-keepers, tobacconists, wine merchants, "*et id genus omne.*"

To be deeply in debt is a great advantage to a young man in any profession in life. It causes—one can readily see—a large circle of men to take a deeper interest in your life and prosperity, than can be secured by any other course. It is difficult for a college-boy, however, to see and act upon this truth. Wentworth, instead of growing more cheerful as the term wore on, and his debts increased, became haunted with gloomy fits, which he in vain endeavored to throw off, by increased dissipation. In spite of these, however, his loss of rank and open-handed generosity, had made him a great favorite in his class, and he had, with Van, Bowyer, Rakeman, Sweatrame, and five others, been chosen as the first ten of the Institute of 1770, the great ambition of the Freshman year.

The last few days of the term, Wentworth had felt unusually despondent. Though he tried to forget his misspent months, the retrospect was continually forcing itself upon him. As he sat in his room this last evening of the term, the contrast of what he had done, with what he had hoped to do, of his idle waste of time and talents, with his high ambition, and proud aims—"Don't think of it," he said to himself—"Regret but doubles evil. No one can say I have not enjoyed myself. Pleasure at least is a reality. Hang it! I keep thinking of Hamilton to-night. I wonder whether he has got back from Philadelphia. I hope his father is better. Somehow I don't feel as though I knew Lewis as well as I used to. These religious fellows never can be friends of men of the world. Hallo! what's this? A letter from father, and one from Hamilton!" he exclaimed, catching sight of two letters on the table.

"My dear son," began the letter which Wentworth first opened—"You will regret to learn, as I to write, that owing to the crisis from which the country is suffering, I have been obliged to greatly curtail my expenses. My property, as you know, consists mostly of manufacturing stocks. These have paid no dividends during the past six months, and it is impossible to tell how soon they will recommence. I can easily allow you $500 for your next year at college, without injury to your mother and sister. If you can live on that sum, you may make arrangements to return to Cambridge next year. Otherwise, you must wait till our affairs look up a little. Your mother sends her love to you.

"Your affectionate father,

"HENRY L. SAULSBURY."

"Heugh!" cried Wentworth, "'*fuit Ilium.*' What next!" and he opened the other letter—

"My dear Wentworth," it began, "I returned to Cambridge to-day. Father died three days ago, after a great deal of pain. It was found on his death that business anxiety had caused his sickness, and that nearly all his property had been lost by the panic. Enough has been saved to enable mother to live comfortably, but I shall be obliged to leave college. My uncle has offered me a place in his store in Philadelphia, as a clerk, which I have accepted. I called to see you twice this evening, but did not find you in. Will you not do me the favor to sell my books and furniture and send the money to my address at Philadelphia, as I wish to start for home early to-morrow morning. I hoped to win a name here, but it has been ordered otherwise. You, my dear friend, will, I am sure, use the golden opportunity, the loss of which fills me with so much regret. Promise to write me often, and believe me,

"Always your sincere friend,

"LEWIS HAMILTON."

"Poor Lewis!" cried Wentworth. "Clerk! the devil! Why doesn't his uncle keep him in college!" and our hero jumped from his seat, seized his hat, and ran toward Harvard Block.

"Why, Wentworth! I'm delighted to see you!" said Lewis, opening the door at his vigorous knocking. "I was afraid I should not see you again for a long time."

"What's this, Lewis, about your going away?" Wentworth broke out with.

"Don't talk about it, Wentworth. It cuts me very much. I have learnt to love the dear old place," and Lewis turned aside from his friend, like all boys ashamed to show feeling. The young fellow looked thin and worn with watching, and the loss of his father had told upon him sadly. "You can't think, Wentworth," he said shortly, with his old pleasant voice weakened somewhat by exhaustion, "how much I thank you for coming round to-night. Sit down and we'll have one of our old talks again. It seems an age since we used to talk together so earnestly, so many things have happened," and a sharp look of painful memories passed over Lewis's face which sent a sudden pang to Wentworth's heart. "But we won't speak of those things," he added softly, "It is of you I want to speak,

Wentworth ; promise me, my dear friend, that you will be true to yourself, and strive to follow the paths your ambition points out, and accomplish the good we so often talked about. I feel that I am taking a great liberty with you, Wentworth. But you know I love you, and I shall not see you again for a long time, I fear."

"Liberty! Lewis? You could not take any liberty with me," said Wentworth, much affected. "It is my fault if any cloud has come between us."

"I don't so much mind it in other men, Wentworth, but you are at heart so full of fine impulses and high aims, that it wounds me to see you waste the talents God has given you for the noblest uses. I only beg you, as you are generous to every one else, to be at least just to yourself."

Wentworth looked down a few minutes in silence.

"Believe me, Lewis, I feel what you say deeply, and thank you kindly for it, and shall always remember it. I may as well," he added with a smile, "make a virtue of necessity. Father writes me that all his property is worthless at present, so I have nothing to do but work."

"Nay, Wentworth, what you do will be prompted by your own honor, not by circumstance, I am sure of that. I am sorry to hear what you say. I never knew the value of money, until I saw my education cut off for the want of it."

"Why do you leave college, Lewis?"

"It can't be helped, Wentworth. Mother begged me to take her money, but of course I couldn't do that. I asked my uncle to lend me some, but he said he would sooner teach a boy to sweep a store, than to go to college. Don't say any more about it, my dear fellow. I must leave."

"But, Lewis, you shan't leave!" cried Wentworth, jumping from his seat. "As for that uncle of yours, I'd cut his tongue out if I had the power, and set him, for the rest of his life, to grinding a hand-organ! Such men are worse than cut-throats—I beg your pardon, old man, I don't mean to say anything disrespectful of your relatives."

"It is hard to take such a comparison as a compliment, Wentworth," said Lewis laughing, "but I'll do my best. Don't say anything more about my leaving. Talk of"—

"But I tell you!" exclaimed our hero, "that you shan't leave. What, are you going to sacrifice your hopes and your future for the sake of a few paltry dollars?"

"Wentworth, you know it can't be helped. Don't talk about it."

"But it can be helped, Lewis. Next year you shall chum with me. Father will allow me five hundred dollars, and I can borrow more, if necessary. We'll take a cheap room somewhere, and board ourselves. We can get scholarships too, you know, next year."

"You are too generous, Wentworth," and Lewis again turned away his head. "I always knew that you had a great soul. If your father had not met with this loss! But now I cannot for a moment think of it except to thank you with all my heart."

"But I say you shall think of it, Lewis. Talk about my wasting my talents! You, who are every way my superior, do you propose to sacrifice your past and future to a paltry pride? If you educate yourself you can make yourself a name, and what you prize more, become a power to advance the cause of truth."

"Stop! stop! Wentworth! Don't talk in that way. You almost persuade me to act dishonorably."

"Dishonorably, Lewis? What do you mean? To refuse to accept a favor from a friend, seems to me to be dishonorable. It shows you distrust him."

"You don't mean that, Wentworth," said Lewis, looking him earnestly in the face.

"Yes, I do mean it, Lewis. Are there no laws of honor, except those of the market? Friendship has its laws as well as commerce. Had you offered me the same thing I should have accepted it, and not nursed a mean pride, at the expense of my friendship. You are not so good a friend to me as I thought you, Lewis."

"Wentworth, you know I am your friend. Would you on your honor have accepted such a favor from me?"

"On my honor, as a gentleman, Lewis."

"And should you not respect me less?"

"I should never offer to do anything for a friend which could lessen my respect for him."

"Wentworth, I will do as you ask me; I feel too grateful to thank you."

"Bravo, Lewis!" cried his friend in great delight. "If you're such a stickler, you can pay me some day—yes, by Jove! with interest—usurious—ten per cent., do you hear?

You know we Yankees are such mean fellows !" and Wentworth fairly hugged his friend in delight.

"Wentworth, you've nearly broken my ribs, you villain. I feel as if I had a new lease of life. How mad uncle will be. Hurrah, old man !" and Hamilton began, to his own surprise, to sing "Old Harvard."

The boys smoked and talked an hour or more, when Wentworth took his leave.

"I shall make something of myself, Lewis, if I have you with me," he said to his friend, as he bade him farewell.

Wentworth was soon sound asleep, but Lewis opened his Bible and a long hour read its sacred pages ; then giving thanks for the new hope this night had brought forth, he said his prayers and went to bed.

The next morning, Wentworth sent invitations to his various creditors, inviting them to call and see him. They came with praiseworthy alacrity, and expressed the most sincere sympathy for the misfortunes of his father. Wentworth proposed that such of his property as remained in its original form, should be returned to its former owners, and said he thought he could pay the balance of the claims in the course of a year or more. This proposal greatly pleased the venders of books, engravings, furniture, and articles of a tangible character. But grief arose in Mr. Gorbold, stable-keeper in breezy Boston, and his heart within his hairy breast was troubled with doubt as to this method of resurrection for his property. The spirit of revolt spread to Mr. Funkhauser, tobacconist, and Mr. Cabus, wine merchant, and others who were unable to see the benefit which would accrue to them from this arrangement.

Wentworth reasoned fairly with them all, and explained his inability to pay them, which he greatly regretted, and most of them took leave of him with friendly feeling. Mr. Gorbold, and three or four others, however, remained after the respectable throng of creditors had gone, and urged their claims somewhat loudly upon Wentworth's attention.

Our hero's strength could have been guessed only by a shrewd observer, and the more angry he became, the more quiet grew his manner. As Mr. Gorbold's voice waxed loud, and almost insolent, Wentworth gently whispered to him.

"My good fellow, I never allow any one to raise his voice in my room."

"You don't, don't you?" shouted Mr. Gorbold, who was a thick burly fellow of great strength, and with this he seated himself in Wentworth's best easy-chair. "I'm not going to leave this room until I'm paid," he added, with a coarse laugh. "I won't be ch"—— The rest of Mr. Gorbold's remark was lost to the world, for no very soft hand closed the channel of his words, and the next moment he was grasped by the collar, and making the best of his unwilling way towards the door. The stalwart stable-keeper and his friends were, however, no cowards, and at once prepared to attack our hero. And now great deeds had been achieved, with which all college had rung, when the door was flung open, and Seaborn entered the room, with

Brandreth and another Soph, who happened to be in Seaborn's room.

"If there's any fighting going on here, you will count us in," said Seaborn, and the young Herculean "oar" placed his hands in his pockets, while Brandreth leaned against the wall, with a happy smile playing round his mouth.

The rebels, cowed by the arrival of these allies, muttered a few threats and left the room. The Sophs laughed over Wentworth's account of the affair, and after a short conversation, also took their leave. Wentworth then seated himself, and indited the following epistle to his father:

"DEAR FATHER:

> 'Quanto quisque sibi plura negaverit
> Ab dis plura feret.'

"I am very sorry to learn what you write on account of your and mother's sake. I hope, however, that the crisis will soon be over, and that you will then be freed from your trouble and anxiety. Do not feel any uneasiness about my education. The sum you mention is more than sufficient. I should have spent a year in college to little profit, if I had not learnt to endure the changes of circumstance philosophically. The older I grow the more I see the real worthlessness to a scholar of more than enough money to support life. A college at least should be a place where learning alone is sought for, and prized, and a student's money should be his ideas. More than this tends to draw his mind from his studies, to which, I regret to say, my course this term is a witness. Truth, you know, loves to dwell in an empty stomach, and the Muses always attack this barbarous world without bag or baggage.

"Next year I shall live after the fashion of the scholars of those good old times, which you so often praise,

> ——'When illustrious men,
> Lovers of truth, by penury constrained,
> Bucer, Erasmus, or Melancthon, read
> Before the doors and windows of their cells
> By moonshine, through mere lack of taper light.'

" 'My room,' I shall then write you, 'is naked and studious; my ragged coat is open to every breath of truth; books are my main food, the fountain of Castalia my wine; for the rest, a cup of pure water and an ear of Indian corn suffice.

> ——'Me pascunt olivæ
> Me cichorea, levesque malvæ.'

"With my best love to mother and Mary, believe me,

"Your affectionate son,

"WENTWORTH.

"*Henry L. Saulsbury, Esq.*"

CHAPTER VII.

"Continuo auditæ voces vagitus et ingens
Infantumque animæ flentes in limine primo,"

THE examination has been terrible, terrible! All men say it has been twice as hard this year, as ever before. Did you get through your Latin Grammar paper? I feel awfully anxious about that. I am safe in Roman History, thank Heaven, I only made one mistake; I thought the Gracchi were one of the Gallic tribes conquered by Cæsar. How did you do in mathematics?"

"Oh, I did everything on that paper. Mathematics, you know, is my strong point. A man who sat next me did not know the answer to a single question. I showed him how to draw a tangent. A tutor glared savagely at me afterwards. I hope he did not report me. But the Greek digamma: I feel all in a perspiration about that. The examination has been terrible, terrible!"

Thus, a few minutes before three o'clock, one day in July, clad in their rustic garments, Masters Solomon Digge, and Solon Grynde, two candidates for admission to Harvard, held high debate, as arm in arm they walked through the college yard.

"Who are those men?" whispered Digge, nudging Grynde, as they approached a substantial-looking old gentlemen, conversing earnestly with one of two boys, standing beside him.

"That is Bob May, a man of our class," returned Grynde; "one of the older men is his father. I don't know the other."

"Are not you Master Digge, and Master Grynde?" asked Saulsbury, the third of the trio, stepping forward as the candidates approached him, and handing them each a printed paper. "I have been ordered by the Faculty," he added, "to summon you to attend a private examination, at three o'clock, in No. 1 Holworthy. That is the room," and with the air of one used to command, Wentworth waved the frightened boys towards the building, and turned to continue his conversation with the old gentleman near him.

"I was not aware that there were two examinations," said Mr. May, père, looking at his son with paternal solicitude.

"It was not so formerly," replied Wentworth, "but it is now customary when, at the public examination, a candidate does not show sufficient proficiency in his studies to allow the Faculty to admit him, but gives so much promise as to make them reluctant to reject him, to grant him a second examination in private, where he will be less embarrassed."

"Certainly a very wise provision, sir, a very wise provision," said the old gentleman, moving his head solemnly up and down, and taking from his pocket a large handkerchief to hide his agitation.

"The appearance of your son," continued Wentworth, looking flatteringly at the blushing face of Master May, "makes me confident that he will find no difficulty in passing this second examination satisfactorily."

"Thank you, sir, thank you with all my heart; you reassure me!" and the old gentleman returned his fluttering handkerchief to its nest, and grasped Wentworth warmly by the hand: then taking his arm, Mr. May bade his son follow them, and the three walked towards Holworthy.

"One cannot," remarked Wentworth, as they drew near the building, "one cannot over-estimate the advantage to your son of becoming a member of Harvard College. Not only will he thereby become master of all ancient and modern languages, sciences, and arts; not only will society of the highest fashion and fortune at once open their doors to welcome him: but he will secure for himself the sure means of future preferment and honor, in any profession he may choose to follow."

"It gives me profound pleasure, sir, profound pleasure," rejoined the old gentleman, pausing to survey the architectural splendor around him," to see our young men, sir, our young men, on whom the hopes of the country rest, appreciate the advantages of the present day, advantages which it was our misfortune to be without. The thought fills me with pride and hope for our country's future, our country's glorious future," and the old gentleman again shook Wentworth warmly by the hand, at which our hero cast his eyes modestly down, and continued his discourse until they reached the door.

"I regret," he then said to Mr. May, "that the rules of the Faculty forbid any friends of the candidates being present at their examination. They fear least their friends should naturally be tempted to give them some assistance, if in difficulty over a Latin or Greek sentence."

"Quite right, sir, quite right! so we should, so we should!" and the old gentleman, who had had but a year's schooling in his life, felt highly flattered by the precaution. Then again shaking hands with our hero, Mr. May turned and walked up and down among the trees of the college yard, feeling the awfulness of the crisis.

Wentworth and Master May, however, passed into the room, where they found a number of persons collected. At its further end were placed two tables, at which several boys, among them Masters Digge and Grynde, were seated hard at work over their examination papers. Pacing up and down before the table were four men, whose sour visages argued them proctors or tutors of the college. The corner of the room, to the right, thronged with venerable scholars, whose long white beards added much to their imposing presence. Two of them, bent with years and wisdom, were buried in huge tomes, from which it required some skill to distinguish them; the rest were debating, with earnestness, problems of great profundity.

Wentworth and Master May, as they passed by, caught the broken expressions—"the connection between the Arrowhead and Choctaw languages at first sight is vague"—"yesterday I dug up a very nutritious Shemitic root"—"my recent researches in Sanscrit literature"—"a minute comparison of all written languages will prove"—"in my late edition of Confucius"—"in committing to memory the body of Greek and Latin poetry, care must be taken"—and other indices of deep discourse.

Master May would have lingered, but Wentworth hurried him to his seat, at the further table, and bending over him whispered in his ear, "My young friend, if you have any dates or mathematical formulæ written down on your nails or shirt cuffs, I recommend you to use them with care, as the officers here are very sharp-sighted."

"I assure you, sir, I should consider such conduct beneath me," returned Master May, blushing deeply.

"If you do not use them with care," urged Wentworth, "you will certainly be found out."

"I mean, sir," replied the boy, blushing more deeply, "that I should think it wicked to use them at all."

"Oh! to be sure," answered Wentworth, kindly laying his hand on the boy's head. "I misunderstood you. Your words and feeling certainly do you credit. Though such arts are often practised here, I think myself that they are very wrong:" and with this Wentworth placed his examination papers before the boy, and left him to his work.

Master May took up his first paper, entitled "Ancient and Modern History," and with growing earnestness, read among others the following questions.

"Trace the connection between the Eleusinian Mysteries, the Destruction of Jerusalem, and the Holy Alliance."

"What inferences do you draw as to the cultivation and use of tobacco among the Greeks, from the prayer of Ajax for a light? What information is derived from ancient coins upon this subject?"

"Show how the expression A No. 1, sprang from the death of Ajax."

"What, if any, was the difference between the ear of Dionysius and the ear of Dionysus?"

"What, if any, is the difference between Jacobins and Jacobites?"

"What relation was Hecuba to Hamlet?"

"Describe the religious ceremonies of the Mohawks, Cyprians, Pantagruelists, Bohemians, Alsatians, and Brobdignagians."

"Was the conduct of Rhea, in giving Saturn a stone when he asked for his child, Christian? What is the allusion to this in holy writ?"

"Why was Hannibal called Barker? Prove from this the custom of the Romans to libel their enemies. Show the connection between the words Hannibal and cannibal. What deductions do you draw from this similarity, as to the carnivorous habits of the Carthaginians? What light is thrown upon your inquiry by the sacred page—' your fathers did eat man-na in the wilderness,' etc. ?"

"Show by historical instances, the advantages of employing negro troops in night attacks."

"Which of the three Horatii was the famous poet? Give the peculiar turn of the foot by which he tript up the third of the Curiatii. How did this give the name to the Horatian metre?"

"Show how the murder of the sons of Ægyptus has given rise to the modern movements for women's rights."

Master May with a sigh laid down his first paper, and taking up a second, entitled Latin and Greek Grammar, began to read.

"Trace the derivation of the name Hellenes, from Helen of Troy. Show the relation of both these words to the Latin word heluo, and the English word hellian. From the identity of the roots of the two words, prove the existence of an Indo-Germanic family."

"Translate and scan the following lines—

Ligo gallina Tartarus cur
Fœnum
Corvus glandarius altus apis illo."

"Show the derivation of the expression lynx-eyed, from Lynceus."

At this point Master May's attention was attracted towards his classmate Grynde, who, hurrying past him, stopped one of the tutors and exclaimed—

"Is there not some mistake here? Is it possible that

my mathematical paper was unsatisfactory? Mathematics, you know, is my strong point. My old teacher, Whaleham, calls me the mathematical phenomenon. I answered all the questions in ten minutes, and I feel sure that the answers were correct."

"Your answers were correct, sir," replied the tutor, eying the boy with pitiless scorn, "suspiciously correct. Do you remember what was said before the examination about copying from your neighbor's paper? Go to your seat at once, sir!—to your seat!"

Master Grynde recalled his more than Samaritan kindness to the boy who sat next him, in the matter of the tangent, and now, to be himself accused of copying, and from such a paper, it was too much! In silence he returned to his seat, and twining the fingers of one hand deep into the folds of his hair, with the other took up his paper, and with growing earnestness read, among others, the following questions.

"Explain by mathematical formulæ the origin of the Gulf Stream. State what you think of the feasibility of deflecting it from England in case of war, and of leaving that country out in the cold."

"Give the formula by which God prevented the world from moving in a spiral curve. Had such been its course, what would have been the probable effect on modern poetry?"

"Work out the problem called a 'pig's tail in a firkin of butter.' Compare this with 'a cow's foot in a cup of milk.' Illustrate your answer by means of two sticks."

"When is it excusable in an eccentric point to cut an obtuse angle?"

"A man wishing to buy a horse, concludes to draw the money from his creditors. He, however, looks the horse in the mouth and finds that it lacks two front teeth. How many creditors had he, and what was the amount of his debt to each?"

"How does the absence of angles in nature afford the strongest arguments for skepticism?"

"What, if any, is the difference between a monad and a nomad?"

"Calculate the number of throws from a dice-box containing all the words in Shakespeare before they would arrange themselves as at present in his works. State the period of life at which it would be well to begin in order to prove this experimentally."

"Show how, by utilizing the minus quantity, the plough can be made to draw the oxen, the ship to steer the rudder, the mill-wheel to move the water, and the corn to grind the mill."

"Write out the formula by which the world was produced from nothing. Illustrate this by the resemblance of the figure naught to an egg, and the maxim '*omnia ab ovo!*'"

When Master Grynde had finished reading this paper, he groaned in spirit.

"Surely," he exclaimed, madly seizing a pencil, "the little finger of this examination is thicker than the loins of the former. What will old Whaleham say if I am conditioned in mathematics?" and although almost a college boy, Master Grynde seemed to feel the familiar whack of Whaleham's ruler.

During the next half hour, there was no further interruption to the examination. The boys with lengthening countenances bent over their tasks: the sour tutors paced to and fro before them: the learned professors devoured their books, or engaged each other in earnest debate. At short intervals each of the college officers passed through a side door to refresh his mind by a consultation with some work of reference.

After a short half hour, Wentworth was attracted by various noises, and finally, by the gently whispered word "Mister," towards Master Digge, near whom he was seated. Glancing up, he saw the boy looking imploringly at him, and asked him what he wanted.

"Will not the Faculty, sir," begged the boy humbly, "allow me the use of a dictionary for a few minutes? There are two or three words here, which I have never met in all my reading. 'Long nine,' I suppose is *longum novem,* and 'brandy smash,' *concursus vinarius,* but for 'bosh,' and 'gaffer,' I can't think of any corresponding words in Latin."

Wentworth kindly looked over Master Digge's paper, which contained the following paragraph to be rendered into classical Latin.

"The great god Bosh, having wined with gaffer Buncom, and dined on the American peacock, smoked a long nine, drank a brandy smash, and said 'a small piece of soap makes a great many bubbles.'"

"It is not usual," said Wentworth, after reading the sentence, "but since you have translated the rest of the exercise so well, and the words are rare in Latin, I will endeavor to obtain the favor from Professor Horace." Our hero thereupon walked to a grave scholar, buried in his book, and urged his request. The professor at first shook his head solemnly, and taking up a copy of the college laws, pointed out one of them to Wentworth. Our hero, however, persevered with word and gesture; the professor's head moved slower and slower, and at length began to nod up and down. At this Wentworth hurried with his prize to Master Digge, the anxious witness of his efforts.

"Thank you, sir, thank you," whispered the boy, "I shall never forget your kindness."

"They are very strict here," remarked Wentworth, as he passed the book to the boy. "I had myself to pass ten private examinations, before I was admitted. But you must make haste: you have only a few minutes more to write."

Wentworth had scarcely returned to his seat, when Professor Horace rapped on a table, and informed the candidates that they had but five minutes more to complete their work.

Then indeed more sharply heads were scratched, more swiftly pencils flew over the paper, and the whole building rocked to and fro with the movement of the students' brains.

Again the fatal mallet was heard. "The time is up," proclaimed the professor. "Mr. Brown, will you and your Freshman collect the answers?"

"Cannot you allow me five minutes more?" begged Master Grynde, as the tutor demanded his papers. "I am just finishing my last question—four minutes, I implore you—one minute—oh Whaleham!—one word—my mother! oh!"

"It is impossible! Justice requires the Faculty to be impartial," replied the inexorable tutor, as he gathered up the papers.

These all collected, Professor Horace told the boys that they might now go, and bade them, as before directed, to call at the President's room at five o'clock to learn whether they had been successful.

At this announcement, the anxious candidates hurried from the door, Master Prym to join his father, the rest to hover about the Green, awaiting from the President their summons to honor or disgrace.

Scarcely had the boys left the room, when a strange metamorphosis took ptace. Peals of laughter shook the walls: dictionaries, wigs, spectacles, and beards flew about the room like things of life, as grim professors and frowning tutors were transformed into jolly students.

"This has been a most glorious sell!" cried Van, who was no other than Professor Horace.

"Look at all these answers!" exclaimed Rakeman, who but a moment ago was Brown, the most savage of tutors.

At this every one eagerly claimed his share, and Rakeman divided among his friends the choice spoils, of which many are preserved as college transmittenda to this day.

"Come, fellows, we may be caught. That Pym, I think, was a little suspicious," suggested Ayres, leading his friends into one of the back rooms. There all refreshed themselves with one more reference to an exhilarating library; they then climbed from the window, and spread the glory of their class far and wide throughout the college.

CHAPTER VIII.

> "Sit mihi mensa tripes et
> Concha salis puri et toga quæ defendere frigus
> Quamvis crassa queat."

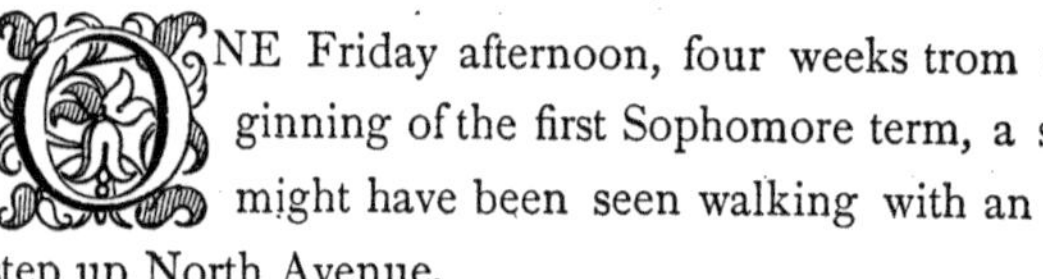

NE Friday afternoon, four weeks trom the beginning of the first Sophomore term, a student might have been seen walking with an elastic step up North Avenue.

His coat, which was threadbare, and of a color to blind the analytic eye of science, was closely buttoned around his neck, a veteran hat, with many scars in front and not a few behind, covered his head, while a pair of boots which might well boast their ancient birth, adorned his feet.

The right hand of the lad carried a bag, in which lay half a dozen eggs, and from his left hung a basket containing a blue-fish, a pound of butter, and a dozen pears. Wentworth, for the boy was no other than our hero, nodded pleasantly to a few of his classmates whom he met, and was turning the corner of the college-yard, when he was aware of three carriages, filled with ladies and gentlemen, driving past him. Suddenly one of the ladies leaned forward and made Wentworth a bow. "Miss Campbell!"

he exclaimed half audibly, and raised his hand to his hat, at which motion the bag followed the great law of gravitation, and by an ill-fated marriage, six eggs became one. The carriage drove on, and for a moment our hero stood watching it disappear. The smile he had worn gave place to Plutonian gloom. "To be seen by Miss Campbell in this plight!" he muttered, as he slowly walked along Kirkland Street, revolving many memories. "Confound it, I would rather have been shot! She'll know, now, why I didn't accept her invitation to her party to-night."

Arrived at the lane on which Divinity Hall fronts, Wentworth turned down it, and soon reached his room, which was on the lower floor of that gloomy building.

This bore but little resemblance in size or circumstance to his former apartment. It was about sixteen feet square, and had on one side an alcove and a small closet.

The alcove was filled with an iron bedstead, projecting from beneath which the mouth of a hat-bath preached the virtue which is next to godliness. A sofa bedstead stood on the opposite side of the room, and in the centre was a pine table, around which were a few wooden chairs. The floor was bare and unpainted. Near the fire-place, surmounted by a tin kettle, was a gas stove, next which stood a cupboard, which boasted six plates, the same number of cups and saucers, two tin cans marked tea and coffee, a salt cellar, a French coffee-pot, a pewter cobler-shaker, and an immense cavernous crock, standing like an after-dinner alderman among starving apprentices. A few of Wentworth's books, which had not been stolen from him by his creditors, rested in an old book-rack, and hanging opposite the fire-place was his engraving of the Madonna, which, like an eye, lit up the entire room. Underneath this Wentworth had burnt with a poker the words,

> . . . . "reliquias Danaum atque inmitis Achilli."

The wall opposite also discovered the aphorism,

> . . . . "Multa petentibus
> Desunt multa : bene est cui Deus obtulit
> Parca, quod satis est, manu."

While before the door, the visitor, on entering, caught sight of the stirring couplet,

> "Aude, hospes, contemnere opes, et te quoque dignum
> Finge deo ; rebusque veni non asper egenis."

Other shadowy maxims were placed at hand around the room, as sops for the intellect to throw to the hungry stomach.

The old building of which our hero's room formed a part, may itself well repay a moment's glance from the profane or pious reader. The Hall was built at a time when funereal gloom was deemed essential for the perfect development of the Christian character. Its situation, however, is in one of the pleasantest parts of Cambridge.

Before it then stretched a green, unbroken except by a snake-pen, the only omen by which the forecasting mind could have predicted the birth of the immortal Museum. Now a foot or leg of this child of the great foreigner's brain has projected itself into sight, and the fossils there heaped together reflect comparative liveliness upon the Divinity School opposite. North of the Hall creeps a lazy brook this side a grove, in which lie hid the houses of fair-daughtered professors. Behind, stands the janitor's house, and a pump which justly grumbles from overwork, while beyond these rise Norton's Woods, the Unitarian Dodona.

Within this old rookery small rooms open into dreary entries. There pace the mild-eyed melancholy Divinity students, who can be heard by the curious at all hours of the day and night rehearsing their prayers, and exhorting each other with fervor.

This spot Wentworth and Lewis had, after long deliberation, chosen as their most secure retreat from the world. Here they lived, cooking their own meals, and devoting themselves to study, in monastic seclusion. Wentworth's allowance, as soon as it arrived, was divided into three equal parts, one to be used for the purchase of luxuries, one of comforts, and one of necessaries. Every morning the baker left a dozen rolls, and the milkman a quart of milk at their door, and on alternate days each boy ordered and prepared dinner for himself and his chum. The rest of their time, except an hour for exercise, was given to study and a generous rivalry for the first place in the class.

Besides their regular lessons they had marked out for themselves a course of English literature, and had enlarged their old custom of learning Latin verses by the addition of fifty lines a day from the best English prose and poetry. Most of their class, and the entire outer world, that they might pursue their studies without interruption, were banished from their room. The exceptions to this general proscription were the members of their old club-table, Van

Courtland, and Hayward, a friend of Hamilton, and a "thinker," who were given the countersign of four knocks. These few friends, however, kept them well informed of the great events of college life. Van unfolded to them the splendor of the world of fashion; Ayres rehearsed to them what the warbling world poured forth; Bowyer gave them the news of the progress of muscular Christianity, that Seaborn's arm had gained a quarter of an inch, or that Brandreth had lost an eighth around the chest; while Hayward instructed them in the new truths discovered by himself, Gowan, and other college thinkers.

The social position of neither of the boys was injured, and their characters were much improved by their new mode of life. Poverty, though it crushes the weak, strengthens the strong. If a man grapple bravely with the subtle enemy, and bear himself with the same dignity and pride in adversity which he has shown in prosperity, he loses in but a slight degree the respect of the world, and gains a self-respect independent of circumstance. Wentworth and Lewis soon found that they had more time to themselves, were in better health, worked harder, and on the whole enjoyed themselves more than ever before. They loved, indeed, to compare themselves to Jerome in his cave or Socrates with his annual cloak, and boasted thorough knowledge of the secret passes of Bohemia, its caves, and fastnesses, and the "pure serene" of its rocky summits. They were, however, only wandering among the pleasant valleys and sloping hills on the confines of that Alpine region. Bohemia proper! far beyond them shine its blue mountain tops, clad with the hue of enchantment which distance lends—far beyond them yawn its hungry ravines, and precipitous steeps inaccessible to less than heroes.

Wentworth on entering his room found Lewis seated at the table, reading a volume of Mr. Grote's interesting history.

"Lewis," asks our hero with a hollow voice, "Lewis, how much money is there in the bag?" Hamilton, as the more economical of the two, had charge of the finances of the partnership.

"Twelve dollars, old boy; you remember we gave ten to that poor devil up stairs."

"How long will it be before we have any more?"

"One week; your allowance came just a week ago."

"Lewis," continues our hero, "I want you to let me have ten dollars and never to ask me what I did with it."

"What shall we do next week?" asks Hamilton in a tone of anxiety.

"We will 'wrestle,'" replies our hero.

Lewis, without further words, handed his pocket-book to Wentworth, who took from it two five dollar bills and returned it.

"You have a recitation at five, have you not, Wentworth?"

"Yes, but I must go into town—*au revoir,*" and Saulsbury ran from his room to the horse-cars, and was soon in breezy Boston. There he hurried to a florist's, ordered a basket of tea-roses to be sent to Miss Campbell's that evening, and returned to Cambridge, relieved in mind and pocket.

Wentworth reached his room a few minutes after six, and found that his chum had already set the table, and was engaged in frying the blue-fish, the savory odor of which saluted his nostrils as he entered the door.

"You know, Wentworth," said Lewis, as they sat down to dinner, "that you invited Van Courtland to breakfast next Sunday, and we have only two dollars in the bag."

"Did you never, Lewis," returned the former, "read the story of Elijah and his ravens? I feel in my bones that there is food in the air, which will be given us in due season. Why do you look so solemn? You resemble a Greek, who, after a life of labor, has amassed not a single obol, and rejected of Charon is forced to flit about the banks of the nine-fold Styx.

"I was thinking, Wentworth, that that breed of ravens had died out. The 'twa corbies' are the ravens one sees now-a-days."

"They shan't theek their nest with a lock from your *caput*, old boy," said Wentworth, looking kindly at his friend's bright face. "I could myself, in this dress, turn an honest penny as a scarecrow. How far have you read in Grote?" he added, as they cleared away the table to begin their evening's work.

"I am just finishing the eighth volume. What a glorious history it is, is it not? How well it refutes the attacks of Mitford and other conservative writers on the Athenian democracy. Athens did more for humanity in one century, than the rest of the world has done since its creation. The Athenian mind seems to flash across the past, "as the lightning" that "cometh out of the east, and shineth even unto the west."

"What a noble exhibition of power it is, Lewis," said his chum, "to see a man like Grote or Gibbon become the Autocrat of the centuries of which they write by a title no one can contest. I am still in my third volume of Macaulay. His history, I think, is much inferior to his essays. He seems in that to have no eye for perspective, and to be innocent of so much as a suspicion of a first principle. I learnt something out of Sir Thomas Browne to-day, which I want you to hear me recite—'I cannot contemn a man for ignorance, but behold him with as much pity as I do Lazarus. It is no greater charity to clothe his body than apparel the nakedness of his soul,' etc."

"I have got something from Fuller—on memory," said Lewis after hearing his chum. "'Overburden not thy memory, to make so faithful a servant a slave,' etc."

After finishing their prose, the boys recited their verse, Wentworth having learnt a piece from Otway,

> "I'm thinking, Pierre, how that damn'd starving quality
> Call'd honesty, got footing in the world," etc.

and Lewis reciting Chaucer's Clerk,

> "A Clerk ther was of Oxenforde also,
> That unto logike hadde long ygo," etc.

"It almost makes a man a critic, to learn pieces from the finest authors," said Lewis on finishing. "The mind so abhors to commit anything to memory, which is not written with art."

"The only way in which you can appreciate the style of an author, is to learn passages from him by heart; style is such a subtle essence,"—added Wentworth, and the two boys then settled down to their regular studies, one reading Terence, and the other Demosthenes, until eleven, when they went to bed.

The next Sunday morning, Lewis, on looking into the cupboard, saw there, to his great surprise, the elements for breakfast.

"Why Wentworth!" he exclaimed, "where did you get all these things?" and a suspicion seizing him, he ran to the closet. "You wretch, what have you done with your best, I may almost say your only suit of clothes?"

"The articles of dress to which you allude, Lewis," replied Wentworth, with proper gravity, "are at present in the possession of a gentleman of the Jewish persuasion, who is engaged in an extensive woolen business. They are, to speak properly, pledged, pawned, hypothecated, soaked, or waiting to be lifted."

"'Lifted!' Wentworth, what do you mean?"

"Since your question, Lewis, proves you to know nothing of political economy, I will begin at the beginning. When a Bohemian wishes to seize a favorable opportunity for investment in a dinner, a ride, a wife, or a novel, and lacks the ready money, the banker whom he patronizes not infrequently allows him to give certain securities of value, before making the desired loan. The banker has of course perfect confidence in the Bohemian, but the Bohemian does not wish the banker's other patrons to be offended by an exception in his own case. A coat, a dozen shirts, a handkerchief, or a paper collar, thus frequently find themselves in the possession of the banker, as a greater or less loan is forced upon the Bohemian. When the latter's ships have arrived, or the rents from his houses are due, and he is eager to repay the loan, the process by which the above securities are returned by the banker to the Bohemian, is technically termed 'lifting,' the coat, or collar, or what-not. Don't look so grave, old boy. Nothing is lost in this world; matter merely undergoes a change. That coat warmed me once from the outside; now transformed by the wand of commerce, it will warm us both more pleasantly from within, '*Ecce signum*,'" and Wentworth takes up two tender chickens by the legs, and gazes lovingly at them. "We are no Chattertons, Lewis. We die hard."

"What would your mother say, Wentworth," asked Lewis somewhat shocked, "if she saw you with a hole in your elbow, 'soaking' your last coat?"

"'Oh, it would kill my poor mother, Lewis.' But we must give Van a good breakfast. Besides, clothes are really the badge of our fall. It is a sin to spend money on anything but innocent pleasures, food, wine, or tobacco. Van is a devilish good fellow, too. The other day he offered to let me have five hundred dollars for as long a time as I wished; but I told him I was not going to get any more in debt. There arn't many men who would do that sort of thing."

"He must be a good fellow," said Hamilton, "but I could never get on with him. He is so fast, and talks in such a skeptical way about everything."

"He likes you very well, Lewis," insinuated his chum, "and has often praised you to men who spoke of you as a dig."

"Come in," shouted our hero an hour later, as he heard four knocks at the door. "Welcome!" he cried to Van, who entered the room, "welcome, thou descendant of royal ancestors, to our more than Sabine fare.

'Victum infelicem, baccas lapidosaque corna
Dant rami, et vulsis pascunt radicibus herbæ.'

It will do you good, though, old boy, to fast for once in your life. The first time one goes without a breakfast from necessity, he feels the genial glow of a new sensation. Thenceforth he surveys the world, from a new point of view, and with a more kindly sympathy. The first love, the first act of consciousness, the first doubt, the first dress, however rude, each of these opens to us a new facet of the world. But more than all these, not to be able to procure a breakfast places you at the very centre of humanity, and enables you to see from within, all sides of many sided life."

"Take him off! take him off!" Van calls to Hamilton, "he's mad, or has written a paper for the Institute, or both. Wentworth, you lazy dog," he adds, "you cut prayers to-day."

"That's true, Van, but how did you learn it?"

"In a way you could never guess. I was there myself."

"Breakfast is served," announces Lewis, placing two straws in Van's tumbler.

"By Jove, fellows! that's the best sherry cobbler I ever drank!" exclaims Van, drawing the nectar through the pipes. "Hamilton, you ought to take a little wine for your stomach's sake."

"Lewis is an odd fish. He has sworn off drinking while he is in college," Wentworth answers for his chum.

"That smacks of atheism," returns Van; "St. Paul is explicit on that point."

"You know more and act less Scripture, I suppose, Van, than any man in college," remarked Wentworth, pouring out for him a cup of coffee.

Van made no answer, but, with a twinkle in his eye, surveyed the table, which had been arranged with skill. In the centre, filled with divine chicken pie, towered the earthen crock, the stomach's arsenal, in which one could hear Plenty winding her merry horn. A bottle of Crosse and Blackwell's pickles stood on Wentworth's left, second to the crock alone in dignity, but second at a vast distance, as Ajax the Less paled before Ajax Telamon. Flanking the pickles were a jar of orange-marmalade, a pot of Yarmouth bloaters, and a dish of devilled kidneys. A coffee-pot, with a bottle of sherry, and two of Bordeaux, stood on the opposite side of the table; while on what had been formerly a hat-box, but was now a side-table, shone bunches of Hamburgh grapes, tempters of the lips.

"Van," asked Wentworth, helping him to some kidneys, "do you see anything peculiar about that crock?"

"I don't know what your ideas of peculiar may be, Wentworth," replied Van; "for myself, I have seen the Mammoth Cave, the Coliseum, and the crater of Vesuvius, but for vastness, for profundity, for grandeur, I don't think I ever saw anything that quite comes up to that crock. Why, old boy, if you were to transport that crock on the Great Eastern to Italy, two millions of lazzaroni would fall down and worship it. It would be canonized shortly, and have masses said to it. What delicious kidneys these are! How did you do them so nicely?"

"Van," answered Wentworth, a look of humor passing over his, and Lewis's face, "in the matter of kidneys, nothing is unknown to us. As your remark implies, there are kidneys and kidneys, and thereby hangs a tale. The doctrine of total depravity one never thoroughly believes until he purchases kidneys. A week ago I called at the butcher's, and ordered him to send me half a dozen lamb-kidneys for dinner. 'I have no lamb-kidneys to-day,' the butcher replied, 'but I have an article,' he added obligingly, which I think will suit you much better. I have just received some very fine ox or bull-kidneys, which are in every respect superior to lamb-kidneys. They are much larger, cheaper, and more nourishing, and are preferred altogether by the boarding-house keepers of the vicinity."

At six o'clock, Lewis returned from recitation, and found dinner already served. Chief of dishes stood in the centre of the table an immense, brown, fragrant kidney, sizzling and stirring, as if eager to leap the barrier of your teeth. Lewis and I were famishing, and as soon as he was seated, I seized a knife to divide our beloved kidney into two equal parts. Van, you know I am a strong man, for I have often punished you severely. The knife had just been sharpened. 'Lewis,' said I, after a few minutes' effort, 'Lewis, to confess the truth, I have dined to-day, and feel no appetite: you may have the kidney entire."

Van laughed heartily at the dolorous tale of the bull-kidney, as Wentworth heaped a plate for him with pie from the wealthy crock.

"Rather an odd thing happened here yesterday, Van," the latter remarked, as he passed the plate to his guest. "I was seated in my room reading, when down rushed a theolog, named Gandy Stubs, and nearly broke open the door. 'What do you want?' I yelled at him in great rage. 'Come quick,' he cried, 'brother Sallows has a fit. I heard him groaning in his room, and I can't get in. I'm afraid he's dying.' I opened the door, and in a few minutes we had a ladder against Sallow's window, and I was climbing up it, when Gandy twitched my coat. 'I forgot to tell you,' he whispered hesitatingly, 'I looked through the key-hole—you may not like to go into the room—he is stark naked.' 'Naked!' cried I; 'in these costly times, would we were all naked!' At this Stubs fainted dead away, and I ran up the ladder into Sallow's room."

"What was the matter with Sallows?" asked Van.

"Oh he only had a fit caused by over-discipline. The doctor came in a few minutes, and brought him to. By the way, Van, wouldn't you like to attend a spiritualists' meeting? Lewis and I have discovered that we are mediums."

"Hamilton may have some affinity with a better world," answered Van, "but I should hate to place much confidence in the spirits you would summon, Wentworth."

"This levity, Van," returned our hero with dignity, "is suited neither to the person nor the subject. If you will call here to-morrow in the broad daylight, we'll prove to you that there's no humbug about the matter. We hold a *séance* with one or two spirits almost every day at about twelve o'clock. Last Thursday we had four or five rapping together, and it seemed as though all Heaven had broke loose. I have learnt to distinguish them very readily now. 'Ah,' I say, as I hear a sullen knock like the kick of a horse, 'that's brother Reynhold's spirit. It has come to instruct us touching the prices of tilburies and high-stepping steeds in our Freshman year. 'That,' I exclaim as a dapper little rat-a-tap follows, 'that's brother Scissors' spirit. It can tell us about garments of price and the fashions of the good old times.' One can learn a great deal from the spirits; but it is all about the past; it is a mistake to suppose that they ever prophesy."

"More than all the other vices which I see in the world," said Van, "that love of money which drives men to seek the payment of the debts due them fills me with sadness. This is the great bar which prevents the free interchange of property, and brings about that stagnation in business, which political economists hold to be the *summum malum.* An American gentleman especially should never, by base payments, pander to that love of gain which has made our name a reproach among the nations."

"One would scarcely, without experience," mused Wentworth, "believe the extent to which the morals of the ignorant classes have been undermined by this vice. With most men it is more than a vice; it amounts to a confirmed passion, like drinking or gaming. Creditors have been known to interrupt one's study of the true, the beautiful, and the good, to urge their ill-timed claims."

. . . . "Quid non mortalia pectora cogis,
Auri sacra fames?"

cried Van, aghast with horror. "It is lucky, old boy," he added recovering his self-possession, "that you are not living a hundred years ago. Then the lower classes of society, tradesmen, creditors, and the like, could clap a scholar into prison to gratify their mean envy. Those infamous laws almost strangled literature for hundreds of years; I don't see how it survived them. However, I suppose Hamilton will tell us, the blood of the martyrs is the seed of the church."

"After all, Van," said our hero, who was a generous fellow, and like Uncle Toby could not hate even the Devil with proper fervor, "creditors serve certain useful purposes. They are no snobs, and cling to you in adversity even more closely than in prosperity. As they do this from self-interest, you have the cheerful feeling so long as they seek your society, that your affairs cannot be desperate. While there is a creditor, there is hope. How truly wretched the life of a debtor abandoned by all his creditors. Yet even then a religious man might strengthen his faith by thinking of debts which he could never hope to pay. 'If a material hat, or the vulgar matter of a pair of trousers,' he could reflect, 'can by the holy touch of credit be spiritualized into an immortal claim, surely there must be more than hope for the human soul.'"

"I am afraid, Wentworth," said Lewis, "if you jest about sacred subjects in that way, your immortality will not be a happy one."

"I have a plan for you, Wentworth," suggested Van. "Why don't you adopt a Rothschild or an Astor for your father. Yet, on the whole, I would advise you not to do it. Why should you be charitable? It doesn't pay. Let them die in their poverty. Next to an Alexander who has all things, the richest man is a Diogenes who wants nothing."

"'Next to rooming in Holworthy, it is best to room in Divinity Hall,' I suppose a college-man would put it, Van. Let me help you to some more pie."

"Not for the world, old boy; I haven't eaten so much for years; even Ayres would swell with envy."

The table was then cleared for dessert; after which the boys filled their cups afresh with coffee, and lighted their cigars.

"Your old teacher, Whaleham, examined us in Trigonometry Friday," remarked Van, as, cocking his heels upon the window-sill, he aimed to unite comfort with grace. "What a muscular Christian he is!"

"I should like to have seen my dear preceptor, Van," mused Wentworth. "I can remember, as though it were yesterday, the years I spent at his school. Just one week after I entered, Whaleham came running down into the room of our usher, dragging after him a little beggar, whom he had thrashed nearly to death. He made the boy tell his story to us, and then asked, 'Who believes that boy's story?' We all pitied the little devil, and stood up in assent. Whaleham's face at once assumed the expression of a baffled tom-cat. He raved, howled and tore himself for five minutes, and then yelled, 'Who believes that boy's story now?' No one rose except me. The gentle Ascham glared around savagely a minute, then pointed at me a finger of scorn, and hissed out, 'Henceforth that boy's word can never be believed.' He had spoken, and from that moment until I left school, he never ceased on all occasions to revile me like a pickpocket."

"I thought you stood at the head of your class," said Lewis."

"So I did generally, and that provoked him more than anything else. It obliged him to somewhat limit his abuse to my character, when it would have been so much more gratifying sarcasm to call me a fool. 'I confess, Saulsbury, you are not so great a dunce,' he would complain bitterly, 'as I once thought you, but your moral turpitude grows blacker and blacker.' Urging one day the advantage to a boy of standing well with his teacher, he spoke of an old scholar of his, who had committed a forgery, but who had been pardoned by the injured persons, on account of his good character at school. I well remember the prophetic manner in which he eyed me during the narrative, as one sure to commit the crime, but against whose punishment no such bar could be interposed. He used, in his leisure moments, to amuse the class with drawing pictures of my future career, and my probable mode of ending it, which were much more graphic than flattering. A gallows I came to look upon as my only means of gaining a higher sphere; though in the flood of youthful spirits, I at times indulged the fond hope of dying quietly in a prison or the work-house. Once at least every day, Whaleham used to start from his seat, make the letter V with his two fore-fingers, and poke it towards me. 'Saulsbury,' he then shouts, 'which horn do you take?' 'What is the dilemma?' I inquire humbly. 'Acknowledge yourself to be either a boor or a knave.' 'I should prefer to take neither horn.' 'Then take a thrashing,' he shrieks. 'In that alternative,' I answer meekly, 'the attractions of each epithet seem so equally balanced, I will willingly allow you the choice.' 'Choose,' he thunders, gnashing his teeth, and shaking his shaggy mane. 'If I must choose myself, I prefer the former horn; no, the latter; no, on the whole I will take the former.' With each doubt, Whaleham advances a step, brandishing a huge ruler: at my decision, he throws the ruler on the table, shakes the building with a pacific frown, gives a contented grunt, and takes his seat victorious."

"What made the fellow dislike you so?" asked Van.

"I never knew till one day, a short time before I left the school, he gave me a sudden look of hatred, and said, 'that boy prides himself on being a gentleman; who doesn't think he is the worst boy in the class?'"

"What did they say?" asked Van, who looked on Wentworth as too moral a man to live long.

"They all agreed with him, every one of them, and I have never cared to speak to any of them since."

"I don't wonder. It must have been hard for a gentleman to breathe in such a den."

"I remember, Van, I used regularly every night to pray God to strike Whaleham dead in his bed. Yet the next morning there he was, seated at his desk unblushingly alive. It made me a skeptic for some years, to find my prayers unanswered."

"You like to make yourself out as bad as possible," said Lewis, looking at our hero with generous admiration. "Have you heard, Van Courtland, what Wentworth did the other night? Sweatrame invited him to meet a party of men to organize a scheme for hazing. Wentworth went to the meeting and told the fellows that as he had thought it low in any one to attempt to haze him, when he was a Freshman, so he thought it would be now equally low in him to attempt to haze any one else. He came near having a row with Sweatrame."

"I heard something about it from the other side," replied Van, "Sweatrame is in our club-table, you know. Still, I don't more than half like him; I don't see why they elected him among the first ten. You must each of you, now I think of it, promise me a piece for my paper next Friday. I have as yet nothing but some verses from Ayres, and an essay by Bowyer on the Athenian trireme."

"How does Ayres write?" asked Wentworth, "He is such a good-natured, pleasant fellow. Last term I remember the only question which seemed to give him any great concern was the relative social position of your and our club-tables. 'Though Van Courtland's table,' he used to repeat daily, 'may stand better with fast men, yet, if you were to take the opinion of the whole class, I think it would be greatly in favor of our own.'"

"His verses draw a different character for himself—a proud, reckless, blighted heart—a man who has drained the cup of pleasure and found it wormwood, and all that sort of thing. By the way, Wentworth, don't you want to go on an adventure some night with Brandreth and myself? We are running an opposition to the Med. Fac., and have hired a house behind Hill's stable, where we keep our lanterns, tools, and dresses. The situation is capital. You can reach the house through the street, or through the stable, which is open all night, or through the churchyard lane. You must go with us some time, old boy; it is really exciting."

"There's nothing I should like better, Van; do count me in, please, on your next expedition."

As Wentworth finished speaking, the second bell for morning service began to ring, at which the three boys strolled over to the chapel, and were soon fast asleep.

CHAPTER IX.

"Noris nos," inquit; "docti sumus."

HE blossoming of the Freshman worm into the Sophomoric butterfly is a beautiful spectacle. The Freshman is too near the base world, not to be somewhat tainted by its traditions.

The Sophomore! what happened to him before he entered college floats behind him as vague as the antenuptial dreams of our parents, that hover about our infancy. Memory, shod with seven league boots, can scarcely reach that distant time.

This great change finds its best opportunity to prove itself in the "Institute of 1770."

The members of this Society, as in all clubs in Harvard, literary or otherwise, except the Φ. B. K., are chosen on account of their social qualities, and number about half the class.

Class feeling receives a severe blow from this division, and the two factions view each other with a repugnance which deepens into hostility in the Junior and Senior years.

The Friday following the breakfast given to Van, Wentworth and Lewis took tea with their friend, and shortly after sauntered with him into the "Institute" rooms. There they found a large audience, and Hayward at the desk in the middle of an oration, the first exercise of the evening after the secretary's report. The subject of the oration, Bowyer whispered to Wentworth, was "The Man," and Hayward was pronouncing himself with earnestness against the masses, and asserting that all truth, all power, all good, sprang from the individual.

Rounds of applause interrupted the course of the oration, and at its conclusion Rakeman, who was President, announced as Editor of the evening Mr. Schuyler Van Courtland.

Van rose amid a great clapping of hands, and opened his paper. His first piece, which, at the risk of tediousness, we shall quote at length, was entitled—

"THE COLLEGE PUMP."

"A few days since," it began, "I was returning somewhat late from Boston, to my room in Hollis Hall. My friends, with whom I had been having a very pleasant evening at Parker's familiar rendezvous, had preferred to remain there during the night, so that I was alone. There was a turbulent fellow in the horse-car with me, who made a great disturbance, and two or three respectable old gentlemen cried 'Put him out.' This seemed to sober him down, for I looked carefully all about the car, but could not find who it was.

"On reaching Cambridge, I passed through the gate

by the old President's house into the college yard, and strolled towards Hollis. Everything around me seemed to be under some mysterious influence. The sky was wide awake, and winking in the most knowing manner with its thousand eyes. I couldn't make out at what, till I saw the moon reeling half soaked out of a cloud. The old elms in the yard swayed this way and that, and some of them followed me as though I were an Orpheus. Their leaves were coquetting with the wind, and now shadowed, now disclosed troops of golden-haired elves, who displayed pairs of very pretty ankles, as they danced over the tops of the grass. They looked for all the world like dandelions, and their shrill voices you could hardly distinguish from cicadæ. Even old University Building stood uneasily on his stout legs, and leaned toward Holworthy, the youngest of the Dormitories, with as soft a glance as can kindle in the eye of hoary granite. He longed, no doubt, to clasp his manly arm around her buxom waist and cut pigeon wings with her over the quiet town.

"Suddenly I heard a noise overheard, and looking up, beheld flying through the air, the long line of college Goodies, headed by the Regina, each bestriding a besom. You would scarcely have believed they were not a flock of geese flying one behind the other, but I recognized the voice of my old goody Lovedust, and knew the careless swing of her broom. They were steering northward, doubtless towards the witches' Mecca, Salem, there to perform their hellish rites. I thought I saw a Freshman in the claws of the Regina, and shuddered at his fate," [immense applause with hand and heel,] "but that may have been mere fancy.

"I had now reached the pump, and feeling thirsty, put my lips to its mouth, and took a long drink. As I turned to go away, I felt a cold hand seize me by the collar. My blood froze, my knees knocked together, and looking at the pump, I was horror-stricken to see how like a human being it had become. It bore a startling resemblance to the portrait of my great grandfather, who lost an arm at Bunker Hill.

"'Unhand me, sir!' said I at length, mustering courage, and I was about to strike him, but his venerable appearance checked my blow. Soon he dropped his arm, but held me spell-bound by his glassy eye. Then a deep voice, which nearly frightened my ears off, issued from him.

"'My friend,' he said, 'I have been warned by many unlucky omens that my end is drawing near, and wish to leave behind me some memorial of a long and eventful life.'

"'You are blue, old boy,' said I with affected cheerfulness, 'and no wonder, you are such a confirmed water drinker. If you will only take a glass of some more generous liquid, you'll grow more hopeful.'

"The old gentleman shook his head despondently, and looking at him more closely, I saw that he bore the marks of violence. The top of his head was laid bare, as by a scalping-knife, and every little while he seemed convulsed with pain.

" 'My friend,' he continued, after a short pause, straightening himself up by a great effort, 'it may be the idle presentiment of age, but I dare not indulge such a belief. Your bright eye, and firm step, proclaim you a Sophomore,' [renewed applause,] 'and you may possibly preserve my life a few years longer.' 'Believe me,' interposed I, placing my hand on my heart, for I was touched by his confidence, 'anything which I can do to oblige a gentleman holding so useful, though ancillary a position in society'— 'I will tell you my history, that you may plead in my behalf,' returned the pump with a chaste smile of gratitude.

" 'I was born on Waverley Hills, and can but just remember the pleasant time of my youth. It was passed in innocence, and the quiet pleasures of a country life. I knew nothing of the world then, and could not have told a Sophomore from a Freshman,' [exclamations of horror,] 'and of Latin and Greek, I had not even heard the names. Yet I was very happy in those days, and can still recall the songs the larks used to sing me in the mornings. I thought them very fine then, though of course they were nothing to your Glee Club—but I grow garrulous.

" 'One day I was stunned by a heavy blow, and when I awoke from my swoon, found myself stript of my bark and leaves, and with only one of my branches left. Looking around me, I saw several large brick buildings, and a stretch of green shaded with trees, under which were hurrying to and fro, a number of men in long black dresses. Presently a strange object, something like a woman, placed a pail before me, and seizing my branch, moved it up and down. I felt a sudden stirring in my bowels, and then first learnt that I had become a pump. After a few days I caught from the men who came to drink from me, that I was a member of Harvard College, and in a few months I knew all about the place, and became a very fair scholar. At first I had but little time to study: they were just finishing that large white building yonder, and I had to work hard to give the 'hands' water. It was very painful for me I remember, even then, to water plebeians, for I have always had a student's pride, and hate and avoid the vulgar.

" 'Kirkland was President of the college when I entered, and a very good President he was, too. Though a learned man, he was even more distinguished for his wit and genial humor, than for his scholarship. I remember him distinctly, and all the men of his day. There was Frisbie, who first taught me Horace: poor fellow! he could scarcely see to read, and used to recite me the odes from memory. Farrar was professor then, and such a wonderful mathematician I have never met since. Before he took a drink, he used always to calculate, from the last rain, the exact number of strokes required to bring up the water. One of the best men I have ever known was Henry Ware, who took a friendly interest in me, from the moment I entered college. He woke in me a sense of my reponsibility as a moral agent, and ever since his first draught I have pumped from purer motives than before. Hedge was another professor to whom I have always felt greatly indebted, through for different reasons. When he first introduced himself to me, he asked me solemnly, 'What is a pump? or rather, a pump is what? This question gave me a strange sensation, as though I had taken an emetic, and first taught me to look below the surface of things. I owe to Professor Hedge, more than to any other man, my critical knowledge of myself, and the rest of the Universe. But Popkins, of all the professors of that time, was my most intimate friend. He used to drink from me regularly, two or three times a day. 'It is so refreshing,' he would exclaim, 'after my long nine!' Poor old Pop! what pleasant chats we have had together! If what I hear some students say now-a-days is true, that men who smoke here, burn hereafter, how I wish I could give you a long drink from my spout now.

"'After some years, Kirkland resigned his place, and a new President was elected over us, named Quincy. He was not so clever or social as Kirkland, but he was a very brisk man, and secured a new handle for me in his reign. By-and-by Quincy also went away, and Everett ruled in his stead. When he first came for a drink he frightened me by his manner, it was so grand. Shortly afterwards, however, I had a new trough made, and Everett delivered the oration on the occasion, in which he compared me to Arethusa. I always respected him highly after that, though we were never familiar.

"'I could tell you a great deal more about the officers and students of those old days—stories which would interest you very much—if I had time. Men late at night, have often made me their confidant, and leaning upon me in the most friendly way, have whispered in my ear secrets about Boston, and the sights one sees in that great capital.

Only the other day Toughnut and Bird—they are Sophomores, you know—came reeling up to me, and told me of many strange adventures with which they had met. Toughnut then, in the coolest manner, sat down in my trough, and asked Bird to pump on him. I gave him a good drenching, you can wager my handle; for I am a pump of humor; and often when strapping Sophomores come for a drink, I make them sweat a long time: but tender little Freshmen, I give them a drink at once;' [tremendous applause,] 'for I pity the poor boys, so far away from their mothers;' [heels and hands, and cries of "Good!" "Good!"] 'Then their breath smells so sweet, and not like college men's. Why, when Toughnut takes a drink, he leaves a fiery taste in my mouth which makes my head grow dizzy, and my arm move up and down, like one of our public speakers. I have witnessed a great many wild scenes in college, and if I chose to let the Faculty know—but a pump is more honorable than men when alive, and never tells tales.'

"The old gentleman here gave a gurgling sound so like a death rattle that I was seized with fear, lest he should die suddenly and I should be hanged for his murder.

"'Do not be alarmed,' he soon reassumed me by saying, 'that was a hawk, nothing more. We pumps are peculiarly subject to colds; it comes from our wet feet and long throats. I have still some hours to live; but I must finish my history. Two nights ago I was awakened by some students out of a sound sleep, and looking up saw a brilliant colored light in the centre of the yard, which made the trees and buildings look all golden. I heard a man near me say that '5— had set off a Bengal light, and that the Sophomore class was now acknowledged by every one to be the greatest class that had ever been at Harvard College.

" 'I had never seen anything so beautiful before, and was enjoying it greatly, when suddenly I heard a terrible noise, and felt something burst within me. The same moment I fainted dead away from pain and fear. When I recovered consciousness, I found that the top of my head had been blown off, and that my arm was nearly paralyzed. I have also received severe internal wounds from which I have little hope of recovery.

" 'I do not wish to say anything to the Faculty, but will not you, who are a Sophomore, tell your class the story of my life and implore them not to treat me in this cruel manner. One more such blow would be hopelessly fatal. Since I first came to college, I have never done or said anything to injure the students, and my highest pleasure has been to give them water with which to duck wicked tutors. I do not deserve such a return; it breaks my heart; ingratitude more potent than gunpowder is wasting me away.'

"The venerable sufferer here became so affected that he could do nothing but sigh and groan.

" 'My dear friend,' said I, 'your words command my deepest sympathy. I respect you; I will defend you; I will beg—nay I will command the class of '5—never again to injure you, but always to hold you in the highest honor.' My voice here choked with emotion, and I rested my head on the old man's shoulder. At this he gave a sharp cry of pain.

"'Pardon me,' he added, 'but I suffer from an attack of acute rheumatism under my arm, brought on by my exposure.'

"'My truest friend,' sobbed I, still more deeply moved, 'your wrongs wring my very heart of heart. I love you; I will die for you; whoever seeks again to harm you, must pass over my lifeless body.'

"The poor pump burst into tears at my words of kindness, and throwing his solitary arm about my neck, long hung there weeping as though I were his long-lost child. At length I tore myself away, and walked to my room, revolving this sad tale in my mind."

Long and loud applause followed Van's first article, and he next read, "A letter from a Freshman to his mother," which was heard with convulsions of laughter. This was followed by a more serious effort, "A night among the Ogres," in which the practices of the College Faculty were unveiled and their custom of feasting on stewed Freshmen after each meeting justly denounced. (We have been requested by the President of the college to state that these accounts were in many of their details grossly exaggerated.—The Author.) A number of other pieces followed, entitled "Character," "My Chum and I," "Alone with my Pipe," "The Grumbler," "The Athenian Trireme," "A game of Billiards," "Remorse, a poem," "Can a Law-Student be a gentleman?" "'A Night in Town," "Whether complete blindness in one eye should be accepted by the Faculty as an equivalent for being cross-eyed in the examination of a candidate for admission to the Vestal Order of College Goodies?" Space forbids our quoting more than the names of these essays, but that they were all marked by the finest culture and rarest originality our readers can take our word.

A vote of thanks was given Van as he took his seat, and his paper acknowledged to be the best of the term. Rakeman then announced as the subject for debate the question, "Whether Prize-fighting is justifiable." Hamilton and Ayres were the regular debaters of the evening in the affirmative, and Bowyer and Sweatrame in the negative, all of whom approved themselves accomplished orators. After Sweatrame had finished his argument Gowan rose and made a brilliant speech in favor of the manly art, closing with a tribute to the great Heenan.

The vote of the Society was then taken and Prize-fighting received a severe check, after which the meeting was adjourned until the next Friday.

CHAPTER X.

"I, fuge ; sed poteras tutior esse domi."

MONDAY evening, the first day of the following December, the College Faculty were seated, as their custom is, around the council fire in University Building, engaged in earnest consultation, touching students, their studies, and moral discipline.

"Much has been said with force and reason on both sides of this question," said the President in summing up a lengthy debate.

"On the one hand, Van Courtland, it has been shown, has omitted to attend a large number, I may say a very large number, of prayers and recitations. He has, for these omissions, twice received a 'Public Admonition,' and, it is well urged, has merited the additional punishment of suspension, if not expulsion from the college. This penalty, it is argued, should be inflicted, not only as due to the gravity of the offences themselves, but also for the sake of a wholesome example, to promote obedience to our police regulations, which have of late been frequently disregarded. If leniency be shown in this case, it has been pertinently suggested, the Faculty cannot, with so perfect justice, punish similar violations of their laws.

"On the other hand, Professor Horace has invited our attention to Van Courtland's proficiency in Latin and other studies, a matter, which, though of less importance than the maintenance of our penal code, should not be altogether overlooked. The arguments seem to be about equally balanced, and I do not wish myself to express any very positive opinion. Since, however, you press me to give one, I may perhaps be allowed to state, without meaning in the least to influence your decision, that I should not be greatly opposed to allowing Van Courtland, in consideration of the excellence of his recitations, a somewhat longer opportunity to reform."

The vote of the Faculty was then taken, and resulted in favor of Van Courtland.

"I am glad," continued the President after the announcement of the vote, "to hear such good accounts of Saulsbury. He has obtained nearly perfect marks in every department, and notwithstanding a few deductions, will probably be the first scholar of his class for this year. Nothing can be more admirable than the influence exerted by such a boy."

We now beg our readers to glance upwards, through two ceilings, and a slated roof, and observe two young men standing upon the top of the building, near the central chimney.

"Are you ready, Wentworth?" asks Van Courtland of his friend.

"Yes," answers our hero; "you, Van, go down the

rope, and as soon as you reach the ground, give it a shake. I'll then light the fusee, and hurry after you."

While Van is making his descent, we will give our readers a brief sketch of our hero's career in the two months just past. Wentworth had studied with his chum through this period, with almost as much zeal as during the first month of the term. After the novelty of exclusive devotion to books had worn away, however, he felt his spirits somewhat droop. He therefore, without neglecting his work, mixed more with his friends, and again enjoyed, though now with moderation, the delightful social pleasures of college life. Nor in his recreations did Wentworth forget what was due to the honor of his class, and the spirit of his Sophomore year. Although he refused to belong to the Med. Fac., on account of his dislike to hazing, he at times joined some of its members, in their attacks against the common enemy of all classes, the Faculty. Most of the enterprises, however, in which he took part, were executed in concert with Brandreth, and their mutual friend Van. Brandreth passed most of his nights upon the roofs of the college buildings, which custom had made as safe for him, as for the nocturnal cat, and had gained the sobriquet of the "lone brave," from his love of solitary adventure. About once a week, however, when some choice scheme offered itself, he would ask Wentworth and Van to meet him at the house behind the stable, which the latter and he had hired.

There our three young warriors put on the war paint, and dug up the hatchet. Thence, anon, in the small hours of the night, they issued upon the war path, each clad in black, close-fitting trousers, light, well oiled shoes, and a black coat buttoned round his blackened face.

The first exploit of the trio was the painting on the wall of the chapel just above the pulpit, the names of their classes '5– and '5–, and underneath them the motto—

"Discite justitiam moniti, et non temnere divos."

The morning following, every one was startled by this work of an unseen hand, and the College Faculty paused a moment in their tyrannical course, struck with the terror Belshazzar's Court felt, as the words of doom burnt themselves upon their eyes. Both classes gained great glory by this achievement, which was increased a week later by the Rape of the Bell.

The students, overtaxed with protracted studies, had long sighed for a night's rest unbroken by the harsh prayer bell. The practical friends of letters in college had often attempted to secure for them this boon by removing the tongue from the merciless crier, who every morning uttered his dolorous summons from the roof of Harvard Hall. But the efforts of these philanthropists had been rendered futile by the young Argus-eyed Janitor and bell-ringer ordinary to the University, who slept in the building.

Undismayed by these failures, our three braves resolved to hazard the attempt. One cloudy afternoon as a division of the Senior Class was going to recitation in Harvard Hall, the boys entered the building with them and remained concealed in one of its upper rooms. About twelve o'clock they stole into the belfry and worked away at their task, each filing as best he might at the stubborn tongue. Three hours they labored with a zeal a sense of duty could have alone inspired. At length its tongue was loosened and the bell became a mute. As Van, however, was giving the tongue a final twist, his hand slipped and the bell, in revenge for its mayhem, gave one loud expiring shriek for help.

"We're caught," whispered Van, as listening a few moments, the boys heard the cat-like tread of the velvet-footed Janitor on the stairs.

"Suppose we attack and gag him," suggested Wentworth.

"The risk is too great," returned Brandreth, he will call the watchman, and we shall all be nabbed. "There is only one way," he added, and nodding to his friends to imitate him, he pulled off his shoes and stockings and threw them with the tongue of the bell over the roof.

The Janitor as he approached the belfry chuckled, but, though chuckling, advanced more slowly.

"Come down," he cried, rapping on the scuttle.

Hearing no noise his courage mounted; he pushed back the scuttle, sprang into the belfry and foamed at the mouth to see three misty objects, crawling away over the roof. The hope of reward for a moment prompted him to tempt the aerial chase. A shudder succeeded the thought, as his imagination painted the natural effect of a fall of fifty feet upon his personal appearance.

"You'd better come back, you can't get off," he shouted, leaning over the edge of the belfry and straining his eyes after the invisible shadows.

"I'll wait till the sun rises," he muttered to himself, "and then I can see who they are." Thus muttering, he again chuckled.

"I wish it were clearer," whispered Brandreth, who with his friends had now reached the corner of the roof nearest Hollis Hall, "I can't see where to jump."

"You're not going to jump without the rope, are you," said Van, who was not such a Dædalus as his friend.

Brandreth made no answer, but seating himself upon the edge of the roof felt with his feet towards Hollis, which is a few feet distant. Suddenly his hand moved slightly on the slippery slates, and the next moment he would have fallen, but Wentworth and Van clutched him, and he himself caught his hand on the lightning rod, which runs from roof to roof.

"Hollis Hall is higher than Harvard, that's what frightens me," he said as he regained his feet; "but here goes," and with a spring the reckless fellow leaped forward into the air.

The same moment the two boys heard his bare feet clasp the slates on the roof opposite, and saw him creeping to the corner attic window. This opened at his knock and one end of a coil of rope which a classmate who occupied the room had in readiness was passed to him. This Brandreth threw to his friends, who in turn made it fast around their waists and leaped across, Wentworth first, and Van next. The boys then hurried down stairs, picked up the spoils of war, and returned to their quarters behind the stable.

But the velvet-footed Janitor through the long hours stood sentinel over the roof. Many prayers like Ajax he offered up for light; many times he breathed upon his frosty fingers; many times he stamped with his velvet feet.

When at length the sluggard Aurora, struggling from her bed of down, opened her dim eyes, their first faint glances discovered the empty roof, and the students 'vanished into thin air."

"I have lived," exclaimed the weary watcher, and gazed stupidly around him. Soon he bent downwards his leaden steps, a man well stricken in years.

The third exploit of our young friends was dedicated to equity.

"It is unjust," urged Brandreth, "in the Faculty to punish men, whose duties engage them most of the night, for not rising to prayers like common idlers in the morning."

One midnight, therefore, the boys opened the southern door of University building, and locking it from the inside, left the key in its place. They then unlocked a postern door to secure a double retreat in case of surprise. Thence passing up stairs they entered the President's room, and took from its hiding-place the key to the college safe. The Regent's room adjacent, where a year ago the world had trembled with the Titanic birth throes of our hero's class, next invited them. There Brandreth opened the college-safe, and taking out the college books, erased from them as many marks against himself and his friends for "cutting" prayers, as a prudent regard for their reputation would permit.

The *mise-en-scène* of this adventurous night, long impressed itself upon Wentworth's memory.

The solemn room with its old safe and Sibylline books, in which the hopes and fears of many aspiring youth lie written; the long table and stately chair once awful with the stern Regent, now, alas! profaned; the old clock ticking angrily at the intruders; the wicked eye of the dark lantern stealing around the walls; and the black spectres busy at their deed of darkness. Without reigns silence, save where the watchman paces around the college to guard it from nightly harm.

At this very moment, perchance, the Regent himself at his happy home smiles in peaceful slumber. He is dreaming of "Private and Public Admonitions" slowly maturing through their allotted periods. Even while he smiles, many of his innocents are dying before their birth by the hand of our young Herods.

Thus passed the golden months of October and November in study and adventure. The weather had now grown colder, and would soon compel even Brandreth to retire into winter quarters. One Friday night, Van musing with pride on what had been achieved, and eager to end the campaign with a crowning "mercy," devised an elaborate scheme, which he at once prepared to execute. The two following days there was a cold snap in which Fresh Pond was frozen over, but Monday, the day chosen by Van to carry out his plot, was warm and pleasant.

About dusk on that day a cart drove rapidly through the yard to the cedar grove behind University Building. The driver took from it a small barrel, which he gave into the hands of Rakeman and Brandreth, who were there stationed.

This and a ladder which shortly made its appearance with Bowyer and Sweatrame were hidden away in the bushes.

About half an hour later a rattling was heard on the roof of the building, and a rope uncoiled itself to the ground. This Brandreth made fast to the ladder, which was then drawn up the side of the building. Soon the rope again fell and the barrel followed the ladder. The unseen agents above were Wentworth and Van Courtland. These late in the afternoon had entered University by a back door, and remained concealed there until the evening. They had then climbed upon the roof, carrying with them a coil of rope, a paint pot, and an effigy of Tutor Brown.

Van's plan proposed nothing less than to burn a barrel of chemicals over the heads of the Faculty, while seated in council, and underneath the barrel to hang in effigy one of its members.

The barrel had been prepared by the ablest chemists in College, and all danger of its setting the building on fire had been guarded against.

Our friends as soon as they had mounted the roof had painted the name of their class in large white letters upon the chimney.

They had then by the help of the ladder hung their victim by the neck to the chimney-top, and had again let down the rope for the barrel.

"Confound it," whispered Wentworth, as they lifted the barrel upon the roof, "I've knocked out the fusee."

"Never mind," answered Van, "stick it in again, it will go all right," and he helped Wentworth place the barrel in the chimney.

The boys below meanwhile separated and took up their positions as scouts, one on each side of the building. It was at this point that our own attention was called away from the proceedings of the Faculty, to observe what was going on over their heads.

"Are you ready, Wentworth?" asks Van Courtland of his friend.

"Yes," answers our hero, "you, Van, go down the rope and as soon as you reach the ground give it a shake. I'll then light the fusee and hurry after you."

"All right," replied Van, and glided swiftly down. He had reached but half way to the ground, when he heard Rakeman's warning whistle, and swung himself into the shadow of a window.

"By Jove, it's the college watchman," he muttered, catching sight of a figure pacing along the path.

In a few minutes the watch had passed out of hearing, and Van descended to the ground.

"Ready!" he said, as his scouts gathered round him, and he gave the rope a shake.

The next moment a loud report was heard upon the roof.

"The devil!" cried Van, "he has lit the wrong end of the fusee," and looking up he saw Wentworth sliding with reckless speed down the rope.

"Run," said Van, as Wentworth touched the ground. At the word, the six boys leaped from their covert in all directions.

Wentworth ran towards the north, and was passing the corner of the building, when—crash! he was hurled violently back by some one dashing against him at full speed. A blue coat and brass buttons disclosed the infamous character of the new comer.

"The pogy," muttered Wentworth, and stood divided in mind, crest-tossing Mars urging him to seek safety and glory in victory, but the azure-eyed Maid persuading prudent flight.

The next moment he darted through the trees and ran towards the Delta. Close upon his heels trod the swift-footed watchman, chosen for his speed. Avarice and rage lent him their aid, but he followed as light a pair of heels as ever winged their way over the green at sight of prowling proctor or wolfish watch. Wentworth's hands were pressed against his chest, his teeth clenched, his head thrown back. Disgrace sat behind him and spurred him on his course. Fast flew his feathered feet over the sear grass. The trees rushed past him; the ground sprang upwards to meet his step. He reached the spot where the new Chapel now stands; suddenly he gave a high leap in the air. The watchman stopped to look for the obstacle and lost precious moments in finding none.

"I'll tire him out yet," he growled with an oath, and with redoubled rage, pursued the crafty "collegy."

They leaped over the bars of the college yard; they ran across the Delta; Wentworth was rapidly nearing the sanctuary of Norton's Woods. As he turned down Kirkland Street, he was aware of a man walking towards him: he threw his arm over his face, and ran on the other side of the street. "Stop him!" shouts the policeman, now some rods distant, and Wentworth hears two new feet in pursuit.

"Podasocus!" he mutters—"Podasocus! the one dangerous tutor to have upon your track. A shudder of despair passes over him, but he will die game. Hotter and faster comes his breath; his new pursuer is fresh; he is nearly exhausted; the sweat pours from his forehead; his face burns like a ball of fire; his head grows dizzy with the terrible strain. The picture of his father and mother swims before his eyes—their anguish at his expulsion. He makes a desperate effort; he gains a few feet upon his enemy. The few feet close slowly up; he almost feels the tutor's breath upon his neck.

Swiftly his mind explores all ways of escape.

Suddenly he gathers himself like a snake coiling for the spring. The tutor's foot strikes the barrier; the tutor himself is projected into space. A thousand stars shed their influence over him for a moment; the next he is shrouded in darkness.

Wentworth, with a grateful heart, crept through the

hedge, which here bounds the street, and was soon lost to sight.

> "'Per varios casus, per tot discrimina rerum
> Tendimus in Latium,'"

he exclaimed, a few minutes later, breaking into Van's room, which he found filled with his friends, refreshing their wearied virtue.

"Glad to see you, old boy! we were afraid you were caught," they all cried, as Wentworth entered the door.

"The rest of us are safe," said Brandreth; "Rake had a close shave of it, though."

"Probus chased me," broke in Rakeman, "and he would have caught me if I hadn't tript in the grass. I lay perfectly still, with my nose buried in the ground, and Probus ran past me; he must be in Roxbury by this time."

> ——"I'll tell you a tale without any flam."

sang the rattling Southron, who valued all things at a song.

"The Faculty came out like a nest of hornets," said Van. "They were wild with excitement. Every one says there hasn't been so good a thing tried for years. But what's the matter? you look pale."

Wentworth told his story, which was received with great applause, and at its conclusion, all his friends drank his health, standing.

He remained an hour later chatting with them, and then feeling very tired, returned to his room.

"Why, Wentworth, what ails you?" asked his chum, anxiously. "You look as though you had been through the wars."

Wentworth repeated his adventure to Lewis, at which the latter laughed at first, but soon answered with seriousness.

"You ought not to do this sort of thing, Wentworth. Every few days you frighten me by some dare-deviltry or other. If you're caught, they'll expel you from college, and you can't always count on good luck. Besides, you may break your neck, dancing on the tops of roofs and chimneys."

"I can't think what is the matter with me to-night," he added, after a short silence; "I feel out of spirits."

"I don't wonder at your feeling blue, Lewis," said his chum, "your prayer-meeting met to-night, didn't it? The prospect of going to heaven with such scrubs as one meets at a prayer-meeting, would make any one gloomy. Don't look hurt, old boy, I only spoke in jest."

"No, no, Wentworth, I'm not hurt," replied Lewis, quickly; "you wrong yourself when you sneer at men because they profess their belief in spite of ridicule. Whatever they may be in other respects, for that, at least, they deserve your esteem."

"You know, Lewis, I never misconstrued your manly assertion of your convictions."

"Your only fault towards me, Wentworth, is too great regard," and Lewis turned his face towards his friend with a look of affection, long remembered,—"but it does cut me to see you repress all expression of the faith which I know you feel in your heart. Truth, that does not seek the light, is but half truth. Dread of ridicule is only a refined form of cowardice and is as base a trait—— What am I saying? It is only because you know I like you better than any one else, that you allow me to be so unjust."

"You're not unjust, Lewis, I feel that I ought to do as you have done, to take my stand before the world, but I hate so to set myself up as a model. One seems to claim to be better than other men if he makes a profession of religion. You are so, Lewis; it is all right for you."

"You can't stop me by flattery, Wentworth. If you wait until you are at the top of a mountain before you take the first step, your ascent will not be rapid. If you wait until you are perfect before you begin to do right, you will not make great progress towards the kingdom of Heaven. You know how much vice there is here, how much drunkenness, profanity, and licentiousness—not so much I don't mean as elsewhere—but enough to fill one with sadness. You know, too, how much influence a man like you can exert in college. Even though you are not vicious yourself, if you do not oppose vice in others and unite with those who do, your influence is not on the side of right."

"I cannot deny it," answered Wentworth, after a few minutes' thought, "what you say is true. It is cowardice: I will do what you wish, old boy, next Sunday, I promise it."

Lewis said no more, for he was a strange boy and knew when to advise and when to stop advising. Soon he moved to the table, on which was lying a somewhat miscellaneous collection of authors, among whom, if we remember rightly, were Jeremy Taylor, Gray's Botany, Boccaccio, Cook's Chemical Physics, Rabelais, and George Herbert.

"I often grow homesick among lifeless books," Lewis shortly remarked, in order to change the conversation. "Men laugh at the feeling in college; it is so strong, they try to disguise it by a sneer, as Thackeray does his finest feelings,—a cowardly fashion, I think."

"One needs to keep the sacred office of letters clearly before him," he added, "to study on cheerfully day after day, although after all it is our own ignorance that makes any thing seem dull to us. The wisest men find nothing stupid: the commonest word is to them the open sesame to the treasure-house of the ages. What an all-important part literature plays in our life! does it not? Without it man is a point in the ocean of eternity, with neither past nor future, clipped about with darkness; its aid has conquered for him a broad island from the reign of night, and built upon it a gorgeous temple set with golden suns shedding light and heat. The Classics are the Propylæa of this Temple of Time, a bulwark against which the waves of oblivion have dashed for two thousand years, and will dash forever in vain.

"What a pleasant time we have had together, Wentworth!" he continued musingly. "I never knew a term pass so quickly before. Yet I confess I shall be glad when vacation comes. You are going to Philadelphia with me this winter, you know. Mother will be so delighted to see you!" and the picture of his home rose before the boy's mind.

"There is nothing, Lewis, I should like better," answered Wentworth. "But I must go to bed, I feel fearfully used up. Hallo! what's all this?" and he took up a solemn-looking roll of papers.

"That's the sermon Plummer preached two Sundays ago—an old lady asked me to borrow it. Do you remember that last sentence? 'My young friends, if that truth of truths that you are immortal souls could fill your hearts but for one moment, then, at once and forever, would all sin fall from you like the scales from the blind man's eyes. Then would you feel the dignity,—the sacredness of this life, and make it the fit beginning of that life hereafter of which it is a part. Your souls would dwell in your bodies as priests in the temples of God. Death you would look upon not as the king of terrors, but as the angel of life sent to lead you hence into the celestial kingdoms of our Father Almighty and our Lord Jesus Christ.'"

"The Doctor draws it strong, sometimes, Lewis, does he not?" said Wentworth yawning.

"By the way, we shall have some skating in a few days, I think; it is growing colder again. Good-night, old boy."

CHAPTER XI.

" Manibus date lilia plenis."

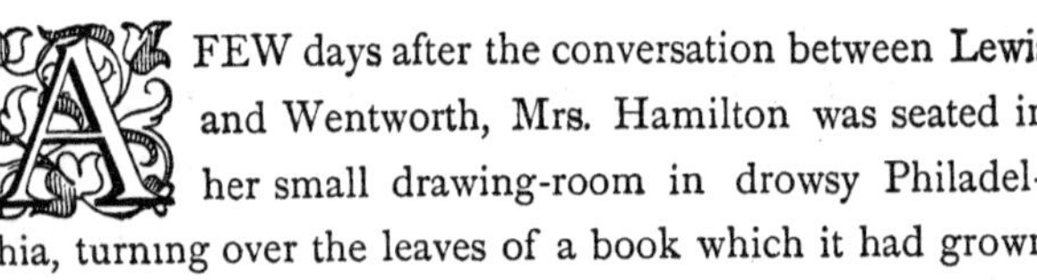

A FEW days after the conversation between Lewis and Wentworth, Mrs. Hamilton was seated in her small drawing-room in drowsy Philadelphia, turning over the leaves of a book which it had grown too dark to read.

Lewis's mother was of middle height, with clear blue eyes, light golden hair, and that tremulous look about the lips which acquaintance with grief brings.

She was thinking of the spot where the hopes of her life were garnered. "It will be time to have a letter from Lewis to-morrow! How long the days seem!" as she mused, the bell rang, and a telegram was handed her.

"Please come on as soon as possible," she read, her anxiety increasing to terror. "Lewis has been taken sick."

It happened in this wise. The Saturday after Wentworth's escape, the two boys, with a party of their friends, went to Fresh Pond to enjoy the first skating of the season, and peradventure a flirtation with some fair-ankled beauty of breezy Boston. The pond has long been famous for this double diversion, which is well suited to the temperament of our New Englanders.

Wentworth and Lewis skated a short time, and then stopped to talk with Van, a few rods from the shore, by the hotel. Suddenly the ice gave way, and they were all struggling in the water. Their friends formed a line by linking themselves together, but the ice was too thin for its success. Rakeman then ran for a ladder leaning against a tree near by, but its top was frozen too hard to be moved. He rushed to a boat-house, a few feet distant: here he found a long mast, which he dragged along, and pushed over the ice.

The boys had now been some minutes in the water, and were fast losing their strength. Wentworth and Van had each one arm resting on the ice, and with the other supported Lewis, whose consciousness was nearly gone.

"Hurry up, fellows! this water is not so warm as it might be," said Van, as Rakeman crept along the mast. The ice creaked and cracked, but the plucky fellow kept on.

"Take Hamilton first," said Van, as Rakeman reached them. Lewis, who was too benumbed by the cold to speak, shook his head, and tried to push himself back, but Rakeman grasped him by the collar, and crying out, "Pull away, fellows," was dragged ashore, clinging to the mast with one hand, and holding Lewis with the other.

Meanwhile, Bowyer had found a rope at the hotel, and thrown it to Van and Wentworth. They, less exhausted, tied it around their waists, and were soon brought to land.

A good rubbing restored Lewis to life, and the three boys then put on the clothes of their friends, and started on the run for the college.

They soon reached Van's room, and at once dispatched a man laden with clothes, for their friends in dishabille. They then opened a bottle of brandy, and drank several glasses. Wentworth and Lewis staid with Van the rest of the afternoon, and took supper with him.

Lewis soon after complained of feeling tired, and went to bed. The next morning, which was cloudy and damp, both he and his chum felt recovered from their fatigue, and attended services at the Chapel. The chapel had this peculiarity—if what is shared by all churches can be called a peculiarity—it was insufferably close. The architect had, by some accident, built a ventilator in the ceiling, but the mistake was fortunately discovered by the Argus-eyed janitor, and the leak stopped before more than a few breaths of air had escaped. Since then, no mishap had lessened the growing sanctity of the original atmosphere.

Hamilton, who was still weak from the strain of the day before, caught a severe chill, by going from the close chapel into the damp air.

He felt no appetite during the day, and in the evening complained of pain and dizziness in the head.

The next morning, Wentworth found his chum worse, and went for the doctor, who looked serious after seeing his patient.

Lewis's pulse was high and feeble, and his symptoms threatened fever. Wentworth in alarm sent a telegram to his friend's mother, and the afternoon of the next day, Mrs. Hamilton drove up to the Hall.

As Wentworth opened the door of the carriage, she gave him that one agonized glance, that searches the sentence of our destiny in the eyes of another. She put out her hand for something to support herself, and whispered "Thank God."

With these words, she followed Wentworth to his room. Lewis had grown worse during the night, and could only be kept quiet by opiates. Wentworth had sat up with him, and in the morning had been shocked by the rapid strides of the disease. The boy's eyes were clouded, his cheeks hollow, and his clear skin turned to a yellowish hue ; his pulse was higher than yesterday ; his young face was emaciated, and his eyes lustreless.

Wentworth gently opened the door for Mrs. Hamilton, and left her alone with her son.

A look of love ineffable beamed from the mother's face at the sight of her child, but was followed by an expression of unspeakable anguish at the change which had come over him.

"Oh, my God ! Thou wilt not !" she cried, in her agony, and sinking unconsciously upon her knees by that beloved bedside, "Save his young life, oh God!" she prayed, "take mine, but oh, save his young life!"

Suddenly Lewis awoke.

"Let me get up," he exclaimed, deliriously, and strove to rise. "I tell you I will get up. Oh, I am in such pain! If you only knew in what pain I am! My head is bursting! Wentworth, you go first. It is very cold!"

Lewis's mother placed her hand softly on the boy's head, and kissed his poor parched lips. "Don't you know me? I'm your mother, Lewis! Oh, my darling!"

"Yes, I know you. I'm choking! Let me get out; what do you mean by holding me down! are you going to leave me to die here? Promise me you won't leave me, Wentworth. I tell you I can't stay in the water!"

The boy struggled, fell back exhausted, and burst into tears.

"I am going to die to-night! It is so cold! I won't go first! I don't like you any more, Wentworth; I don't like any one any more. Go! leave me—leave me here alone!" and Lewis impatiently pushed away his mother's hand, tenderly pressed upon his forehead. The poor boy ran on in this way a few moments longer, when he again fell into a feverish sleep.

Thus passed nine weary days, during which Lewis hung between life and death. Night after day, and day after night, his mother watched his every breath with a suspense a mother alone can know, sleeping only when exhaustion closed her sad eyes.

With the tenth night the fever passed away, but the danger had only changed its form : Lewis lay scarcely breathing, half sleeping, half waking, lifeless from its fierce attack. His skin had grown deadly pale, and the veins were distended on the lids of his sunken eyes. Towards noon the fever again set in, but under the influence of opiates the boy slept restlessly an hour or more : suddenly he opened his eyes.

"Dear, good mother!" he said in his natural voice, trying to reach out his hand. Mrs. Hamilton's mind had been so strung with care, that she had not before shed a tear, but at these words her self-command gave way and she sobbed aloud. "Don't cry, mother dearest!" whispered Lewis, his old sweet smile hovering over his face, "I must have been a great care to you." Even while he spoke his lips grew purple, and sent a thrill of horror over his mother's heart.

"How beautiful you look to-night, mother! Lean down and take my head in your hands and kiss my eyes, as you used when I was a boy. Bessy, dear, why have you been so long away?" he adds, thinking of his sister, long since dead. "Don't light the lamps yet, pet, it is so pleasant in the dark—give me another kiss, mother," and as the lips of the dying boy part to meet his mother's, a look of love hallows his face, and he falls asleep.

The childless mother sinks upon her knees by the lifeless form of all she loved and lived for on earth. A moment ago her darling was, now all is silent, all is still. But it were impious further to lift the veil, for God, himself, is standing in the room by her side.

They buried Lewis with his father and sister. Wentworth, as he listened to the grand old service that has given faith to so many hearts, felt even then how beautiful is the death of the pure in spirit. In after days, when time had taken the sting from his grief, he learnt the holy office of death to touch the soul with a finer influence. A friend dying does not die but incarnates our ideals, and gives them a human presence. The radiance of the Sun, the painting of the landscape, the sweet voice of music, all things of majesty and beauty are informed with a more life-like power by the sympathy of grief for the loss of those whom we love and reverence. With what peace and joy their faces shine upon us from the clear sky, lit with heavenly light from the bright world above. "I heard a voice from heaven, saying unto me, Write, From henceforth blessed are the dead who die in the Lord : even so saith the Spirit; for they rest from their labors.'

Wentworth's room on his return to Cambridge looked gloomy as he entered it, and grew gloomier every day. The ghost of past pleasure flitted about it, and seated itself in the vacant chairs. The books, the old fireplace, the half conscious pictures were all mourners with him for their friend.

"I'll tell you what, old boy," said Van to him one day, "it won't do for you to live in this tomb; you're growing as lean as a divinity student. Come and room with me the rest of the year, there's a good fellow."

Wentworth accepted Van's offer with thanks, and the next day moved to Brown's.

There, through the rest of the term, he sought forgetfulness in work. Yet every now and then, as the mood seized him, he wandered back to his former haunts, and with a silent prayer in his heart, looked again for the familiar face of his friend, again listened for the sound of his sweet voice.

CHAPTER XII.

"Nec tamen undique corporea stipata tenentur
omnia natura; namque est in rebus inane."

"Cum autem finitus fuerit totus usufructus, revertitur scilicet ad proprietatem, et ex eo tempore nudæ proprietatis dominus incipit plenam in re habere potestatem."

NE forenoon shortly after the celebration of the Sophomore class supper, which was held at Point Shirley the first Friday of the second term, Wentworth ran from the Post-office to Brown's in a state of great excitement. Van was in his room reading one of M. Gautier's moral tales, and commenting on the story to Rakeman, who, seated nearer the fire, was enjoying the ambrosial humor of Henry Fielding, Esq.

Van's rooms, which took up half the first floor of the building, were furnished with rich carpets, seductive lounges, well filled book-cases, and whatever else was suited to a luxurious child of the great metropolis. His centre-table offered you the works of Balzac, Dumas *fils*, and other novelists; and his walls exhibited much taste in their collection of pictures. Among them we recall a favorite painting, with many of Van's friends, by a famous French artist, in which a frolicsome girl, struggling to check the naive admiration of a young soldier, discovered no little beauty. The most noticeable feature of the room, however, was the main door, which was covered over with slips of paper. These were part of Van's correspondence with the College Faculty, through which he had been kept informed of the deductions made from his marks for smoking, grouping, and the like, and of other matters of current interest.

"I thank Heaven, fellows!" exclaimed Wentworth, breaking into the room, "that I can now look on my fellow-beings with respect. Two months ago, wherever I went I saw creatures in the livery of creditors, who followed me, and hung upon my words like the slaves of an Eastern despot; now I have set them all free, and made men of them."

"How?" inquired Van, amused; "by an edict of emancipation?"

"No," answered Wentworth, "I have bought their liberty with hard money. I have just had a letter from the governor; he is all right again, you know, which says that my last debt has been paid. Let me invite you both to a cutlet, some fried brains, a veal pie, or anything in the line of the Prodigal Son. Seriously, fellows, you don't know how much sweeter it makes your life, to have all men able to look you honestly in the face and say—'You do not owe me a single penny.' Down! down!" he added, as a ferocious looking dog leaped upon him. "Down, you beast, confound him, whose dog is this?"

"Huc, huc, Romule," called Van, laughing at his

chum's vain efforts. "That's the dog I spoke to you about the other day. He arrived this morning with a letter from my old tutor. He is a splendid classical scholar, and doesn't know a single word of English—a cross between the Molossian and Spartan breeds."

"Did you bring him here to teach you Latin?" asked Rakeman.

"Not me, but my teachers. I tell you he knows more Latin, than any other professor in Cambridge. Old Rome herself has entered into the belly of that dog as the Devil into Faust's puppy.

"Ganni!" Van ordered the dog, and the dog begged.

"Arripe!" and the dog tossed a piece of cracker from his nose into the air, and caught it in his mouth. "Which of our professors," exclaimed Van triumphantly, "can do that?"

"By the way, Rake," remarked our hero, after applauding Van's exhibition, "I haven't spoken to you since the class-supper; have you recovered from that, entirely?"

"Your inquiry is equivocal," returned the Southron with hauteur.

"What became of you, yourself, Wentworth, about the middle of the supper," asked Van. "You remember when Nutkins wanted to fight you, for knocking a glass out of his hand, and Rake clapped a punch-bowl on his head as a helmet. I couldn't find you for an hour after that; you must have run away."

"I went to take a walk on the beach," replied Wentworth, and a look of painful memory passed over the face of the boy, in whom the revelry of his comrades had heightened a sense of isolation, and excited feelings most in contrast with itself.

"You should have seen Rake's retreat," said Van quickly, noticing the expression of his friend. "Nutkins pursued him thrice around the table with all the wrath of an Achilles."

"You should have seen Sweatrame's little game of duck, that was very humorous," added Rakeman. "As I was congratulating myself on my escape, I heard a noise at one end of the room, and saw Sweatrame, with Dummer, and half a dozen other men, throwing plates at a bottle on the table. This added greatly to their own amusement, but also to the item *sundries* on the supper bill. I was on the committee, and ran up to stop them. As I reached the spot, the polished pate of a bald-headed waiter, whom fatal curiosity, or too great love of plates, inspired, lit up the scene. Sweatrame was just aiming a platter at the bottle, when the waiter's shining crown offered a more inviting mark. The victim gave one loud yell, as the platter broke over his head, and darted from the room in mortal terror. Once only he looked back, and saw Death shadowing him with his wings—Death! who spares neither the 'hand,' nor the 'boss,' neither the prigging waiter, nor the lordly proprietor of a hotel. Your mind follows him as, with the wings of a dove, he flies to his ethereal cot in the attic. There first he pauses, to breathe a short prayer for fair Harvard, and her free-handed students. Anon a co-waiter plasters his head, and whispers words of hope in his ear.

Together they thus sit trembling, till the lame night has halted off; our revels ended, the ghouls descend, dig up the corpse of the jolly supper, and pledge themselves in countless heel-taps."

"I returned to the room," said Wentworth, "just as Gowan was finishing his response to the last toast, 'the Union;' did you hear that, Van?"

"No; there was such a noise in the room, then, that I only caught a word or two, where I was seated; was it good?"

"Very fair. First he drew a picture of the American eagle, with its beak buried in the Atlantic Ocean, and its tail shadowing the Pacific coast. 'Gentlemen,' he then burst forth, 'there is but one danger which threatens our happy, our united land, with discord and ruin. Need I name it? The Maine liquor law! Too well you know the baleful words. Ah! gentlemen, when my eyes shall be last turned to behold my beloved country, may they not, like the dove first sent from the Ark, see every where water, every where clouds. Impious, to whom the Flood has brought no warning! Ho! waiter! bring me some of the 'red eye.' Wine for Freshmen, but the 'red eye' for Sophs! Saulsbury," he shouts, catching sight of me, "you're a nice, elegant, superb, little white-headed boy; give a rouse."

"Gowan is a comical fellow," returned Van, "but he is a man of talents, and will be one of our great political leaders one of these days, I have no doubt."

"He can place himself outside of more whiskey, in less

time than any man in the class, I reckon," said Rakeman. "Yesterday, I remember, he complained to me, that we were getting to be so moral a class that a man was ashamed to be seen drunk; 'it was not so under the old regime,' he sighed."

"It seems to me there is almost a touch of coarseness about our class suppers," mused Van, after a few minutes. "We ought to be able to get up something better in college. By Jove! I've an idea: suppose we have a Roman dinner."

"Capital!" "Bravo!" shouted both his hearers.

"These rooms are just the place for it," added Van. "We can get six more good men. I'll come down on my uncle for the wines; he's a Harvard man, and a great connoisseur."

Wentworth and Rakeman entered heartily into Van's plan, and soon the work of each of the three had been marked out, and five other men selected.

"Did your fellows accept my invitation to-night, Rake?" then asked Wentworth, who, on his return to prosperity, had invited his old club-table to a supper in town. "I tried to induce Van to go with us, but he says he is engaged; I'll call for you all about seven at Mrs. Green's. I think I shall join you again next week, if you are willing."

"We could not possibly think of it, old boy," returned Rakeman, slapping his friend on the shoulder. "We shall all of us be ready at seven. Suppose we take in our instruments with us; it will be good fun to wake up the old town."

The twelve o'clock bell now rang and the boys hurried to recitation.

About dusk the same day in the drawing-room of one of the quiet houses on Beacon Hill, a bright looking girl was laughing and talking with a gentleman some ten years her senior. The girl, in whom ruddy health and delicate beauty vied for mastery, was no other than Miss Campbell. The gentleman whose manner expressed great admiration for his fair listener, was Mr. J. Endicott Otis, a man much sought by men for his personal traits, and by mothers for his great wealth and alpine social position.

After some minutes of casual conversation, Mr. Otis leaned forward with that look which women well know precedes the critical occasions of their lives—observe, my fair readers, the delicate flattery of the plural number.

The animated girl at once became perfectly still; her ivory neck, mantled with crimson, which mounted and stained with livelier color the roses in her cheeks; her hand trembled, and, to hide its embarrassment, broke a bud from a bouquet on the table by her side.

"Miss Campbell," whispered Mr. Otis, bending nearer, "it cannot be a secret to you that I have long loved you passionately." The girl's lips quivered and she cast down her eyes.

"I —— you surprise me—," she answered in sweet confusion. "Believe me, I never thought —— I feel deeply flattered—but— "

"Do not deny me, Miss Campbell—Nell! may I not call you so? Tell me that my love is returned. My life"—

At this auspicious moment the harmonious voices of Rakeman's cornet and Bowyer's flute awakened the sleepy street, and the words of Schubert's serenade, gliding from Ayres's lips into the room, put a truce to further amorous argument. Mr. Otis started back and swallowed two—what shall we call them ?—ejaculations, with great difficulty.

"They are serenading me—how charming ! " exclaimed Miss Campbell, after listening a minute. "They must be college boys : I wonder who they are ?"

Mr. Otis was himself a graduate of Harvard, but had he then heard that the college with all its students had been buried in the ocean, he would have received the news—dare we record it—with resignation. So deeply is the New England Brahmin leavened with all Christian virtues.

Scarcely had Ayres finished singing, when Rakeman began that rattling ballad, which has always been justly a favorite at Harvard.

"It was a tall young oysterman lived by the river side—"

Rakeman was in good form, and the winged words of this Sapphic song flew right and left with brilliant effect.

"I must see who it is !" cried Miss Campbell, with that fine spirit of inquiry which marks her sex ; and with these words, tne arch beauty jumped from her seat, opened the folding windows, and stept softly into the balcony, which was closely covered with woodbine.

"You will catch cold, I fear, let me put on your shawl," urged Mr. Otis, with something too much of fatherly concern in his voice.

"No, I thank you," replied Miss Campbell, and leaning forward she peeped through the leaves.

As Rakeman finished his tearful strain, a slight rustling caught Wentworth's ear, and looking up he saw the glimmer of the girl's light dress, and her coquettish face shining through its reluctant veil.

"For heaven's sake, don't sing any of your negro melodies," he whispered to his friend, who was tuning his throat for a soft lay of the South. "Ayres, sing what you sang the other night; don't you remember it? about the pale moon, sweet face, windows, and all that sort of thing."

And without further entreaty, Robin began that lovely song,

"When the pale, pale moon arose last night."

"How exquisite! did you ever hear anything prettier, Mr. Otis?" said Miss Campbell, and she clapped her hands in enthusiasm.

"Never," answered her admirer, though from his manner, one would hardly have guessed it.

The boys sang a few more songs, and then mounted their tilburies to drive away. Wentworth, however, remained behind a moment, and glanced admiringly at the sunny-eyed face above him for recognition. Miss Campbell's hand had stolen through the foliage, and was resting on the railing of the balcony, holding the rose-bud she had just taken from the table. As she bowed to our hero, through some accident unseen by Mr. Otis, the rose dropt from her hand. Wentworth caught it, pressed it to his lips, and joined Rakeman in his tilbury.

When Mr. Otis ordered a bouquet to be sent to Miss Campbell that morning, little did he imagine the base use to which one of its fair flowers would be put by its fairer recipient. So dangerous is it to have any dealings with the fickle sex.

Did Wentworth preserve this flower for long months in a secret drawer, to be gazed at with fond memories? Alas, no. Fiction would have so represented it, but plain history must set down the fact. Ayres would have done so. The warbler had a drawer consecrated to ribbons, fans, a slipper or two, and a Gehenna of dead flowers, over which, after a pint of claret, he would sigh by hours together. But Wentworth placed the rose in his pocket, and in the evening, finding it faded, threw it away.

The boys drove off; Miss Campbell returned to her seat, and Mr. Otis to his suit, though with less heart. "Do not," he said at length, "do not Miss Campbell forbid my hoping in time to win your love."

"You embarrass—there is no one, believe me, Mr. Otis,—" and the girl's tempting lips again trembled, "there is no one whom I respect more. But I—I am not in love with you: I ought to tell you the truth."

"Can I ask, Miss Campbell, if your affections are engaged?"

"Certainly, you may: I should have told you had that been the cause."

"I may then hope?"

"No, no, I don't mean that," and Miss Campbell grew more confused, and looked prettier than ever; "I—do let me—I must be frank with you, Mr. Otis. I am not in love with you, and I fear—I mean I feel that I never can be."

Mr. Otis rose, took Miss Campbell's hand, kissed it passionately, and left the room.

What could have been the reason that induced Miss Campbell to refuse Mr. Otis, to whose attentions she had not, perhaps, been altogether averse? Was it that he seemed older than before, or could it have been the handsome face of the boy who had piqued her vanity by his neglect, or that a victory won is forgotten, and she already sighed for new worlds to conquer? Who, through the mazy labyrinth of a woman's mind, can trace the thread of causation? We, humble chroniclers, merely write down the results, nor stop to search the cause, or point the moral.

"Why, Wentworth," cried Van in astonishment, on entering their rooms about three o'clock the same night, "what are you about?"

Wentworth was seated at the table, his coat upon the sofa, his collar on a chair, and most of the rest of his dress in different parts of the room. Before him lay Tennyson, Coleridge, Spenser, and other poets without number. Our hero himself was wild with thought, his eyes rolling, his hair hurled back from his brow; one hand rested on the table, the other warned back his friend.

"Hurrah, Van!" he at length shouted, "it is done; bliss rhymes with kiss, dies rhymes with eyes," and Wentworth handed Van a sheet of paper, on which four stanzas were written.

"By Jove, they're capital!" responded Van, glancing over them, "just the thing for my Institute paper to-morrow: I'm much obliged to you."

"Institute paper!" cried Wentworth in a rage, "do you suppose I would sit up all night to write verses for the Institute; do you think I am mad?"

"Since you ask me, old boy," returned Van, "I confess I never saw any good reason to doubt it. So it's a real sketch, is it? Well, I wish you luck. My night has been better spent than in rhyming about a girl in a balcony. I have been giving a lesson in disinterested philanthropy."

"That's a new line for you, Van. What have you been doing?"

"We have been making a night of it, Brandreth, Seaborn, and I. We started for Boston after recitation, and took dinner at Destre's—by the way he is just the man for our Roman dinner, he says he will get it up on 'tick.' After dinner we went to Parker's to have a game of billiards, and then dropt into the theatre to see the ballet. That troupe you saw in New York last winter are here now. You remember the première Tiptonini, what a ravishing 'limb!' as you Bostonians say. We went behind the scenes and I introduced the fellows to her. After the second dance we dragged Brandreth away, and drove to the National to see a sparring match between Heenan and the Bowery Pet. We stayed till they broke up, and about eleven walked to the Revere House, where we ordered a champagne supper. When we left the hotel the last car had gone long ago, and we found ourselves caught in a heavy rain. At length we routed out a hackman, who was willing to drive us, and all tumbled into the coach." Here Van became convulsed with laughter.

"As long as I can remember," growled Wentworth, still sore from his friend's cruelty to his verses, "I never heard anything to compare with this story of a night in town, though I have been all my life in the habit of hearing similar narratives! Why don't you publish it? You could make your fortune."

"Stop! stop! wait till I finish," cried Van.

"We were some distance past the bridge, when the thought struck me that the gentleman on the box might be driving us, not for pleasure, but from some base motive. I had spent my last penny; Brandreth and Seaborn had together but twenty-five cents. Swiftly the hack wheeled over the road; nearer drew the dread moment of liquidation. The position was indeed critical; some Napoleonic stroke was needed; the Time called for the Man, and the Man responded to the Time.

"The hack had reached Quincy Street, and was driving over the soft ground, when the door gently opened and discovered the dark form of Brandreth gliding to the ground; him followed Seaborn, and lastly appeared the god-like proportions of Van Courtland.

"The innocent hackman drove on through the driving rain, and left us masters of the situation.

"When the driver reached the centre of Harvard Square,

he stopped his coach and waited a moment for us to get out. Then, whistling a merry tune, and thanking the good God, maker of night-wandering Harvard spendthrifts, he dismounted, opened the door, touched his hat politely, and was brought face to face with the great Void.

Then, slowly, the awfulness of the occasion forced itself upon him; then slowly he realized the absolute emptiness of all things. Unable at first to breathe in that fine atmosphere, he staggered and supported himself upon a wheel of the coach. Recovering his strength, he searched through the hack, under the seats, behind the cushions, in every corner, and found three cigar stumps. He looked up North Avenue: not a step echoed along its peaceful sidewalks; he gazed down Main Street: it was buried in happy slumber. The feelings of the hackman lay too deep for oaths; in silence he mounted his box, turned his horses' heads, and drove towards the city, a sadder and a wiser man. Soon he whipped his horses madly, if possible to catch some belated train, and *rattraper* the coin his carelessness had squandered."

"All persons who come to Harvard gain wisdom," said Wentworth, laughing; "anything else it is a sin to attempt here. Is that what you call giving lessons in philanthropy? I hate to think how eager that hackman will be to drive the next student that asks him."

"It sets my teeth on edge to think how little oil he will put on the doors of his coach after this," replied Van, gaping. "Come, we must go to bed, it is past four o'clock.

CHAPTER XIII.*

"Sed nec post primum legat hæc summumve trientem."

ARRAH! be gorra! D'ye mind the binches, and the bot, and the plasther of parish images, and the tobaccy boxes, (and if I only had me dudeen to suck meself!) and this saucy phanix, and this villainous baste! Sure it's a strange thing is larnin."

Thus, about the ninth hour of a pleasant summer's day, in his rude vernacular, muttered the *ostiarius* of Van Courtland. This door-keeper, who, on account of his immense size, was nicknamed the Infant, had been captured several years since, in a barbarous island, and sold as a slave. His former master had employed him as porter and private watchman, but Van Courtland, on purchasing him, had appointed him to his present position.

The Infant, as he spoke, lazily rattled his chains, and shook his *virga* or rod of office at the dog, Romulus, who was fastened near him, with the warning words, "CAVE CANEM," written in capital letters above his head.

While thus diverting himself, his ear caught the sound

(* Published by permission from the MS. of the M. & M. Club.)

of guests, whom his master had that day invited to dine, approaching the house.

A moment later, eight stalwart slaves halted before the door, bearing a covered *lectica*, from which Rakeman dismounted. Close behind him was Sweatrame in a *covinus* followed by a *basterna* on which Ayres was seated, and a *rheda* containing Bowyer, and one Pippins, a shade from breezy Boston.

The guests, as they passed through the door, examined with interest a new mosaic *salve*, worked upon the threshold, and a parrot of rare beauty in a cage above their heads, that saluted them with the same word of welcome.

After entering the *atrium*, they again paused, to study the frescoes upon its walls, which represented Prometheus Bound, the Rescue of Andromeda, the famous Plea of Hyperides, and other scenes of beauty and grandeur.

The shade, Pippins, who was a stranger, lingered a few minutes over the beautiful symbolical marriage bed, which stood opposite the door, and then read, with awe, the titles of honor, underneath the long row of *imagines*, which, crowned with fresh laurel, attested the dignity of the house of Van Courtland.

He was interrupted by an usher, who led him and his friends through the *alæ* of the *atrium* into the *cavum ædium*, and turning to the right of the *impluvium*, conducted them to the door of a small *triclinium*, built facing the west, to command a view of the sunset. Upon this was fastened a door-stud with the following inscription—

> "Worthy guests, my name's the Crumb
> But I give you large welcome;
> Gently on your couch repose,
> Let your locks with balsam shine,
> Scatter with free hand the rose,
> Crown the brimming cup with wine;
> Drink! while age and care delay—
> Drink! and seize youth's golden day."

"Enter with your right foot foremost!" cried a slave, stationed at the door for the purpose, as Rakeman, after reading the inscription, led the way into the dining-room.

"Hail! Rakeman!" exclaimed Van Courtland, coming forward, and saluting each of his guests with a kiss. "Hayward and Dummer, as you see, have already arrived, and we have now made up the full number of the Muses. How well your violet-colored *synthesis* becomes you, Pippins," he added turning to the latter, "though I prefer scarlet for myself. Dinner will be served in a few minutes; till then, I hope you can find something with which to amuse yourselves."

The guests were glad of delay, which gave them time to examine the contents of the *triclinium.*

The dinner-table was made of rare wood, beautifully mottled, and the three couches around it were ornamented with purple coverings, and divided by cushions of the same color.

The pictures upon the walls, though different in character, rivalled those of the *atrium* in genius. Among them you saw Ajax slaughtering the Trojan sheep, Io metamorphosed into a heifer, Jupiter changed into a bull, the companions of Ulysses transformed into swine, Actæon pursued by his hounds, Ægle binding drunken Silenus with his own garlands, and Pelias boiling in the sterile pot, all the work of artists of the very first rank.

The pictures were, however, dwarfed by the antiquities displayed upon the side tables.

Among the rarities there exhibited, you beheld almost with incredulity, the tortoise which killed Æschylus, the tortoise of Mercury, the grape-stone that choked Anacreon, the dagger with which Dido stabbed herself, the pearl of Cleopatra, condensed with difficulty, the horn of Amalthea, a horn of Marcus Aurelius, the goblet of Nestor, the bag of Æolus, the ring of Gyges, the helmet of Pluto, the cup of Circe, a stone of Deucalion, the stone of Sisyphus, the apple of Paris, the apple of Atalanta, the girdle of Venus, the thread of Ariadne, a labor of Hercules, a labor of Leda, the spindle of Clotho, the scissors of Atropos, a leaf from the Cumæan Sibyl, the kettle of Dodona, the sandal of Empedocles recently discovered, some fleas found on the body of Jason, after his death, a bean, the grandsire of Pythagoras, the gad-fly that pursued Io, a chaste piece, the sword of Ulysses, marked "U. S.," the lost books of Livy, the eye of Polyphemus, restored, a primordial atom, a hair of Berenice, a hair of Alcibiades' dog, a serpent from the head of Medusa, still living, one of Socrates' demons, stuffed, a smile of Democritus, preserved in a bottle of Chian wine, a tear of Heracleitus, changed into amber, the golden mean of Epicurus, one of Aristotle's shoes, found near Athens, a hoop of Diogenes' tub—but perhaps the gem of all the curiosities, was one of Plato's divine ideas, sealed in a transparent glass bottle. Over this treasure the college professor of metaphysics often pored for days together, and grew wiser and better the more he studied its mysterious qualities.

The host, who had stepped from the room, now returned and conducted his guests to their couches. Sweatrame was given the highest place upon the highest couch, with Dummer and Hayward below him. With Bowyer, and the shade Pippins, Rakeman occupied the middle couch. Rakeman, himself, had the seat of honor, next the host, who reclined upon the lowest couch, with Saulsbury and the *scurra* Ayres, an object of humor to the rest of the table, for his power of devouring whole loaves at a single mouthful.

As soon as the guests had taken their places, slaves removed their sandals, and poured water, cooled with snow, over their hands and feet. While they were enjoying this agreeable service, a boy with a look of terror ran into the room, and throwing himself at their feet, implored them to intercede for him with his master.

"What was your offence?" inquired Rakeman, kindly.

"My master told me to take his old *toga* as a present"—replied the slave, "and I sold his new one by mistake."

Rakeman and his friends joined in begging their host to pardon so natural an error.

"It is the impudence of the jail-bird, not the loss of the *toga* that provokes me," returned Van Courtland. "The *toga*, to be sure, was of the finest Milesian wool, but it had been worn once, and had a spot upon the inside. What matters it, however! The boy is yours; you shall cast lots for him at the *comissatio.* My stomach barks with hunger, and my teeth are so well shod, that they would win a prize in a race course."

As Van Courtland finished speaking, he clapped his hands, and a band in a corner of the room commenced playing a stirring air.

At this signal, a slave entered bearing the *gustatorium* which he placed upon the table. In the centre of this tray, the dishes of which showed no little ingenuity, was a large platter, on which stood a miniature market-stall. Within the stall appeared an old woman selling various kinds of vegetables. Before her lay baskets of radishes, asparagus, carrots, sliced onions, and beets, dwarf lettuce, noble-hearted cabbages, hiccoughing mint, and other spurs to the weary stomach. Upon the floor of the stall were groups of three dormice, (the parasites of Diogenes,) sprinkled with honey and pepper; one, lying upon his back, was holding an egg in his feet, while two accomplices were dragging away their comrade with his prize, by the tail.

In a second dish was a sow made of paste, wallowing in a trough filled with delicious sauce, the ingredients of which were oil, pepper, vinegar, native wine, and the juices of sea-fish. The breasts of the sow, which were real, and as numerous as those of Diana of Ephesus, had been cooked while unsuckled, and the sow herself was gazing, lost in wonder, at a boy who was pulling from her mouth a string of dainty sausages.

The appearance of a third dish, which bore an olive tree,

was even more singular. The upper branches of this tree were thickly hung with light and dark olives, the pips of which had been removed and replaced by anchovy paste, while its lower branches bore snails, muscles, oysters, scollops, and a variety of small fish.

"This olive tree," said Van Courtland, in answer to an inquiry from Pippins as to the cause of so strange a crop, "was in existence as far back as the flood of Pyrrha,

'Piscium et summa genus hæsit ulmo,'

at which time it was growing upon the summit of a high hill. The waters of the flood reached above the lower branches of the tree half-way to its top, and it has ever since borne olives upon its upper branches, and shell and other fish upon its lower.

The guests were amused at their host's explanation of the miracle, and helped themselves to their choice of the whets to the appetite before them, while two slaves offered them *mulsum* made of honey and old wines.

"The Egyptians eat cabbage before their other food," remarked Hayward, helping himself to some of that dish. "Nothing except sudden grief is a better preventive to drunkenness. The vine, it is said by Theophrastus, runs away at the smell of the cabbage."

"The vine," said Rakeman, "is not the only thing that flies from the smell of boiled cabbage. I take an onion in self-defence, as you work off one wine by another."

"Yesterday," said Pippins, extracting an oyster from its shell with his cochlear, "I saw a hardy Westerner, who was reclining next me at a dinner party, served for the first time with a dish of oysters upon the half-shell. He was very hungry and at once clapped one, shell and all, into his mouth, and began to masticate it. Soon detecting a certain grittiness in the delicacy, 'What coarse food you eat here,' he whispered to me, 'I will not be so effeminate as to spit this one out, but I trust I shall never taste a second.''

After a few minutes' further conversation, the guests expressed themselves satisfied, and the *gustatorium*, at a sign from the band, was quickly removed. Two crisp-haired Ethiopians then entered, one of whom wiped the table with a purple cloth and picked up the crumbs, and whatever might offend the guests, while the other offered them water for their hands.

While they were thus engaged, cup-bearers brought into the room *amphoræ* made of green glass, and carefully sealed with gypsum. The necks of these had attached to them labels which bore the following marks :

"*Falernum. C. Julio Cæsare. IV.*"
"*Cæcubum. Cn. Pompeio. III.*"

The guests read the inscriptions, and the slaves then opened the vessels and poured the wine through a strainer filled with snow into the *crater*.

"We will drink Scythian draughts to-night," said the host, as the slaves passed glasses around the table. "This is sweet Falernian; I warrant it pure. The grapes were pressed when the south-wind blew through the vineyard, which you know makes wine mellow and wild boars tender. Boy!" he then commanded a slave, "fill my cup with wine *cyathi* of Cæcuban."

The slave hastened to obey the order of his master and to pass him a cup, which was curiously fashioned out of a human skull.

"Good luck to you! good luck to us! good luck to our mistresses!" cried the host, "may this draught, my friends, take away all restraint!" and tasting the cup he passed it to Rakeman.

"So may the Gods love me!" exclaimed the latter, handing the cup to his neighbor. "This Cæcuban has a drop of the divine spirit in it."

"I feel obliged, by long custom," said Hayward, "to mix water with my wine. When thus taken, it is more healthy. Indeed, certain philosophers have held that water, even when pure, is nutritious, since grasshoppers live upon that alone."

"It affects grasshoppers more favorably than men," rejoined Rakeman; "the one it makes merry, the other morose."

"How old do you say this Cæcuban is?" inquired the *scurra* Ayres, looking ruefully at the small quantity remaining in the cup. "Many centuries? May I perish, if it is not very little for its years."

"You speak like a cask that thinks only of how much it can hold," responded the host with a laugh, and bade a boy fill the cup anew.

He then again clapped his hands, at which a stalwart slave entered bearing a *repositorium* containing the first regular course of the *cœna.* Within this tray in their several dishes were capons, stuffed hares, a long-breasted lobster, hedged about with asparagus, and delicious eels with shrimps swimming in their sauce.

"What a tail your lobster turns up at us all," observed Saulsbury as the slave deposited his load upon the table. "You, Van Courtland, who hang the world upon your nose, do you not wish you could give that as contemptuous a curve."

"By Ceres!" cried Ayres, enthusiastic at the sight of food, "this is a dinner fit for the Salii. What a godlike eel! One would die content after tasting it. How easily could I win any old woman, by the present of such a treasure, to write me down sole heir!"

While Ayres was talking, the *structor*, keeping time to the music with many artistic flourishes of hand and foot, had deftly carved up the dishes.

"Do not," the host warned his guests, as the slaves passed round the different sorts of food, "waste your forces upon the outworks;" and, after no very long interval, he again gave a signal to the *structor*, at which the main dish of the feast, a huge wild boar, made its appearance upon the table.

The band then sounded a charge, and a slave, dressed after the fashion of auburn-haired Meleager, rushed into the room with a spear, which he thrust into the side of the boar. The stroke discovered numerous bodies of men and dogs made of rich paste, which, with others, impaled upon the tusks of the monster, or lying by its side, were given to the guests to carry away as *apophoreta*.

"That was a terrible contest," mused Van Courtland, as the boar divided itself under the rapid knife of the carver. "had Ayres been there he would have ended it by devouring the creature, tusks and all."

"Milo," observed Rakeman, as Ayres helped himself to no small portion of the dish, "is said to have devoured a whole ox at a single meal : to you, Ayres, he must appear to have been a poor starveling."

"Did you never, Ayres," asked Saulsbury, pursuing the pregnant theme, "hear of Cambles, king of the Lydians? You would have found in him no mean competitor. Though a great epicure, he was also like yourself an admirer of women. These two passions led him one day after a generous dinner, to devour his wife for dessert. Her hand was seen by a friend the next morning protruding from his mouth, and Cambles, who was over sensitive, hanged himself by reason of the disparaging reports to which the affair gave rise.

"Cambles," he added, "was less lucky than Dummer, when he came to college, though he only escaped hanging by a thread."

The rest of the students, at this, turned towards Dummer, who arose and would have left the room in anger.

"Do tell Pippins of your humorous adventure ; that's a good fellow!" urged his host, and the rest joining him in the request, Dummer at length yielded.

Stretching out his right hand, the last two fingers closed, the rest extended, and the thumb upturned, he began.

STORY OF DUMMER, THE STUDENT.

When I first came to college, I cherished the deepest affection for an old woman in town, who always furnished me with the best of good cheer. One night returning from her house to my room well sprinkled with wine, I heard a noise within. Excited by what I had drunk, I drew a dagger and sprang through the doorway. The moment I had entered, I was attacked by a number of men. One tried to hamstring me, a second made a thrust at the middle of my body, while a third seized a table to hurl it at my head. By a downward stroke I disabled the rascal at my feet, then, with a lunge, I ran through the leader of the band before me, and the rest giving way, I pursued and slew them all. Heavy with wine and blood, I then crept to my bed and fell fast asleep.

Aurora's rosy fingers had long since drawn back the veil of night, when I awoke.

Seeing myself covered with gore, I recalled the horrors of the previous night, and burst into tears of regret at having killed so many men.

"Where are the corpses? I then asked myself, not without alarm, when suddenly my door was burst open, and my room filled with lictors, officers and students, who loudly accused me of homicide.

"I am innocent," I protested, but in vain. They dragged me to the forum before the judgment seat, in front of which lay a covered bier, which I doubted not, bore the bodies of the slain.

"Fellow citizens," then began my accuser, who was one of the night watch, "you see before you a murderer who has killed seven citizens in a single night, and who was prevented from killing more by exhaustion rather than humanity. This morning I found these seven bodies lying hacked and bloody, and the prisoner sleeping hard by as peacefully as if he had killed seven fleas.

"Let all men who value their own lives, deal just punishment to the monster, who has deprived our neighbors of theirs."

The people loudly applauded this speech, and the crier then bade me answer.

"My friends," I faltered, struggling to find words in my terror, "I am paralyzed, not with guilt, but with astonishment at this charge. That I killed these robbers I admit, but I killed them in defending myself against their attempt to complete the plunder of my property by the murder of its owner. I beseech you, at least not to punish a man, who, at the risk of his own life, has preserved from danger the lives and fortunes of you all."

"Bravo!" shouted the people, and I should have been at once set free, had not an old hag, whom Death had scorned, made her way through the crowd to the bier, and beating her breast, screeched out, "Pity, my countrymen, I implore you! pity a childless widow. Since you cannot give me back my children, at least give me vengeance. Bid the murderer remove the pall from the bier: the sight of his victims will either strike him dumb or extort a confession."

"Excellent," exclaimed the people, and I was led reluctantly to the bier, and forced to remove the pall, when, oh, ye Gods! what a sight met my eyes. Before me lay seven swine, stabbed and gashed like the body of Cæsar! The sight froze me to the ground, but caused the whole assembly, and the solid earth, to shake with laughter. Many of the spectators rolled in the dust in an agony of mirth; others clasped themselves tightly two and two for safety; not a few burst asunder, and the bulk of them became corpulent from that very moment.

"Do not, friend Dummer," said one of the judges, at length enforcing silence, "think that this jest has been played upon you from any ill will. This is the day of the festival of the god of Laughter, the tutelary divinity of the students, which is always marked by some conceit. It is to propitiate that deity, and not from any want of respect, that you have been offered as a temporary sacrifice."

"By the quiver of Cupid, had you been in such real peril as I myself incurred the other day, you would have cared little for such a jest," said Van Courtland, and his friends urging him, began the following story:

STORY OF VAN COURTLAND, THE STUDENT.

I have, as you know, been long enslaved with love for Galatea, a roguish girl, fresher than ivy, and fairer than the swan. Her father, Damœtas, is a rustic, whose humble turf-covered cottage, smokes behind a scanty field of corn —his little kingdom. Hard by, a brook paints its banks with purple flowers, while overhead, trees and vines weave a pleasant shade.

Damœtas had long since forbidden me to visit his daughter, but what can avail against the power of love, who, with ease, can blind the eyes of Argus, or outwit Mercury himself in cunning?

This simple rustic had two tunics of different colors: one of these, whenever his business would detain him and his stout son, Thyrsis, late from home, Galatea hid, which forced him to wear the other, a well known sign.

A few days since, seeing Damœtas bringing me the message of his absence, I hastened to the cottage.

Entering, I found Galatea alone, and strove to win a kiss from her coy denial. She, eager only not too easily to yield, at length clasped her arms around my neck and exclaimed, "Thus! thus! I forge for you the chains of Venus. Tell me, how long will you wear them?"

"So long," I answered, "as the bee shall love the wild thyme, or the cicada feed upon the dew."

Scarcely had I spoken, when the step of Damœtas and Thyrsis was heard drawing near the door, followed by the bark of their mastiff Scylax, who had run on before them.

Galatea turned pale, and looked anxiously around for some means of escape. Seeing none, she led me into the room next to the one in which we were seated. "This," she hastily whispered, "is your only hiding place," and bade me conceal myself in a large ash-box, which stood in a corner.

In this filthy kennel I crouched, while my mistress ran to the door.

"I was busy cooking," she said, as she opened it, "and did not expect you back so soon."

"Nor should we have returned," replied Damœtas, "but as we approached the market place, a viper ran across our path, and we hurried home, fearing least some evil might befall us."

Without more words, Galatea prepared dinner, and the three sat down to their meal of bacon, gruel, lentils, curds, and mellow apples; for so I heard the old man joyfully tell them over.

Meanwhile I knelt, cramped and covered with ashes, feeling like a mourner at my own funeral, nor in my wretchedness did I believe that the gods any longer heeded the sufferings of us mortals. Suddenly I felt a treacherous cinder eat through my tunic, and burn into my flesh. The pain made me writhe, and the sound caught the too sharp ears of Thyrsis.

"By Silenus!" he cried. "Here's rare sport! A rat in the ash-box! We'll scald it to death!" and springing from his seat, he ran to the fire-place to carry out his purpose.

This suggestion was so far from giving me any pleasure, that with the same breath consigning the boy to the cross, and myself to Good Fortune, I leaped from the box, and sprang towards the door.

"Thieves! thieves! May Jupiter protect us!" shrieked Galatea, and throwing her arms about her father, favored my escape.

I had, however, but reached the centre of the corn-field, when, as the wolf pursues the wanton kid, Scylax bounded upon my track, and in a moment more had seized my toga in his teeth. This I at once threw him as a sop, and before he had devoured it, I was far on my way home, where I arrived, covered with sweat, and foaming at the mouth.

My fellow students, to whom I told my story, showed me no sympathy, but eyed me askance, and muttered to each other, that I had doubtless caught the hydrophobia! One of them soon proposed a most horrible test. Filling two goblets, one with choice Falernian, and the other with water, a beverage I abhor, he whispered to his comrades, "If he drinks the water, he will prove that he is not mad."

They then all left the room, and fastening me alone within, watched my movements through a crack. I was forced, therefore, in order to free myself, to drain a large goblet of water. This, though it proved to my friends that I was sane, almost convinced me that I was indeed a madman."

"You were safe," said Rakeman, "in any event; for they who die for virtue's sake, do not perish."

"So may the God Belly-full love me!" exclaimed the Parasite; "I pity the persons who had tried to stop you. You would have set them all hunting for their teeth and bones. Do you remember that day at the circus, when with one blow of your fist you broke the fore-leg of an elephant—fore-leg, did I say! I meant the thigh—and by a careless stroke. By heaven! had you made an effort, you would have gone through his skull. I drink to your escape: drink deep my patron, a *rex* should never die by a dry death. Had you been lost, what would have become of us parasites," he continued sadly. "Alack-a-day; this business of dining out, is not what it used to be. Those holy words, 'do dine with me to-day,' are growing obsolete in this profane age. Were it not for the few hundred farthings I pick up by way of *sportula*, I should long since have become a hungry shade. I am thinking of making an auction of my mots; whoever bids most dinners shall have them all; I will then retire from my profession, and hang up my tongue in the temple of Ceres. You, indeed, Van Courtland, are a gentleman of the old school: I never make you smile, but you give me *a smile* in return.

"Boy, fill Ayres's glass again; give him another piece of the boar! Look at our friend!" cried the host, admiringly. "How many more pounds he weighs than Hannibal or Cæsar. One continent cannot satisfy him; you must cross the seas and ransack the lakes and forests of the world. Nature opposes to him the rocky shell-fish and the savage boar in vain; he washes them down with a draught of Alban wine. 'Nothing,' he exclaims, 'has been eaten while anything remains that can be eaten!'"

"Speak, Sweatrame, that I may see you," he added, turning to the latter, "you look more gloomy to-day than the solitary tooth of an ancient virgin when she smiles. A painted cheek in a rain storm is more cheerful, or false hair when it feels the caress of a lover."

"No one could have better reason to be sad," replied Sweatrame, "than myself. For three weeks my childless old uncle had been coughing violently. I thought he was about to do the polite thing and that my fortune was made. God help me; this morning I met him hale and hearty; he had been only flattering me. Once I believed what the poets tell us was true, that all men are mortal. Now I have ceased to cherish even such a hope."

The guests were silent for some minutes in pity for the sufferer, when the host nodded to the *structor*, at which slaves entered with a charger which they placed upon the table. This was filled with a figure made of rich paste, which represented the citadel of Rome, guarded by six fat geese with their feathers still upon them.

"How can we eat fowls unplucked?" asked the disappointed faces of the guests. The host smiled at their confusion, when the carver, without using a knife, took hold of the tail of each goose and lifting it back, disclosed the insides filled with stuffed geese's livers, truffles, more costly than Sicilian granaries, pieces of cranes sprinkled with salt and corn, limbs of pregnant hares torn off, rare fish, blackbirds, and pigeons without their haunches.

"That hare will make you handsome for seven days," said Pippins, a man famous for cutting men's throats with a mot, as Saulsbury was helping himself to a piece of that dish. "Eat it quickly that we may see the change."

"If eating a hare makes one handsome," returned the

latter, "it is clear, Pippins, that you have never so much as tasted one."

"Geese often cackle when there is no Rome to be saved," rejoined Pippins, at a loss for a repartee.

"By Ceres!" broke out the belly of Ayres, "how happy this fish looks for gracing the table of our *rex*. 'I was eager,' it seems to say, 'to be caught!'" and the parasite grasped a whole fish with one hand, while with the other he took the last piece of bread from the bread-basket.

"May the gods confound you!" muttered Hayward, angrily. "At least, Ayres, leave food enough in the world to furnish your own funeral feast. Your mouth seems the breathing hole of Hell! Oh, the morality of this age! We are devoured by diners out and parasites. What can be worse than these flatterers? Smile, and they break into a horse laugh; weep, and they drown you in tears. I wonder, Ayres, that you have never left your soul sticking in the gravy, like the shoe of a horse that has been lost in the mud!"

"Cease your barking, you crabbed cynic," exclaimed Sweatrame; "you swim through the conversation like a cuttle-fish that turns all the water around it into ink. The stomach is the fountain of all good. My sole prayer to the gods is that they may keep mine always full. I have made me a Bacchus out of a sponge, to which every day I pour out—I mean I pour down libations."

"You should rather pray," said Hayward, "for a soul that is unmoved by anger or desire; that prefers the labors of Hercules to lust, or luxury, or pomp. What do you think will be your end with your purse still shrinking as your throat widens, when you have sunk all your property in a belly large enough to contain horses and houses and broad acres?"

"By Bacchus, I will then go and live in my belly if it is so large and well furnished."

"May the gods," cried Rakeman, "give you a barber, Hayward, for your advice! Do you accuse Sweatrame of extravagance? Whatever its price, who can pay less for anything than he who pays nothing? 'The thief,' he teaches his creditors, 'will break open your money chests; the flames will devour your houses; the waves will swallow up your ships. That which you give your friends is alone out of the reach of fortune; that alone you will possess for ever; 'and no human creature,' he reminds them, 'should be other than a friend and a neighbor.'"

"What one obtains on credit," said Pippins, "is indeed the gift of the gods."

"Extravagance!" shouted Sweatrame. "Blame me for extravagance! What can be lower than to dispute the price of anything? There is but one possible combination of circumstances when it is not base, and that is when you intend to pay for it."

"Though to borrow," urged Hayward, "is human, to pay is divine."

"Have done with your strife, my friends!" begged the host; "Again rest your elbows on the couches! Fill up your glass Hayward! Even great Socrates loved jovial dinner parties, and went so far as to wash his face and put on his shoes when he went to them."

"Whoever wishes," continued Rakeman, not to be moved, "may undertake the labors of Hercules: for myself I do not disdain to while away the morning with draughts of good old Falernian, while my mistress, seated by my side, spins out for me the golden thread of life."

"Your philosophy is partial, Hayward," said Saulsbury, "my aim is to fit myself for any station, to be equally at home in a palace or a hovel, and equally well dressed in purple or in rags."

"Give me," mused Bowyer, "a moderate fortune, a hearth always burning, health, strength, a few books, and a wife not over learned, and you may have all the palaces and hovels in the world."

"Why has the band stopped playing?" called out the host. "Drain your glasses, my friends! Boy, do you not see Pippins' glass there is empty? Fill up all your glasses again! When drinking does not keep lengths with talking, a dinner is a sorry cripple."

The slaves, hastening to obey their master's order, tipped over an *amphora* of Chian wine.

The sight of so much good wine spilling made Ayres faint away.

"Give him a kiss!" cried Sweatrame, as Saulsbury in vain to strove to bring back the parasite to life. "Close up his eyes. *Conclamatum est.* Take him down and throw hot water over him!"

The host, however, shrewdly nodded to the *structor*, and the smell of the fourth course, which consisted of two noble peacocks, at once awoke Ayres to life and hunger.

When this course was finished, slaves removed the trays, and sprinkled the floor with sawdust mixed with saffron and cinnabar.

"Do not," said Ayres to his host, "allow your slaves to approach too near the cynic: they will be bitten, and dog days are near."

"Have you no sulphur?" retorted Hayward, "to purify us from this pestilence;" and the dispute would have waxed warmer, had not the guests been attracted by the singular device of the *mensæ secundæ* which were now served.

A miniature vineyard and orchard divided a large platter. In the vineyard, vines covered with clusters of grapes, clung to their marital elms. The trees in the orchard were hung with a variety of fruit; apples, olives, plums, pears, dates, figs, and quinces stuck over with almonds. Among the branches were perched small game birds stuffed with paste, raisins, and nuts, while suspended from the largest tree two Priapi watched over the orchard and warned off intruders. Lying on the grass was Mercury with the spoils of a thieving excursion spread out before him.

"This little dog," said the host, taking up one of them, "is yours, Pippins; it has more tricks than would fill a page. Let me present these dumb-bells to you, Bowyer, though I think you would find it a healthier exercise to dig in the vineyard than to use them. These barber's instruments are for you, Hayward. Both these Priapi you may have, Sweatrame; though you eat every bit of them you will not be less pure."

The guests wrapped their *apophoreta* in their napkins, Ayres receiving a gridiron and two cheese cakes, Dummer a parasol and a box of pomatum, Rakeman, a set of *tesseræ*, and Saulsbury some Vitellian tablets.

"Whoever wishes," said the host, as a slave was passing around tooth-picks made of lentisc wood, "can now bathe. You need not fear sudden death and intestacy; the bath, I assure you, is well tempered." Then bidding a slave watch a *clepsydra* which marked an hour, and summon them when it had half run out, Van Courtland followed his guests from the room.

"How sweet your flowers smell!" exclaimed Ayres when the guests had reassembled in the *triclinium*, brilliantly lighted with candelabra. "Would that I were all nose, (saving my belly's presence,) that I might enjoy them the better!"

"Give me a crown of ivy," cried Rakeman, as he reclined upon his couch; "I will foil Bacchus with his own weapons."

"I prefer the myrtle sacred to Venus," said Sweatrame.

"I shall wear a garland of violets and hyacinths around my neck after the Greek fashion," said the host. "You, Wentworth, will pull your wreath in pieces, we all know why. Who shall be master of the feast?" he added, when the rest of the guests had bound their perfumed hair with chaplets of roses. "You, Pippins, make the first throw," and he passed the dice-box to the latter.

"May my mistress favor me!" prayed Pippins as he

made his cast. "By the three mouths of Cerberus, it is the dog."

"Give me the dice," cried Rakeman. "See I have thrown a Venus," and luck favoring none of the rest, Rakeman was confirmed as Lord of the Cup.

"Drink," he commanded, "as many *cyathi* as there are letters in the name of our host! Good-bye to all water: What we drink to-night shall be unadulterated. Now, my boys, as many *cyathi* as there are letters in the names of our mistresses!"

"Remember the saying," urged Hayward, "the first cup for thirst, the second for mirth, the third for delight, the fourth for madness; we should drink with moderation."

"A farthing for moderation!" returned Rakeman. "Nothing great was ever accomplished by moderation. Æschylus was well soaked when he wrote his tragedies. Alcæus and Aristophanes were never sober. Immortality is a tippler. We will make Bacchus himself envious. Boy, strain the wine more quickly!"

"Drink deep!" cried Sweatrame. "The just enjoy an immortality of intoxication in Hades, as a reward for their virtue. Rakeman, my good fellow, since we cannot hope for that, we will make the best of our present life."

"Even Plato," observed the host, "that pink of propriety, allowed his disciples to get drunk on sacred days."

"Then," added Sweatrame, "I will so live that every day shall be a Sunday—I mean a sacred day."

"Silence!" enjoyed Rakeman, "while each of us sings a song in turn. I will begin, to give your confidence.

"Fill full the cup, my boys,
Each drop we sup, my boys,
Floats our hearts up.
  Joy's wings quickly clutch,
  Cast the cripple Care a crutch ;
  And while a health goes round,
  Let bright To-day be ivy crowned!
  In dull delay what pleasure's found?

Fill full the cup, my boys,
Each drop we sup, my boys,
Floats our hearts up.
  Let the poor miser measure
  For a fool's heirs his treasure ;
  We'll bid a health go round ;
  Let our To-day with gold be crowned!
  In hoarded wealth what pleasure's found?

Fill full the cup, my boys,
Each drop we sup, my boys,
Floats our heart up.
  What's war?—but a rattle,
  And fame?—but vain prattle ;
  Then bid a health go round ;
  Our brows with ivy shall be bound!
  In thirsty bays what pleasure's found?

Fill full the cup, my boys.
Each drop we sup, my boys,
Floats our hearts up.
  Where gloomy Styx flows,
  Nor grape nor kiss grows ;
  Then bid a health go round ;
  Let live To-day in joys abound!
  In Death's dark realms what pleasure's found?"

"Bravo!" cried Ayres, and clapped his hands. "Catullus himself is outdone. But in Bacchus's name, let us drink between songs; the gluck of wine is the sweetest melody to my ear."

"I have some verses about Danae and her child," said Saulsbury, upon whom Rakeman next called; "Let me recite them in place of a song.

"Sleep! Beauty, sleep! thy head upon my breast,
Ah! burden of delight! is gently prest;
Thy rosy eyelids closed cannot all hide
Thine eyes' soft light; the rays their veil divide
As sun-beams clouds: on thy sweet lips a smile
Is brightening of magic to beguile
The raging night of gloom. Sleep! beauty, sleep!
While o'er thy sacred form, my prayers keep
Vigil. Without, I hear the angry wave,
The cruel wind, and man more cruel rave;
But thou, Darling, clasped in thy mother's arm
Sleepst calmly on, what shouldst thou dream of harm?"

"Would to Jupiter," sighed Sweatrame, "some one would turn herself into gold for love of me! I would clap her into my girdle before she could be retransformed."

"I have a surprise for you," said the host when the guests had finished their songs. "What would you not give to see Nania as Ariadne!"

At these words a curtain drawn across one end of the room fell, and unveiled a beautiful danseuse. A turban was bound about her head; an eastern robe hung loosely from her shoulders, her lips were parted, her hands stretched forth in supplication. The band began to play a plaintive air, and the chorus to sing the *canticum*,

"Siccine me patriis avectam, perfide, ab oris,
Perfide, deserto liquisti in litore, Theseu?"

as Ariadne, with sinking steps, moved slowly across the stage.

The flutes then quickened their measures: the dancer's step grew light; her eyes flashed through their mask; her hands, feet, and body, spoke the eloquence of wild despair; her robe seemed reluctant to hide so many charms.

"'Tis Tiptonini," cried Sweatrame, "as sure as I'm a Roman citizen," and he drained an Allifanian cup.

"Brava! brava!" shouted Rakeman, and threw his wreath at Ariadne's feet.

Ayres placed his hand upon his belly, speechless.

Suddenly wild and inhuman shrieks broke into the room, and called all the guests to their feet.

Our readers, to learn the cause of this interruption, must turn their eyes towards the *ostium*. The slave there fastened, had, during the main part of the evening, continued sober. As the weight of his chains increased, however, time began to drag heavily with him.

"Be me sowl!" he muttered, "if I only had a dhrop of poteen! sure it's myself knows the ould smack of it. Musha, acushla macree," he called to a young slave passing by, "may the ould boy keep a cool corner for you in Hell! will you not give me the smallest dhrop of somethin' to keep out the cowld o' the evenin'?"

The boy was won by this rude eloquence, and the Infant drained goblet after goblet of choice wines, which in the absence of poteen he pronounced "foin dhrinks."

The conflict of these children of Bacchus among themselves, soon kindled a kindred spirit of warfare in the Milesian. The dog Romulus, who had grown restive at the noises about him, offered a ready occasion for its display.

"Arrah! bear yourself asy, ye crooked cur!" hiccoughed the Infant, as the dog gave a low growl. "Is it myself you'll be after bitin', ye dirty orangeman! How do ye like the douse o' this switch, ye bluthy heretic!" and he struck the dog a smart blow with his *virga.* "Is it giving back talk ye are, ye spalpeen!" a poke with the rod, and a deep growl from Romulus. "The curse o' the crows upon you, ye devil's limb! Is it sich a baste as you that shall be after aggrawatin' a dacent man like myself! Do ye think I'm a beggarly nager?"—more pokes, and fiercer growls.

Thus, by gentle banter with Romulus, the Infant strove to solace his weary minutes. The pleasure of the dog, however, in this diversion, did not seem so keen as that of the Milesian. Romulus's growls grew deeper, and a row of teeth displayed themselves, which even with one of the Infant's race, when sober, would have pleaded feelingly for peace. The sight of them, in his present mood, only spurred the slave with greater zest upon his sport. He again poked the dog with his rod, then snapt his fingers near his nose, and at length stooping down, blew in his face. At this, Romulus drawing back a few inches, leaped at his tormentor's throat.

The Infant had just reason enough left in him to spring back for dear life, when snap went the dog's chain: and as the slave, forgetting that he was bound, turned to run, the dog's teeth buried themselves deep in the fleshiest part of his person. Romulus's earnest gripe acted like a charm to restore the Infant to soberness, but not, alas! to content. As the dog's teeth pierced the shield of the slave's skin, he gave a howl, in which the groans and yells of three funerals in his native country, and three meeting together in the Roman Forum seemed marvellously blended.

"Holy Virgin! och! I'm murthered! ogh! be the holy man! take aff the baste! I'm dead! I'm kilt entirely! Saver above! a priest! a priest! och, the rip o' Hell!" such were the undigested words that burst with extreme unction from the lips of the hardened sinner, who doubtless preferred his former drunkenness with all its depravity to the sharp medicine of returning sobriety.

The tumult at once brought all the guests to the *ostium*.

"How happens it?" exclaimed Van Courtland angry at the interruption, "that no one lives content with his lot, whether reason marks it out, or chance throws it in his way? Huc! huc!" he called, seeing the blood upon the floor; but not the eloquence of Cicero could have tempted the stern moralist to let go his hold upon the Infant's mind.

"Mother o' glory!" shrieked the slave, "I'm murthered! och! wurra! wurra! Take him off. Be the crass, it's penethratin' entirely. I'm kilt! I'm kilt! och! ogh! a priest! a priest!"

"Throw water over him, Robin," cried Wentworth, and with Rakeman seized the dog by the throat, while Van Courtland grasped him by the tail, calling "huc, huc!"

"Huc!" repeated Sweatrame, whose state inclined him to construe all things with humor, "hoc! give me some hock. Damn your Falernian. Give a rouse, boys. Cure a man with a hair of the dog that bit him," he added, striking a more practical vein.

The growls of the mastiff, the yells of the Infant, the shouts of Van and his friends, the maudlin advice of Sweatrame, the scholia of the parrot, the dainty cries of Tiptonini—"What does all this mean?" demanded Tutor Brown, suddenly entering the door.

"Save me, save me!" gasped Tiptonini delighted at finding some one at leisure, and swooned with abandon into the arms of the ravished tutor.

"Thank Jove! he's off," said Van, as the dog, half drowned by Ayres, let go his hold, and the Infant, unchained by Rakeman, took to his heels at full speed after a priest.

"Is that the way you treat a lady, sir?" exclaimed Tiptonini, leaping with a single bound from the floor on which she had been deposited, and eying the tutor with indignation.

"Gentlemen, I shall have to report you all to the Faculty," growled the tutor, "give me your names."

"Will you not, Mr. Brown," inquired Sweatrame courteously, "before you make haste to take your leave of us, have a glass of choice old Cæcuban wine, sealed in the consulship of——"

"Wine, sir!" barked the tutor, scratching his right ear in anger. "Have you been having wine, in your rooms! Your offence is rank, sir, rank!"

"The very last offence of which I should have suspected myself," returned Sweatrame, who stood at the foot of the class.

The tutor made no reply, but snapt his fingers,

slapped his right thigh, and with a malignant smile left the hall.

"I feared as much," mused Van, gazing after him, "for yesterday, as I was turning into Concord Street, I beheld perched upon the steeple of the old Unitarian Church an ill omened crow, that cawed hoarsely at my approach, boding evil. However, what matters it? '*nunc vino, cras ingens,*' and returning with his friends, to the room, they continued their revels until the morning.

Two days later, Van learnt that his dinner, added to numerous other offences, had been made the occasion, by the Faculty, of his banishment to the town of Stockbridge for six months.

| "*Vos valete et plaudite.*" |

CHAPTER XIV.

"Nomen tamen haud leve patrum
Manibus hoc referes, telo cecidisse Camillæ."

"Columbarum fera natura est."

LEASE pull off my gloves for me, Mr. Saulsbury; my hands are frozen," said Miss Campbell, with whose charms the quaint old window-seat in Wentworth's room was blossoming.

The girl, as she spoke, reached out her hand to our hero, who was seated at her feet alone ——

"Explain yourself!" cries Mrs. Grundy in her severest voice; but we enjoy keeping that censorious duenna in suspense.

"What a cheerful fire you have!" continued the girl, looking around the room. "See how the light leaps over the beams in the ceiling, and plays hide-and-go-seek in the carvings of your book-cases. What a clever idea of yours, that picture is!" and she pointed to a painting of Wentworth's new room in Massachusetts Hall, in which the photographs of his friends had been ingeniously set.

"Where can mother and Amy be!" she added, with an impatience that gratified Propriety more than her other hearer. "How did we get separated from them? Is it not too provoking? What a charming song your friend, Mr.

Ayres, sang at the concert ; it has always been a favorite of mine :

> 'My soul I bid thee answer,
> How are love's marvels wrought,
> Two hearts to one pulse beating,
> Two spirits to one thought.
>
> And tell me how love cometh,
> It comes unsought, unsent ;
> And tell me how love goeth,
> It was not love that went.' "

Miss Campbell had as sweet a voice as ever fitted the hearts of men for stratagems and treasons. As she sang, Wentworth stole a glance of admiration at the picture before him, whose beauty flattered the gray old room, and won from its sombre walls a smile of pleasure. Miss Campbell sat closely muffled in a thick, white cloak, which set off the delicate hue of her cheeks, which is the pride of the girls of our Eastern coast. One dainty foot crept from beneath the waves of her dress ; an arch smile had escaped from her dimples to sun itself upon her rosy lips ; the gentle movement of her breast gave eloquence to her imperial form. She sang with rich feeling, but without effort, like some magic instrument that voluntarily pours out its notes.

"If I were not an angel," she said, as she ended her song, "I should not have come with you this evening. You have treated me in the most brutal manner : last winter you did not even make me a party-call ; and you have only been to see me twice this year. I have half a mind to revenge myself upon you," and she gave Wentworth a glance, half-humorous, half-earnest, which would have made a mother tremble for her son."

"My enemies," replied our hero, "could not wish me

a worse punishment than the thought of the pleasure I have thus lost."

The boy had now completed half his long task, and drew one dangerous hand from its tiny sheath. The hand was cold, but at its touch a sudden fire of mingled pain and rapture ran through Wentworth's veins, and with soft flame played about his lips, and eyes, and temples.

"You sing, do you not, Mr. Saulsbury?" asked Miss Campbell, drawing back her hand. "You are such a Crichton, I thought you must. Yes; women like men who sing and dance, but they never think of falling in love with them. Is not that a picture of the Harvard Boat: you are in the crew, arn't you? Mrs. Morris tells me you are a great student also: how can you find time to be both? I wish I could be a scholar," and the girl's face lit up with enthusiasm. "One would not then waste one's life in idle formalities, but live to some high purpose, arming the Truth of the past to fight for the Hope of the future. See, the moon has just risen," and, with the prudence of her sex, Miss Campbell made Wentworth throw open the window, and leaned out. "One ought always to see a college by moonlight. The sun is a funeral torch; it only lights up the dead. The moonlight infuses the world with life: at its coming the elves dance on the green; the spirits of the forests and the streams glide from their haunts, and the banished gods move along the pathway of the skies.

"How easy it must be to study in these old buildings," she continued, looking back into the room, "and how glorious, when you have mastered your weapons, to go out into the world and compete for its honors. I know you must be ambitious; I had sooner see a man dead than lose his ambition. Tell me what you are going to do when you leave college. I hope you will succeed; success is so important, and yet it is so difficult: even the brightest men often fail."

"Success," replied Wentworth; for at the call of a woman, who of us does not love to tread that narrow path, that, bordering on the ridiculous, alone leads to the soul's heights? "What is education worth, if it does not teach us the rule of life, that makes success certain? What the world calls success is difficult to gain, and when gained is of little worth. Real success is even more difficult, but the path to it is plain; it is the climbing it that is so hard. The highest development of our highest nature—he who makes this his earnest aim through life succeeds, and he alone achieves a success worth living for. Wealth, position, birth!—these distinctions are but the rude attempts of the herd to classify themselves. The largest growth is the truest success; he who strives for that, whether he lives as a prince or peasant, what matters it! to a Man, all places are alike honorable."

"What should you do if you fell in love?" asked Miss Campbell, who listened to the boy with amusement, not unmixed with admiration. "That would sadly interfere with your scheme, would it not."

"My love," answered Wentworth, with warmth, "should grow with my growth; it should be the divine counterpart of every thought and feeling, the life of my life, the soul of my soul!"——

A loud knock, worthy of the ghost of Malthus, interrupted this gentle discourse, and made Wentworth spring to the door.

"I'm so glad to see you," he said, with the earnestness of insincerity, as Mrs. Campbell, with her niece, Miss Leigh, entered the room, under the protection of Rakeman, the brave Southron; "I was on the point of running out to look for you; how did you escape us; we thought you were just behind us. Shall I not take your cloak, Miss Leigh?"

"I thought we were going to Mrs. Morris's," said Rakeman, "and didn't find out my mistake till we were some distance from your room."

"We seem to have reached a very comfortable harbor, at last," said Mrs. Campbell, whose serenity returned with her breath, and was not dispelled by the sight of a pleasant supper spread upon the table.

"What luxurious rooms you have!" she added, seating herself upon the sofa, and loosening her furs; "Carpets, pictures, curtains! how college has changed since my time!"

"It must have changed very quickly, then," returned Wentworth, a remark which shook for some months the good lady's belief in the degeneracy of the present day. "You can't think, Mrs. Campbell," he continued, "how the sight of ladies in college touches the heart of a student.

——'O brave new world,
That has such people in 't!'

Most of us have never seen a woman, except a College Goody, who is a sort of she-Caliban."

A stalwart Ethiop, who answered to the name of Ariel, now passed round supper, after which Rakeman made a short speech, of which the burden was the contrast that this jewelled hour of delight offered to the grim rigor and Herculean labors of college life.

"Is not that the sign of the Mush and Milk Club, Mr. Saulsbury?" asked Miss Campbell, as Rakeman ended. "How I should like to belong to a secret society! Do tell me all about it."

"We are bound by the most solemn oaths, Miss Campbell"——

"Oh, you know it is no crime to perjure yourself for a woman."

"Well, if you insist on it, but remember that I risk my life for you: treason, by the laws of the Club, is punished with death. The initiation is very warming; compared to it, the tortures of the stake, the rack, the cross, or even your frown, Miss Campbell, are but gentle pastimes"——

"How ungallant! you don't know; you underrate me," returned the girl, justly incensed.

"Nonsense! Mr. Saulsbury," broke in Miss Leigh, "you can't deceive me. Mr. Brandreth once showed me a photograph of Mr. Bowyer as Titania, and told me all about your plays and suppers; he said you had nothing but ortolans and Lafitte."

"He broke his oath," said Rakeman, gloomily. "Were

it not so natural, Miss Leigh, to break anything for your sake, I should inform against him."

"How nobly your Oxford cap looks!" cried Miss Campbell, who had been again examining the contents of the room; and going to the wall she took it down and placed it upon her head. The learned cap cast a shadow of wisdom on the girl's fair face, and chid the laughing waves of chestnut hair that mocked its authority.

"*Exspectata oratio a* Campbell," cried Wentworth, imitating the voice of the worthy President.

"'*Quousque tandem*——'" began Miss Campbell, shaking a threatening finger at our hero.

"Hear! hear!" cried Rakeman, rapping with his knuckles on the table.

"Stop! stop!" interposed Mrs. Campbell, good humoredly, "this is very improper."

"Do allow her to finish the oration, please," begged Wentworth; "'when you are at Rome, do as the Romans do.' Portia herself could not have been a better orator."

"I think, on the whole, mother is right," said Miss Campbell, with a puzzled look. "It would be improper to go on."

"Are those brown things the sign of a secret society, too, Mr. Rakeman?" asked Miss Leigh, looking at the table on which Miss Campbell had laid the cap. "Boxing gloves! Do teach me how to use them," and springing up, she buried one little bunch of fives in the recesses of a pugnacious glove.

The gallant Southron helped his pupil arm herself, and

with what to an observer seemed over-care, placed her hands in position, and taught her to poise herself, to draw back her head from the blow, and to strike from the shoulder.

"Miss Campbell, will not you be umpire?" he asked, drawing on the gloves himself, and challenging his fair foe to mortal combat.

"I'll hold the bottle and sponge for Miss Leigh," cried Wentworth. "Mrs. Campbell, you will do as much for Rakeman, I am sure," and he passed a champagne bottle to the startled but good natured matron. "Miss Campbell, you give the word."

Rakeman, as Wentworth spoke, turned his head from Miss Leigh towards him for a moment, when suddenly the treacherous Amazon unchained the beauty and terror of her arm, and Rakeman's nob received a declaration of war, and a fierce attack at the same moment.

"Victory!" exclaimed Miss Leigh, for women have no principle and enjoy a triumph, however won.

"A foul blow!" said Wentworth. "You must pay Rakeman a forfeit by all the rules of the prize ring."

"I have only a glove," replied the blushing Penthesilea. "I thought all means were fair in war as in love."

"Why, Mr. Saulsbury!" exclaimed Miss Campbell, who had been looking over his books, while Rakeman and Miss Leigh were settling upon the terms of peace. "Are you suchan admirer of Byron? here are three copies of his works?"

"I think him a great genius, but a man of little education. His selfish moral nature prevented him from being objective, or he would have been almost as great a poet as Shakespeare."

"How can you think Byron a genius?" said Miss Leigh, "He was such a brute to his wife."

"Don't you think his influence is as good as Thackeray's?" asked Wentworth. "They both found the world very hollow, and both beat the devil's tattoo upon it; but Byron, at least, made it sound grand and impressive. It was very wrong for him to fall in love with every handsome woman he met; but you all expect it, and feel offended with us if we do not do it; is not that true, Mrs. Campbell?"

"How should I know?" answered Mrs. Campbell, who still retained much of her early beauty, and was not displeased at the inquiry. "I'm afraid, girls," she added, "that it is time for us to start. I don't know, Amy, what your mother would think of me, if she knew on what a romp we had been."

"Who would have thought," said Miss Campbell, "tha. you, mother, who are the most respectable woman in Boston, would ever be a——what do you call it, Mr. Saulsbury? a bottle-holder in a prize-fight."

"Do not hurry; you have plenty of time to catch the last car. I wish I could urge you to stay longer," said Wentworth, as with Rakeman he helped the ladies put on their cloaks; after which they walked to the cars, and rode into town.

"I will tell you a secret," said Miss Campbell to oui hero, as they drew near her house; "it is only known to a few dozen of my girl friends : you must promise not to tell it. I am engaged to Mr. Otis : it is coming out next week when he returns from the South. He said he knew you."

"I congratulate him," replied Wentworth, whose face did not seem to echo his words.

On reaching the house, Mrs. Campbell asked the two boys to come in, but they excused themselves, and walked together to the favorite haunt of men of wit in breezy Boston, where they spent the night.

"My dear Van," Wentworth wrote his friend the next morning, "I feel blue to-day, and write to you in order to cheer myself up. Ever since your banishment, I have done nothing but study and write : I am editor of the *Harvard Magazine*, you know, with Gowan and Hayward, and have to furnish an article a month, which is hard work.

"Rakeman and I were elected last week into the Sausage Club, where I now spend an hour every day after dinner, reading : we have a capital library. They called on us for a speech at the initiation, and Rake made a very good one, in which he said that a gentleman was a man who used more water on the outside of his body, and less on the inside, than any other man ; a sentiment which was received with great favor.

"The whole college for a month past has been dedicated to music : the dancing fiddle, the cathartic trumpet, the pious harp, have been all tuning themselves for the Glee-Club concert, which was given last evening.

"Most animals, even women, when dead, are silent ; the

cat alone, who makes night musical in life, in death, though with a different organ, prolongs his strains. I wrenched four tickets from Rake and Ayres, which I sent to Miss Campbell, and in the evening I escorted her with her mother and cousin, Miss Leigh, to the concert. I introduced Rake to them, and he became very sweet on Miss Leigh. As we were going to our room, where I had ordered a spread, Miss Campbell and I got separated from the others and reached it some time before them. The girl perched herself in the old window-seat, where she looked very pretty. After leaving the ladies at their house in town, Rake and I went to Parker's, where your health was not forgotten.

"Nothing else of great public interest has happened, except that a few days since some silly Sophs set off some fireworks in our favorite professor's room.

"By the way, I never wrote you about the Mock Parts; you had three or four.

> —— 'Are not these woods
> More free from peril than the envious court?'

was one of them, I remember. I think that these personalities are low, don't you, and should like to see the custom abolished.

"Do write me a description of your place of exile, and of the people you are with; you have never told me any thing about them; and tell me how you stand the cold in Siberia, now that winter has come. Oblige me by giving my love to all the pretty girls whom you meet, and believe me always your sincere friend,

"WENTWORTH SAULSBURY."

"My dear chum," replied Van's letter a few days after, "Your favor of the — came duly to hand, as our worthy governors write. I weep at its contents, and the reports I hear concerning thee. Grievous complaints are abroad; 'tis rumored that thou hast become a dreamer, a dig, an editor. Villainous company, 'tis said, thou consortest with; scrubs, who know not the brush; theologs who make long prayers; once 'twas whispered—my hair whitening at the tale—thou wast seen walking with a law-student.

"And yet there is a virtuous man, whom I have often noted in thy company; a man with a fine leg, a pleasing eye, and a most noble carriage: and, now I remember me, his name is Van Courtland. He knows how to handle the ribbons, and to lead the mazy dance: he is skilled to blow the purple rings, to mix the stealthy punch, to strike the ivory ball. There is virtue in that man, or he deceiveth me. Keep with him, you are safe—banish him, banish hope.

"You ask me to give you a description of Stockbridge. It is a beautiful place, even in winter, and I have been thankful to the Faculty ever since I came here for my suspension. The society is as agreeable as the scenery. Every other person you meet here is, to be sure, as in Boston, a genius; but as they think that a member of Harvard College must be also a genius, and as I am at no pains to undeceive them, we get along bravely together.

"I am living in a pleasant house set back from the road, surrounded by a dozen acres of land, and shielded from the sun or wind by fine old trees. My teacher, who is, as you know, a clergyman of reputation, is an admirable scholar, and the most courteous man in the world. He has, also, a most charming wife, who is surrounded by a 'brood of darlings,' with lovelier faces than Raphael ever stole from heaven.

"I wish you could look in upon us to-night. The family gathering-place is a large, comfortable room, hung with a few portraits, and a painting of a deer killed by the parson's grandfather. A snow storm is blowing without, and we are all at home. A hale old black servant, who has been a great many years in the family, has just brought in some logs with which the hearth is blazing merrily. A sweet child with motherly ways is seated before the fire, and whispering to her doll the stories, which her dry old crony, the andiron, has been telling her. The poor doll bruised his finger badly this morning, and a piece of muslin dipt in arnica, has been carefully wrapped about it. Nearer the fire basks a gray tabby cat, with a face of great benignity, that breathes a benediction over the scene. The mistress of the house is knitting a pair of mittens, and listening to a golden little boy, who with tears in his eyes is reciting to her the ballad of the Children in the Wood. That holy look of a true mother's face! How it steals into the heart like a silent prayer! Pshaw! old boy, I believe my principles are being undermined by these people: they make me fear that I am at heart no better than a domestic man.

"I shall go to New York in a few days: the pure and sacred influence of that New Jerusalem will restore my moral tone. I have, however, a strong presentiment that

I shall be taken physically sick there, and forced by the advice of a physician to remain in the city the rest of the term.

"Hoping against hope, that you will not deteriorate more during my absence,

"I remain, till death do us part, your friend,

"SCHUYLER VAN COURTLAND.

"*P.S.*—Rake sent me a bale of perique the other day: may his sins, which are many, be forgiven him for this charity.

"*Note.*—Don't try to palm off your remorse after a drinking-bout, as grief for my absence."

CHAPTER XV.

"Sed nil dulcius est, bene quam munita tenere
Edita doctrina sapientum templa serena,
Despicere unde queas alios passimque videre
Errare atque viam palantis quærere vitæ."

"Eugepæ : Thalem talento non emam Milesium:
Nam [pol] ad sapientiam huius nimius nugator fuit."

"TIME was, Wentworth," said Van one day, throwing himself back in the old arm-chair of the Sausage Club, to which he had been chosen on his return from exile; "time was, Wentworth, when your laugh outroared the North wind, and your appetite shook the granaries; but thee now, nor the talker pipe delights, nor the athlete ale, nor the oyster, his own dish, nor the coxcomb champagne, nor the hero brandy; and thou, who wast wont to feed on all things, art become thyself a dish for brooding melancholy, pinning thy soul as a bob to the kite of a woman's vanity."

Wentworth had during the term been often rallied by Van for his fits of despondency, and this afternoon had confessed that the cause of his low spirits was that *primum mobile* of evil, a woman.

"'You apprehend a world of figures,' Van," he replied pleasantly, as his chum ended. "I felt sure from her manner that she fancied me; and to flirt with me the very night she told me she was engaged; but I don't believe she would try to make me fall in love with her merely to gratify her vanity, do you?"

Cupid is both a Fury and a Momus, and Van was on the laughing side of the rascally Janus.

"I have read of women guilty of such crimes," he rejoined, "though I am glad to say I never met one;" and the spoilt child of fashion stroked a dangerous pair of whiskers he had grown, and gave his friend a quizzical look.

"I remember once telling her," said Wentworth, "that no woman could make me fall in love with her against my will, and seeing a look of power flash from her eyes."

"Telling her what?" exclaimed Van. "Pique a woman, and not know she would revenge herself: I don't blame her. If I were you, I would learn from my enemy: show her that you are her master at her own weapons; that your self-command is more perfect; that your wit is more dangerous than hers. Love in a woman is a mixture of passion and fear; the girl will soon fall in love with you, if she likes you already: she'll be all the more apt to do so, now that she is engaged; you know you're a good looking fellow enough, and that after all is the main thing."

"How can a man wish to give pain to a woman he loves, Van? I can't think that you are in earnest. I shall throw myself into study and exercise and try to forget her."

"There is philosophy in thee, shepherd," answered Van, more seriously. "But if love some fine day doesn't run off with your wits, before that lean domestic can shut the door, the girl can't be very fascinating. Philosophy does very well to lock the door of the empty stable, or to prove 'no horse,' or 'spavin,' but at bottom he's a quack. Still, if you want to take up the line of forgetting her, read Montaigne, Thackeray, and such writers; they'll draw the teeth from your grief for you."

"I hate your emasculated skeptics," returned Wentworth; "It is better to be the slave of a noble passion, than to be master of such puny ideals as they offer you; such men are fit neither for heaven nor elsewhere."

"That third place is the home for me, too, old boy," said Van, blowing a ring from his meerschaum: "A region where the fierce heat of the infernal shore is softened to a genial temperament, and the frigid virtue of heaven mellowed to a more kindly warmth: that's what this world would be, were it not for you puritanical fellows, who make such a pother with your rights and reforms. But I forgot to ask the name of the lucky man, Mr. Otis? I used to know him in Paris; he's an uncommonly good match, too. He used to be a great friend of Céleste Coralie; you've heard of her, that famous dancer; in fact she left the stage to live with him; I wonder where she is now; those French women are the devil sometimes."

"Miss Campbell can't know know of this," said Wentworth, shocked by the careless manner of his friend.

"No, I don't suppose she does; there's nothing wrong in

it of course, old boy; purely Platonic; but men don't like to mention these *neo-platonisms* to their *fiancées*; women have so little faith in the spirituality of their own sex: but Miss Campbell's dear mamma has heard——So you've chosen me into the Harvard boat, have you?" he added, seeing that his friend was annoyed. "After all, hard work, though irrational, has a certain pleasure in it. Feel of that arm, old boy," and Van pulled up his sleeve, and displayed an arm as hard as ivory, and bound with curving muscles from the shoulder to the wrist: for Van, though he preached laziness, was driven by force of his fine constitution into exercise.

"Come and take tea with us to-night, Van," said Wentworth, after paying his respects to his friend's biceps. "It is Saturday night, and only Rake and Ayres will be there. I am going to meet Hayward at the post-office at six; it's nearly that now; I have seen a great deal of Hayward this year, and the more I see of him, the better I like him. We had an editors' meeting yesterday; what a comical genius Gowan is? Last night, I asked him whether he trusted a certain man. 'I don't think,' he answered, 'that he would steal a grizzly bear, or run away with a red hot stove, but I can't say that I have absolute confidence in him.' He declares that he is going to make the Harvard Magazine the best periodical in the world."

"If you wish, Wentworth," said Van, as the two boys issued into the street, and strolled towards the square; "You can attend a meeting of the B. H. society, which will be held in our rooms, to-morrow night."

"Many thanks, Van: it is a privilege to be allowed to remain in one's own room. What is the B, H. society? I never heard of it."

"You need not be ashamed of that, old boy," replied Van. "It has only been in existence two days: in fact it can scarcely be said to be more than an idea, but it is an idea pregnant with nectar and ambrosia. The B. H. Club, whose object is social rather than literary, is at present composed of six of the greatest swells in our class: every week, however, a Freshman of wealth and position is elected into it, who is obliged by custom to furnish us with a magnificent supper, onthe night of his initiation."

"You are indeed a magician, Van," said Wentworth. "You rub the lamp of your reason, utter a talismanic word, and lo! a sumptuous feast spreads itself before you."

"The joke of it is, Wentworth, that each of these foxes, when he finds that his tail has been cut off, will wear it as a great feather in his cap before his fellows, and make them eager to gain the same honor."

The boys had now reached the Post-office, where Hayward joined them. Hamilton's old friend was a type of the worthiest class of men whom New England breeds. The son of a farmer near Worcester, he had under every disadvantage fitted himself for college, and with the sum of two hundred dollars in his pocket, entered Harvard. After six months he had gained a scholarship, and had since then supported himself by scholarships and teaching. During the Freshman and Sophomore years, Hayward saw little of his class, and was spoken of as a "dig," a man devoted to study, always an unpopular character in American colleges. The third year, however, when the college-boy develops into something very like a man, and brains are more prized, Hayward mixed more with his class-mates, and became as much liked as he had been always respected. It is the facility which New England affords to men like Hayward to educate themselves, that gives her her intellectual superiority over the rest of America.

Wentworth and his friends, on entering the supper-room, found Ayres seated in state, with Gowan opposite him, whom, now that he had achieved greatness, Ayres often honored with an invitation to the club-table.

"I am preparing an article for the Harvard Magazine," remarked Gowan, shortly, "to do away with the study of the classics in our American colleges."

"The study of the classics," replied Hayward, "is the very object for which colleges are founded, to preserve the Past——"

"I don't believe," interjected Gowan, "that colleges should be the mummy pits of old truths; they ought to be the centres of modern thought."

"On the contrary," rejoined Hayward, "nothing is so good for any country, and especially for one like our own, in which all influences tend to concentrate the mind on the present, as to have schools in which the two great classical models are held up for our study. It is a great gain to the world to have another ideal, not antagonistic, but different to the Christian ideal offered it. You find in

Greek literature alone, an ideal of man harmoniously developing himself: nothing stimulates Christianity so much as this, and prevents its becoming a religion of blind authority, to crush out reason, and change its own truths into barren letters."

"I myself don't believe in the Christian ideal any more than the Greek," said Gowan; "I think Modern Times can give us ideals superior to any of the Greeks or Jews."

"What! are you going to overthrow Christianity as well as the classics by your article?" asked Ayres, sadly, and for a brief moment ceased to absorb toast, for the warbler had experienced religion, and was keenly alive to any danger which threatened it.

"Wait until better ideals are given us by modern times," exclaimed Wentworth, "before you ask us to give up our old ones. It does not seem to me that Thomas Carlyle or Auguste Comte are prophets direct from God."

"I don't believe in the study of the classics as they are studied here," said Van. "They should make us study the Greek and Latin literatures, not the grammars."

"It is the stupid system of recitations for four hours a day," said Hayward, "that stultifies both college officers and students. The students are obliged to take about twice as long to show how little they know as to learn that little. If a man after every half hour's hoeing were to be examined as to how much he had done, his day's work would not be worth much. Besides, these recitations cut up the day, and take the soul out of a man."

"What I most object to," said Van, "is that deductions

should be made from your rank, on account of your conduct; I don't see what smoking, or standing on the grass, has to do with my rank as a scholar: and to state, as they do, that rank depends on scholarship alone, is to state what is not true: if it were," he added, good humoredly, "my great talents would place me in the first half of the class, I am convinced."

"That would be rough on you, Robin: it would just push you into the second half," said Wentworth, to the warbler, who held the hazardous position of the last man in the first half of the class.

"The American college system," he added, "secures one of the virtues of the bed of Procrustes; though it cannot expand a fool to the stature of mediocrity, it shows great skill in cutting down those heads which might overtop their fellows. The remedy for the evil is so easy, too; abolish the recitation system, and substitute for it fair written competitive examinations, to excite emulation, and short familiar lectures to point out the books, methods of study, and whatever the student cannot readily discover for himself. Every University which has adopted this system has grown famous for good scholarship, and not one without it."

"Harvard College," said Gowan, "is looked upon by its students as a gladiatorial school, and by its officers as an amateur police station."

"Take care what you say," interposed Van, "there are two boating men here, and you may get into a row."

"If," continued Wentworth, "we had the wit of our

fathers, who founded this college almost before they had pitched their tents in the wilderness, we should build it up to be a great University, and endow it with money enough to educate all the men and women of talents in the country: we should make it not a place for boys to be drilled in, and tutors to air their brief authority, but the centre of American thought, at which scholars and students, young and old, would gather to give and receive inspiration. It is only by such a union that a great literature can be produced; a man, however gifted, cannot grow without sympathy: Shakespeare himself would have been dwarfed, if he had not lived among his peers."

"'Tis oh, the poor vork 'us bye,'"

sang Rakeman, rushing into the room, and looking anxiously about the supper table. "One such man as you, Robin," added the poor Lazarus, gleaning a few crumbs after the warbler, "is more ominous than the seven lean-fleshed kine of Pharaoh."

"You get off more poor jokes, Rake, than any old almanac," retorted Ayres, not over pleased at the comparison.

"I took tea with Professor Robinson last night," remarked Hayward, after peace had been made. "We had a long conversation, about the best course to follow in the study of history, and constitutional government. He said France was the country whose history one should study first, as being historically the most central country in modern Europe, and the only one which had never been in a state of *coma*, from the fall of the Roman Empire, until the present day. In speaking of the different kinds of government, he said that England had received from the world the same award of merit, which was made to Thucydides, that every one gave her the second place after his own country."

"I wish we had an aristocracy here," said Van, "we need a strong government to keep down the modocracy; no man can live long in New York city, and still believe in a democracy."

"No one," returned Wentworth warmly, "can live long in New England, and not believe in a republic. A nation, in choosing its form of government, should aim always at the truest ideal; then all progress is a real progress: on any other plan, the more you build, the more you have to pull down in the end, unless you become fossilized. Every one admits that intrinsically, the principle of choice is more worthy of an intelligent people, than the principle of birth: the means we adopt to put the theory into practice may not be the best, but the principle itself is a true one, and should be carried out boldly without regard to sex or color or nationality."

"I don't believe in the divine right of voting," said Van. "What right have two fools, merely because they know how to count, or can get some one to count for them, to vote down one of us? What right has any one to anything, except to do what he is fitted for?"

"The right of rights," said Gowan, "the right to be educated, to learn for what he is by nature fitted; the man whom birth seems to have designed to be your footman, God may have designed to be your master, and he has a right to know it."

"They do know it in New York," said Van, "without any education. But seriously, what has our homœopathic system of education done for us? The literature of a country is the best index of its growth, and what national literature have we worthy of the name? Do we not steal all our ideas and books from England, swindle her writers out of their just pay, and abuse her roundly into the bargain?"

"America has one excuse for her want of a literature," said Wentworth, "that she has to import her Past. An American cannot merely open his mind, and let the golden-grained current of historical and mythical times flow through it. If you take from the poets of Europe of this century, the thoughts they have breathed in with the stories of their childhood, or which have sprung from their countries' history or traditions, how little would you leave them? Here we have no Mother Goose and Robin Goodfellow to whisper their legends in the ears of our children as they play about the chimney corner. We have no ballads of good King Arthur, or brave Roland, to lead away our thoughts to the enchanted regions of romance, where the Muses love to dwell. There does not move before us, as before the Greeks, the gorgeous panorama of an heroic age, made luminous by poetic genius, now glittering with the pomp and circumstance of the Trojan war, now shadowing forth in darker colors the woes of the house of Œdipus, now glowing with the splendor of Olympus and the cloud-compelling God."

"We, certainly," said Gowan, "make as much as we can of what history we have. Bancroft devotes a volume to a campaign of Captain John Smith at the head of an army of two whites and one friendly squaw."

"The greatest misfortune," said Hayward, "that is produced by the want of a Past and of a literature, is that owing to this want we have no strong national unity; in proportion as an American becomes educated, he becomes denationalized; his thoughts and feelings centre in France, or England, or Italy; he ceases to be an American, and consequently ceases to exert any influence upon his country, or to receive any impulse from it."

"Still," replied Wentworth, with earnestness, "the advantages of our position far outweigh its evils. The Past sits upon the neck of Europe like the Old Man of the Sea; it has bound her hand and foot with its traditions; it has burdened her with the husks of worn-out truths; it has bred up standing armies to prey upon her entrails; it has set her religion and reason at war together; it has planted upon her head a nobility like a crown of thorns.

"America is not the offspring of the night; she was born when the human mind had awakened from its long sleep; in her infancy she strangled church and caste; her society honors, or condemns every one upon his own merits; her law limits the freedom of the individual only where it encroaches upon the liberty of his neighbor; her religion is the spontaneous tribute of the human soul to its God."

"In her charity she has opened her doors to the oppressed of every nation; like the serpent of Moses, her flag has been lifted up, and to it the sick and wounded from the four corners of the earth have come flocking. If the republic perish, she will sink, borne down by the multitudes who have stretched out their hands to her for aid; if she perish, she will die as the physician, the victim of diseases caught in the dens of wretchedness to which his charity has led him. If she perish, may she so perish! But who of us has any fears for our country? Under the influence of freedom, and the discipline of our schools, the children of the foreigner will grow worthy of their adopted home; in time we shall mould these different nationalities into one; in time some great poet, with his golden numbers, will draw all hearts together and call forth from our mountains and rivers the souls that lie imprisoned within them; or a great war will sweep over us with its fiery breath, and we shall come forth from its trial welded into a nation.

"In times past three great republics have lighted up the pages of history, the Jewish, Athenian, the Roman; and to these three republics the world to-day owes all that it has of worth; its law, its mind, its soul.

"Among the nations of modern times, America has come late to the race; but she is the child of the Sun; her feet are shod with the wings of the morning; her veins are alive with the blood of her sire; wherever she moves, she shakes light, liberty, and hope from her locks; she shall not be last at the goal."

"By Jove! fellows," exclaimed Ayres, looking at his watch, and springing to his feet; "I have a special engagement with my dentist this evening; I'm half an hour late."

"To have a tooth drawn?" asked Rakeman, eagerly, and a look of hope ran around the table.

"No, to have a new tooth set," replied the warbler, cheerily, and hurried from the room.

After a few moments of silent gloom, his friends followed him.

CHAPTER XVI.

"Anna soror, quæ me suspensam insomnia terrent!
Quis novus hic nostris successit sedibus hospes,
Quem sese ore ferens, quam forti pectore et armis!
Credo equidem, nec vana fides, genus esse deorum."

"Sunt bona, sunt quædam mediocria, sunt mala plura
Quæ legis hic."

"Phaselus ille, quem videtis, hospites,
Ait fuisse navium celerrimus."

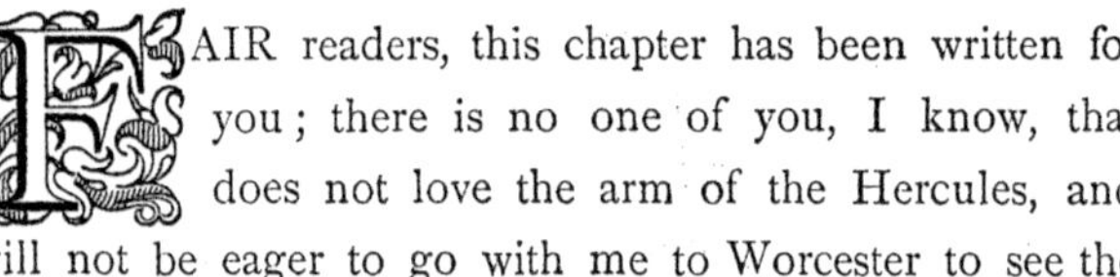

AIR readers, this chapter has been written for you; there is no one of you, I know, that does not love the arm of the Hercules, and will not be eager to go with me to Worcester to see the Great Games.

Wentworth and his chum, during the summer months, had spent most of their time in training for the boat race. O study, during this muscular period, we regret to say they took but little heed; and perhaps it must be confessed that at all times athletes and prize-fighters have not been the Homers and Shakespeares of the world. Do not frown, my pretty readers: you, I know, all love to believe that the strong arm in whose embrace you would be so powerless, is but the symbol of a mind and soul equally dangerous; and I do hate to undeceive you: but I have learnt from your own sex, by long intercourse, to speak the truth at any cost.

Wentworth had thrown himself into muscular Christianity in the hope that religion and absence would enable him to forget the woman whom he had loved with sudden passion. A vain hope—the absence of a woman we love is the presence of an ideal: this may or may not be more charming than the original; in your case, my dear madam, I am sure it could not but be much less so; still it is generally enough.

Our friend, Van Courtland, as good-natured fat gave place to surly brawn, groaned for his lost pleasures, his wine changed to beer and his forbidden cigars, and pronounced Muscular Christianity to be no better than paganism. Absolute goods, indeed, Van held that there were but three, wine, woman, and tobacco, any one of which, he said, led one to the devil: but even Van, though he railed at his lot, viewed with secret satisfaction his lessening waist and growing biceps.

It was the day before the race: Van, Wentworth, Bowyer, Bilger, Seaborn and Brandreth, who made up the crew, were at dinner at the Bay State House in Worchester: half the college was chattering around them: the oars in silence devoured huge "shins of beef" and drained off goblets of ale.

"You must win the race to-morrow," cried Rakeman to Wentworth, "I have staked my last penny on you: if you are beaten, I shall have to walk to Richmond!"

"It is your 45 stroke that will do the business," said our old acquaintance, Morris. "Nothing that floats can stand that."

"Yale has won the first game of chess!" exclaimed Ayres, entering the room, sweating with excitement.

"Come, sit beside me, Robin," called out Rakeman, "and tell me all about it. It's a roasting day; as you melt, old boy, you draw the heat from me very pleasantly."

"Suppose we see what's going on outside," said Van to his chum, finishing dinner, and the two strolled to the billiard-room, where the champion game was being played. Yale was twenty points ahead, but both sides were playing well, and the bets ran even. Among a group of his friends, in another part of the room, was Gowan, who offered to play with any one for any sum, and give him 99 points and discount. "I have never," he whispered to Wentworth as he came up to him, "played a game of billiards in my life; but if I once hit that ball, Heavens! how I shall make it spin!" A flashily dressed gentleman offered to take Gowan's bet, and was surprised to find himself passed out of the room with a *staccato* movement by the students.

On leaving the billiard-hall, our friends met a band of gentle youth pricking over the town in search of adventure.

"Come, fellows, fall in!" ordered Rakeman, who, armed with a billiard-cue, had taken command of the corps; but Van and Wentworth passed by them to their hotel, where by ten o'clock they were fast asleep.

The town, however, at this hour was just beginning to open its eyes. The streets were thronging with rollicking students and citizens dumb with terror. There was Thumpum, the eminent divine, whose large arm and weak intellect had taught him the doctrine of Muscular Christianity. Behind him were two brave bucks from Grafton, who had come to catch a glimpse of the great world. Further on you saw a group of Boston gentlemen, among whom was the versatile Pippins, who lent their sober countenances to the jolly night. Next came the proprietor of a small hotel, beating his breast, followed by two servants bearing a mutton. In an evil hour, for himself and his posterity, he had contracted to board a training crew at the usual charge. "I have fed firemen!" he exclaims, "militiamen! alderman! but these students! famine! locusts! 's death!"

Meanwhile, Rakeman's command rolled on, swollen by stragglers. The Southron brandished his billiard-cue before them, and with it tested panes of glass and ribs of inquisitive burghers. Hovering in the distance around this genial band, like ghosts come to trouble joy, frowned the unwholesome countenances of numerous special policemen, which but faintly reflected the jovial features of the students. They had made two or three efforts to seize some thoughtless loiterer, but the cry of "Yale! Yale!" "Harvard to the rescue!" had brought such a nest of hornets about their ears that they had retreated. At length, Mr. Poplet, a pious young fellow, who had been urging Rakeman to disband his troops, sprained his ankle: Ayres remained behind to assist him, when, in the twinkling of an eye, ten policemen pounced upon them, and before they could call for help they were mercilessly immured in the Bastile of the town: there they passed the night revolving many things in their minds.

"Suppose we build a bonfire!" suddenly cried Sweatrame to his friends.

"Bravo!" returned every one, delighted, and ran to secure fuel.

"Why not burn it before the Mayor's house? He'll make us a speech!" said Gowan, and the students at once marched thither: Gowan staggered under an empty barrel; Sweatrame carried a milliner's sign, Dummer a tobacconist's show figure, and every one had secured his offering. There was standing at the corner of the two main streets of the town, a mammoth wooden boot which might have graced the foot of the prince of the Brobdignagians—the labor of many days and the delight of its possessor. This, at Rakeman's command, six heroic men with violent strains wrenched from its base, and placed before the Mayor's gate. Its owner slumbers far away in the soft embraces of his faithful spouse; him, cheerily whistling with light heart returning on the morrow to his shop, the empty pedestal will surprise, and the ravished boot: ravening, he will scour the town to discover the charred remains of his idol, and never more to smile; but to return to our muttons.

These had now built a fire worthy of Prometheus before the house of the Mayor, and formed in a ring were singing "Auld Lang Syne." The cheerful blaze gilded the streets and houses, and warmed the damp features of distant policemen, and citizens unused to such diversions.

"Give us a speech, Gowan!" shouted a friend to the young orator, who had clambered upon a fence.

Gowan, nothing loath, steadied himself and began—

"Gentlemen, and ladies!" he added, waving his hand to two or three biddies who were hanging upon the skirts of the students. "The flower of the Intellectual and Sporting worlds"—

"What does all this mean! Stop this noise! Police! Seize him! Hang him!" and the indignant night-gown and slippers of the worthy Mayor burst through the door, and a fist brandished itself in great heat.

"The Mayor! The Mayor!" shouted the students. "A speech from the Mayor!"

"Silence!" ordered Rakeman, and he climbed upon the fence.

"Mr. Mayor!" he then began, making him a courteous salute with his cue. "The scholars of America have gathered together on this classic occasion to beg the favor of a speech from your eloquent lips."

"Speech! You drunken rascals! I'll have you all arrested!"

"Bravo! Encore!" shouted the students. "Three cheers for the Mayor!"

Again Rakeman enjoined silence. "If, Mr. Mayor," he said, making him a second salute with his cue, "you are, as you allege, too much under the influence of liquor at present to speak, we will defer our pleasure."

"Police! Jail! Militia! Fire! Charge! My country!" Three domestics removed their master from the night air in the midst of such utterances.

After an hour of further debate the students marched toward their hotels. As they were passing down a sloping street, they saw before them a lawless band of special policemen who had gathered from the whole town to dispute their passage. Our young friends halted behind a heavy dirt-cart and held a council of war. "Let us bowl down the specials!" cried Rakeman, struck with an idea worthy of Hannibal. At once the cart was turned and aimed at the wondering enemy; down thundered the merciless engine, scattering terror and policemen in its course. One leaped through a window-pane; a second climbed a tree, where he perched like the author of evil; the captain of the band dived down a sewer which opened to receive him; the rest took to their heels and left the students to continue their peaceful way to their hotels, where they arrived in safety.

Sweatrame at once demanded a room of the hotel-clerk, who in vain informed him that there was no room.

"Come with me, Sweatrame; I have a room you shall share," said Rakeman, leading him up stairs. "I found the name of a man from Providence," he then explained to him, "on the hotel book, who had a large room which I thought ought to be put to a better use; so I at once went to the telegraph office and dispatched a message to him to return home at once on important business;

the obliging fellow had just time to catch the train and this is his room."

Sweatrame took the latitude and longitude of the room with great care, and left Rakeman to go to bed. Rakeman had but half undressed himself, and was just pulling off his other boot, when he heard a noise in the entry, and looking out saw Sweatrame rapping violently at the door opposite.

Within that room seven American citizens were enjoying a momentary snooze in their trim little bed; as they awoke, a Nile of oaths was poured against the inquirer. "You have taken my room, you villains!" cried Sweatrame nothing daunted; then, without further persuasion, he climbed through the ventilator over the door into the room, unlocked the door, pulled out the key, and jumped from the room: as our seven citizens clasped the door-handle, the click of the key informed them that they were safely locked within. Rakeman waited a few minutes, then stole off a short distance, and cried "Fire! Fire!" at the top of his voice. This magic word filled the room opposite with a legion of devils. Picture to yourself, gentle reader, seven Bengal tigers, each fighting to lead the way through the eye of a needle; you can thus form some dim conception of the struggle of our peaceful citizens to make their escape through the narrow passage over the door. "Next year," said Rakeman, telling the story to Van in the morning, "when the room is again occupied, some lucky waiter will find seven skeletons lying about it, which he will dispose of, with profit to the Harvard Medical School."

Scarcely had this selfish contest subsided, when Rakeman heard his name called from the upper entry. Running up the stairs he found there by a window, a huge pile of boots and shoes, which Sweatrame, Dummer, and Gowan had been at pains to collect from the whole hotel; these they were throwing on wagers at cats, gas-lamps, or, choicest of marks, the blue coat of a policeman. Hence in the morning the tears of many men mourning over their boots, and their curses on the cause of letters, but from the boot-makers of the town (save one) blessings without number. "Thus God keeps the moral as the physical world *in equilibrio*," said Van, "and what is taken away by one person is added by another."

With these careless humors, until morning dawned, our young friends ruffianed it, and made night's rafters ring with songs and wild uproar, that old men fumed over their broken sleep and the degenerate days; mothers clasped their infants to their breasts, and prayed that they might never go to college: serving maids hid their heads beneath the clothes and called on Holy Mary; only the young rosy bosomed daughters of Eve, trembling as they awoke from innocent dreams, felt a strange interest in the young revellers, and a longing desire to reform them by the charm of female influence.

The next day was a glorious day for the race. Lake Quinsigamond lay smooth as a mirror: the boats' course was surrounded by gaily trimmed pleasure boats: on shore the blue and red ribbons of the pretty partisans upon the platform waved like a garden of flowers: their sweet jargoning blended with the manly tones of the students and the salt jests of the boatmen. The Yale and Harvard rested lightly before the judge's boat: Wentworth was pulling two, Van three, Bowyer was stroke, and Bilger bow: their broad backs were almost parallel with the water.

"Are you ready?" cried one of the judges. "Back a little, Harvard."

"Are you ready?"

"Aye! Aye!"

"Ready. Go!"

At the word the two boats leaped over the water. "Harvard! Harvard! Yale! Go in Yale! Bravo, Harvard! Hurrah for Yale! Fifty dollars on Yale! Taken!" shouted the men on shore as the boats glided bow and bow past the seats.

The handles of the Harvard oars spanned the space from beyond the toes of the pullers to their chests, which bent back beyond the perpendicular: the Yale pulled a shorter stroke and feathered nearer the water.

The two boats passed into the silence of the lake; the Yale now drew half a length ahead, now the Harvard; Wentworth heard nothing but the six oars as one striking the tholepins; he saw nothing but the broad back of the stroke and its huge muscles rising and falling: his body seemed turning into bundles of whip-cords: the blood ran tingling from his temples to his toes: a mad thirst for victory possessed him: he pulled fiercely but steadily on. Suddenly he heard a grating sound on his left.

"Hold port: Hard starboard!" cried Bilger angrily,

and drove the rudder to the larboard. Wentworth turned his head : his boat had been accidentally driven in to the shore : the starboard oars were scattering the shingle on the beach : the Yale was a length ahead. A shudder of despair ran through his breast, but a moment later they were steered into deeper water.

"Are you ready, boys?" muttered Bilger. Bowyer gave a savage grunt.

"Spurt her!" hissed Bilger; and Bowyer quickened without shortening his stroke. White drops of foam flew around the boat: she rocked from side to side.

"Steady, confound you!" cried the angry bow; and the boat again ran upon an upright keel. The oars cut the water like knife-blades; they were pulling forty-eight strokes a minute. And now a wild joy filled Wentworth's heart, as his boat under its matchless stroke crept even with its rival : strained ahead, now a yard, now half a length, now a length—and now Bilger had steered them across the bows of the Yale and Bowyer returned to his common stroke. They reached the upper stake, the Yale more than a length behind them.

"Hold port! hard starboard!" cried Bilger; and Wentworth drove his oar into the water and leaned to the larboard, as the boat slowly turned. What was his rage to see the Yale cut in nearer the stake and start on the home-stretch half a length ahead. The boats now nerved themselves for the final struggle. The Yale made for the middle of the lake; the Harvard hugged the shore. The land here runs out into the lake and cuts it off from the view of the spectators on the platform; for a few minutes neither boat could be seen; then darted into sight the blue caps of the Yale; a yell of triumph burst from their friends.

"Where are you, Harvard?" "Two to one on the Yale!" "Three to one on the Yale!" and no takers. Suddenly the light flashed from the shining oars of the Harvard crew as they glided around the point, closely pressing their rivals.

"Harvard! Harvard!" yell a fierce chorus, whose words faintly reach the boat.

The spectators then grow silent; no more odds are offered; swiftly the boats draw near their goal. They are but a quarter of a mile distant, and the Harvard is still half a length behind.

"Are you ready?" whispers the bow.

Bowyer gives an inspiring grunt.

"Spurt her!" growls Bilger.

Again the boat quivers under Bowyer's fiery stroke. Wentworth feels that they are gaining upon their rival; the oars shoot across the water like flashes of light; they are even with her; he would give ten years of his life to win; they have crept ahead of her a yard, half a length, a length; a fierce delight sends strength into every stroke; now they are gliding past the platform full three lengths in advance. The Harvard men are yelling wildly, and hugging each other in triumph; the ladies are uttering their dainty hurrahs, and crying, "Harvard! Harvard!"

Wentworth turns his head a moment to the left: Miss Campbell and her friends are standing on a barge, waving their handkerchiefs, and calling, "Bravo!" Wentworth turns back his head, throws all his strength into his stroke—once—twice—suddenly he hears a loud snap and sees his broken blade floating in the distance; a fierce oath breaks from Van, whose jaw has been nearly dislocated by Wentworth's head; the boat half capsizes.

"Steady!" yells Bilger, beside himself with rage, and drives the rudder to the starboard. The remaining four men redouble their strokes as well as the rocking boat permits; the Yale quickly gains upon them, but it is too late; as the pistol cracks the Harvard is still a length ahead.

"Three cheers for Harvard!" cried the stroke of the Yale, and three cheers for Yale were returned. The Harvard then pulled past the platform, which was ringing with huzzas; from the platform, Bilger steered them to the opposite shore, where the crew disembarked, and were loaded with the congratulations of their friends.

"Come, fellows," said Van to the rest of the crew, "let me invite you to dine with me; it is nine weeks since I have tasted food."

Of all the pleasures of life, a glorious dinner after long training is the most sacred. Far into the night the hungry crew feasted on the ambrosial food and drank the divine wine.

The triumph, the dinner, and to-morrow's separation made Van talk more earnestly and truly with his friend than when he wore the cool habit of common courtesy.

"It always cuts me more, Wentworth," he said after they had gone to their room, "to leave you, than anything else. You are my friend, and a man who would love me the same, rich or poor, in honor or disgrace. The good opinion of the mass of men I count for what it is worth; it can be bought for a cigar; it is lost by a shabby coat: but a real friend—for these men are but spectral—his friendship I value as the choicest treasure of my life. Promise me one thing, old boy, that you won't throw yourself away from a passion for a woman: they arn't worth it: you moral men always overrate them; I remember when I thought as you do," a look of hatred passed over Van's face, "I have half a mind to tell you."

"Stop! stop, Van!" said Wentworth; "I don't wish to hear any secrets, which in the morning you may regret to have told."

"You are right, Wentworth," replied Van. "It is more honorable. Good-night, old boy.

'You must wake and call me early, call me early, mother dear.'"

CHAPTER XVII.

"Qui sapit, innumeris moribus aptus erit,
Utque leves Proteus modo se tenuabit in undas."

"YOU must go with us to-night to Mrs. Morris's mask-ball," said Wentworth's cousin, Miss Saulsbury, at whose house in Newport he had just arrived to spend a part of his Summer vacation. "You will meet the beautiful Miss Campbell and Miss Leigh; the party is given for them: they are from Boston: of course you know them."

"Fate is against me," thought Wentworth, as he heard Miss Campbell's name. "Why should I resist it?"

Fate is a variety of things: she is a scape-goat; she is a ready ally to every wish of doubtful propriety; why is it that we are never fated to do what is right? But I am not equal to an analysis of Fate in this short chapter.

Wentworth had heard that Miss Campbell was at Newport, but he probably had not expected to meet her.

That evening, as Wentworth was offering himself as a mark for the pretty assassins around him, he caught sight of a lady whose step he could not mistake. She seemed a lovely vision of Undine: her dress, of transparent, shimmering sea green, hung around her graceful form in loose, undulating folds, caught up with water lilies, and sprays of coral: her beautiful hair fell in long ripples over her shoulders, and was crowned by a wreath of the same buds; the drapery of her dress was fastened at the waist by a deep belt of tiny shells: her sleeves were looped with the same ornaments, while a single row of pearls encircled her fair throat. As she approached Wentworth, she threw him a little bunch of blue violets. The boy at once followed the lovely mermaid and asked Mr. Morris, with whom she was walking, to allow him to take his lady.

"I know who you are, very well," said our hero. "Who has such grace? who such a swan-like throat? who such houri eyes? Though all the rest of you were concealed, one glance from them would betray you; I read you for Miss Jones."

"The world knows who you are," replied the mask. "The flower of courtesy, the truest of friends, the—but do lead me into a cooler place," she added, dropping her voice from the ear-piercing key of the masks around her.

"Will you not take off your mask, Miss Campbell?" urged Wentworth, when they had reached one of the distant paths which surrounded the house in which the masks were hurrying to and fro.

"Hush!" said Miss Campbell. "There is Mr. Otis looking for me; there is Miss Campbell," she then said, speaking to the latter gentleman, and pointing to a girl of about her own size, who was evidently being fought for by two gentlemen, some little distance off. Mr. Otis walked away, and Miss Campbell returned to Wentworth, elated by her success.

"Take this!" she said, giving him an ivy leaf. "It is the symbol of your constancy; don't you remember that six months ago you promised to be my friend? You have never been to see me since."

"My mother," replied Wentworth, "taught me, when still young, not to walk into the fire."

"Oh, fortunate mother to have so docile a son!" said Miss Campbell, and took off her mask. When Miss Campbell was excited her eyelids quivered, and as they closed, her eyes flashed forth like melting diamonds. For six months our hero had been building a citadel of books, theories, and principles for his soul; one glance from Miss Campbell and down it all tumbled.

"Love," he said to himself, "has its rights as well as convention; I will try and win her."

"I supposed," he said to Miss Campbell, "that when a lady was engaged, all her thoughts and feelings belonged to the beloved object, and that to steal a glance or word, would be a moral theft."

"Miss Campbell's eyes again flashed.

"Belonged! did you say? You are too gallant."

"You would not drive your *fiancé* jealous?" said Wentworth.

"A little jealousy does no one any harm," replied the girl; "it is a spur to keep love on the wing; without it love becomes too tame; but don't think that I wanted to ask you to see me; I merely wished to tell you that my friends have bought you a pillar, on the top of which you can live retired, like St. Simeon Stylites; your mother will bring you food in a basket."

Wentworth, though young, knew the way to conquer a woman in argument.

"What is it, in heaven's name?" I hear a hundred husbands ask, offering me full purses. It is to say nothing.

"Miss Campbell," Wentworth therefore remarked, "how charmingly you are dressed to-night; all the ladies to whom I have spoken have flattered you with their envy." He then asked his fair partner to promenade with him, and for the rest of the evening devoted himself to her exclusively.

"Will you not be at home in the morning?" he asked, as he took his leave.

"I do not know," replied the girl, with a coquettish smile.

The next morning, however, Miss Campbell's fatigue compelled her to permit Miss Leigh to make her calls alone. Wentworth never enjoyed a morning in his life so much, except the next, and the next, and the next.

But Miss Campbell's engagement with Mr. Otis! Of course she kept that constantly before her mind, but you know, my pretty readers, or will soon know, I trust, that nothing so fans the passion of a lover as to have rivals in the field. Your lover, then, not only sees the divine prize of your own charms before him, but feels the spur of emulation. Besides, wit is always something of a radical. Wealth, a high position, and all the social virtues, though they make a man a worthy object to gain, make him rather tedious to keep; there is so little in absolute respectability to touch the heart of an imaginative girl. Miss Campbell thought of none of these things; she was far too honorable. It is, however, the unconscious feelings of women that control their actions. What Miss Campbell did think, was this, that it would not be courteous to refuse to see a gentleman when he called upon her, especially if he were handsome and appreciative.

Wentworth, himself, had a nature which was capable of a grand passion; having once lost the rein, love was his master and must run its course.

Our hero, therefore, pursued his game with the spirit and freshness of youth; he walked at Miss Campbell, he rode at her, he danced at her, he swam at her, he bowled at her, he rowed at her, he drove at her, and in fact attacked her with all the weapons which youth and leisure offered to his hand. After he had been some weeks in Newport, he received a letter from his mother, telling him that he must not allow a woman, whose affections were already engaged, to have any attractions for him. This, my fair readers, of course at once put an end to Wentworth's attentions; he remained in Newport, however, two weeks after his vacation was over, and lost his rank in his class by consequence.

Mr. Otis's business allowed him to come to Newport but twice a week; but his sister, who was very plain, and no great friend of Miss Campbell, kept him informed daily of matters of public interest. You may be sure that she did not omit those delicate personal touches, innuendoes, and *on dits*, which have always won for women the palm of epistolary excellence; and Mr. Otis was at length persuaded by his sister's letters to remonstrate with Miss Campbell.

Now, to remonstrate successfully with a woman, you must use words in which she can never guess that any remonstrance is intended. As remonstrance of this kind produces no effect whatsoever, why, the over-curious may inquire, do you call it successful? Because, my dear sirs, this mode, and this alone, does no harm. Mr. Otis was too honest, and had too little command of language for this Macchiavellian method, and simply told Miss Campbell, that he hoped she would see less of Mr. Saulsbury. At this Miss Campbell became highly indignant; though her pride prevented her making any reply, there sprang up a tacit misunderstanding between her lover and herself, which was heightened by an incident which happened the day before Miss Campbell returned to Boston, and Wentworth to Cambridge.

Miss Campbell, her cousin, Wentworth, and Miss Otis, were standing on the rocks behind Mrs. Morris's house; the sun was setting; the breakers were dashing their spray as near the ladies' dresses as they dared.

"How still it always is at sunset!" said Miss Campbell. "There's not a breath of wind stirring," and she held up her handkerchief to see if it moved. In a moment a catspaw had snatched it away and it lay floating on the top of a wave, a rod from the shore. Wentworth, as soon as he saw the white spot on the water, touched his hat to Miss Campbell, and the next moment she saw him arching the waves and disappearing beneath them; soon he reappeared beyond the handkerchief which he seized and brought back to the rock.

"It was a pity to ruin your clothes," said Miss Campbell, half smiling, and with a heightened color, as she looked with a little feeling of pride and gratified vanity at Wentworth's dripping coat "Ah! Miss Otis, you do not know how dangerous to a woman's heart is a little graceful and rash gallantry."

"Perhaps," said Wentworth, "you would resent it, were I almost tempted to desire that you, and, not your handkerchief, had been in danger." He gave her a quick look as he said these words, that made Miss Campbell's soft lashes shut out all the light of her eyes for a moment.

"Keep it, at least, till it is dry," she said, looking up and laughing a little embarrassed laugh, "I should like to decorate you with it, and make you my chevalier."

Wentworth ran the delicate piece of muslin through his button hole, and said smiling, "It is really *tout ce qu'il y a de plus mouchoir.* I do not think, if that is the condition on which I receive it, that it will ever be dry."

This innocent incident, even when colored by the genius of Miss Otis, afforded her brother very little pleasure.

CHAPTER XVIII.

"Quid enim falsi Lauronia?"

ISS CAMBPELL was one morning, early the next winter, engaged in embroidering, and in meditating on what Mr. Otis had just said.

"If James wishes it," she thought, "I of course ought to do what he says; but I cannot be unkind to my friends; that is a duty I owe to myself. The world, he says, calls me a flirt; but the world is always wrong. If I thought Mr. Saulsbury was in love with me—but I know he is not; a woman can always tell; he is so cold; he only speaks of love in the abstract; and of poetry, and books. Mother says that there can be no such thing as friendship between men and women. What an absurd idea! Look at Madame Récamier, and—and—there's a stitch lost."

While Miss Campbell was debating with herself, a servant brought her a note from a sick woman, who asked her assistance.

Charity is a favorite foible of the fair aristocrats of Boston, and is carried to great lengths. I know of no place in the world where the unlettered novelists and tattered *raconteurs*, who tickle the ears of the rich, receive fairer incomes.

"What! Do you speak of the objects of benevolence with a sneer?" I hear a chorus of clergymen exclaim.

It is not, my reverend sirs, with a sneer, but with a profound fellow feeling, that I speak of these illegitimate members of our guild. In what does the beggar, whose hungry eyes glance from your face to his eloquent hat, and who pours out his tale of want and despair, differ from myself, save in the pomp of type and paper and publisher? His story may be false—so far as I know, it always is—but it is false in the same sense in which Homer, and Dante, and Shakespeare are false: in the highest sense, nothing can be more true. Gentle reader, if you wish to hear fictions told with art and power, at once close this book, run into the highways and hedges, and with a few pennies, kindly entreat the first beggar whom you see, to tell his story.

Miss Campbell, you may be sure, was not behind her fellows in benevolence: she spent an hour or more a day in its exercise, and laid up treasure in Heaven for herself, to the amount of about a thousand dollars a year, and that in gold times: estimated in currency, you will perceive that the sum would be much larger.

On reading the note, she at once hurried to the woman's address, which was at a little house in Myrtle Street. The room into which our heroine entered, was small and squalid: a few sunbeams struggling through the shutters, revealed a bed, a small table, and two old chairs, its only furniture; on the table, which stood by the bedside, lay a bottle of oil, a phial half full of whiskey, and a broken cup which held a few faded rose buds; on the bed lay a woman, at sight of whose face Miss Campbell's heart melted with pity.

"Has the good lady come?" asked the poor sufferer; and as she spoke, she gave Miss Campbell that look of gratitude, which makes one's charity however great, seem to dwindle to nothing.

"You are so good, dear lady," continued the woman. "I have heard of your goodness so often, I dared to write to you; I am very sick; and my friends—I have no friends any more. You will do me a kindness, will you not?"

"It is you who confer a favor on me, my poor girl;" and Miss Campbell's eyes filled with tears, as she bade the woman who had opened the door to run out and purchase some luxuries for the invalid.

Then, smoothing back the woman's tangled hair, which was a chestnut of somewhat darker shade than her own, "Do not speak, my dear girl," she said, gently; "it will tire you: I will talk to you;" and she took one of the girl's hands between her own, and sitting beside her, promised her care and comfort. The poor woman seemed, however, to have something upon her mind. "I must speak, dear lady," she at length said, pressing Miss Campbell's hand to her lips, and then closing her eyes to hide her embarrassment, "I cannot be silent, my heart must speak. I have a favor to ask of you, dear lady; it is not hard, but it will be so great a one to me. I cannot live to repay you; but you are so good; I know you prize the prayer of one who is dying." Then, the tears stealing down her face, she faltered out her plaintive story in her broken English:

She was born in sunny Provence. When a girl of sixteen, she had been taken to Paris by her friends, and placed upon the stage. "I did not look then, as I now do," she said with a sad smile. "Men called me beautiful, and used to throw flowers before me, and whisper soft words of love in my ear: and there was one; ah! he was so handsome, and rich, and good! He told me that he loved me, and would always love me, more than any woman had ever been loved before; and he took me to live with him, first there, and afterwards he brought me here to America: and we lived together one whole year. Ah! those happy, happy days! I know it was wrong, dear lady; I think it is always wrong to be happy; but I cannot regret it; it was so like the sunshine. And I don't know, it seems to me that to love can never be wrong. But one day he was cold; I kissed his lips and he would not kiss mine in return. I asked him what I had done, and he said he was engaged to be married, and could not see me any more. With that I flung my arms around him passionately and cried, 'I am your wife, before God.' He looked coldly at me, and said, 'Do not be foolish, Céleste.'

I did not speak another word; I pressed my hand to my heart and went from the room, and wandered up and down the city, so lonely, ah! so very lonely. There was no sunshine any more, nor any smiles, but all was black around me. I would have killed myself, only I was afraid; and at length God was good to me, and sent me this sickness And now, dear lady, that I am dying, I cannot remember his coldness; I can only think of the happy,

happy hours we spent together. Tell him from me, dear lady, that I love him, as before. Give him this ring for me, which he gave me in happier days. Tell him that I love him, as then : that my dying words breathe a prayer for him, and that when I am dead "——

"Who? where does he live?" exclaimed Miss Campbell, rising to her feet.

"He lives here, dear lady : his initials are on the ring ; his name is Otis—James Otis."

Miss Campbell turned deadly pale ; she took the ring from the woman, placed her purse upon the table, and tottered from the room. She reached home, she knew not how.

"Why Nell, what is the matter?" asked her mother, frightened at her colorless lips and the wild expression about her eyes.

"Nothing, mother dear," she answered softly. "I caught a chill walking ; I shall go to the ball to-night and dance it off ; I've changed my mind."

CHAPTER XIX.

"Arma dedi Danais in Amazonas. Arma supersunt,
Quæ tibi dem et turmæ, Penthesilea, tuæ."

PAPANTI'S! At that word how quickly, as with a pair of compasses, the mind draws the magic circle of Boston society. There fashion has built her University. Around the two poles of Harvard and Papanti's Boston, with what there may be of the world besides, revolves with regularity and law.

Mrs. Morris's was the first large ball of the season, and every one was there. The chandeliers were hung with vines and roses; the walls were gorgeous with duennas, whose charms, as time had mowed them away, art had replaced with perennial beauty; rosy cheeked warriors were skirmishing throughout the body of the hall with their fatal weapons.

"How divinely they play!" said Miss Campbell in a pause of a waltz with Wentworth. "One's heart beats time to the music. You must not tell any one when you engaged me for the German; two or three gentlemen asked me before you, and I told them I was already engaged. There is Miss Otis looking at me; she thinks I am a flirt," and the girl cast down her eyes with a saintly look of forgiveness. "Will you not wear one of these roses for me?"

"A thousand thanks!" replied Wentworth, placing the rose in his buttonhole. "How can your friend so wrong you? If she were right, how I should tremble for my sex; Pandora's box of troubles would be nothing to you; Argus, with his hundred eyes——will you not give me another turn?" and off they whirled.

If I only dared humbly to sketch the divinities of Boston society——

"Rash youth, forbear!" cries Prudence. "Will you, to fly your kite, draw down upon yourself the lightning of the gods? Well, if you will, I've nothing to say; only remember that I told you so!"

Take your place, then, gentle reader, by the door; for I am resolved to whistle Prudence down the wind; and look out with me upon the beauty and chivalry of breezy Boston, which are promenading before you.

First comes no other than our friend Mr. Jonathan Alcibiades Pippins, shining a head above his fellow wits. After five years' gestation, he has just been delivered of his fourth *mot*, the Benjamin of his old age, and mother and child are doing well. 'Twas his third *mot*—I remember it distinctly—"Love is madness, but marriage is hellebore," which, joined to his learning and versatility, gained for him the title of Alcibiades. Pass him by, timid muse; he wears a wisp of hay upon his horn; he is very dangerous.

A few paces behind Mr. Pippins follows Mr. B. S. Pitt, one of Boston's own, very Brahmin of very Brahmin. Mr.

Pitt is the admired leader of Boston's most exclusive set; how shall I shadow forth his character? His ancient birth puts to shame the oldest families of the city; without labor and with few breaks he has traced his line through three generations of men: he unites with his illustrious lineage, a princely income of three thousand dollars a year: who can wonder, then, if there is about his manner a touch perhaps too much of aristocratic hauteur? A noble lord once complained to him of being received in Boston with the caution which one would use in his social intercourse with a pickpocket.

"We are exclusive, I confess it," rejoined Mr. Pitt.

The Brahmin has been to Harvard College, the Brahmin has travelled, the Brahmin has read, but the Brahmin rarely speaks a word: he is too deep, too profound, to need the flippant aid of speech. This silence gains for him the respect of men and the idolatry of the fair; before its awful mystery the most gifted women grow priestesses to an unseen power; should the Brahmin speak, they feel that the talismanic word, the open sesame of universal truth, would drop from his lips.

The coarsest of us are taught by a divine instinct to reverence this oriental reserve, which no combination of circumstances would ever be grand enough to call into action.

But my pen drops from my hand; I am not equal to my task; I will retire; I will fill up the number of the shades; my friends shall tell their story as before.

There was that rich vital power in Miss Campbell, that

her slightest touch awoke in Wentworth a sense of passionate life. "How well your roses become you!" he whispered, as his eye flattered the girl's dress, which was a white silk, hung over with white tulle, looped with rose buds, that matched the delicate coloring that came and vanished on her beautiful neck and fair cheeks as the dance and music animated her. "You dance like the soul of a music, or a Cremona fiddle inspired with life."

"You change from an Achilles to a Thyrsites by your conclusion," replied Miss Campbell, pleasantly. "Will you not hold my bouquets for me a moment? You were so kind to send me these flowers! nothing could be prettier."

"I hope you have saved some dances for me," said Mr. Otis, who had come late to the ball, approaching them.

"I regret that I am engaged for them all," replied his *fiancée*, with coldness; "I was afraid you were not coming to-night. How gracefully Miss Leigh dances!" she added, turning to Mr. Pippins, who had come to pay his respects to her. "I always liked our greatest philosopher for calling Fanny Elssler's dancing, poetry, and religion."

"Natural and revealed religion, he might have styled it," answered Mr. Pippins, who was not over nice in the choice of his words.

Miss Campbell turned to Wentworth without hearing Mr. Pippins.

"I am so glad you liked my dress to-night!" she said. "Do I not seem in good spirits? I never felt so full of life at a party before."

"You must not fish for a compliment, Miss Campbell,"

answered Wentworth, "when so many are eager to come to you without a hook."

"Miss Campbell," said Mr. Pippins, "once told a gentleman, who said that to her, that she should not fish in such shallow water."

"The water is deep enough to drown certain young domestic animals," answered Wentworth, *enragé*. "Miss Campbell," he added, "may I not present my friend, Van Courtland, to you? he has asked me so many times; I have warned him against you, but if he will expose himself, it is his own fault." Wentworth, with this, bowed to Miss Campbell, and walked towards Van, who was talking to his hostess.

It is so pleasant," Mrs. Morris was saying to Van, as Wentworth drew near. "It is so pleasant to talk with a man who has been to England; here persons often say ben for been ——" Van's hypocritical face at once assumed the expression of Job at the lowest depth of his misery, which as quickly disappeared as he turned to follow Wentworth to Miss Campbell, who was now standing alone with Mr. Otis.

"Can you tell me, Miss Campbell," asked Wentworth, after introducing Van to her, "why, your friend, Mr. Pippins, is called Alcibiades?"

"Oh, I believe he keeps a dog," answered Miss Campbell, carelessly.

"Pippins," said Van, "fires his *mots* at people for invitations to dinners and parties, as negroes pelt monkeys with stones, that they may throw back cocoanuts."

"Your friend," said Miss Campbell, turning to Van, "gives you a strange character; he says you have not only the virtues that dignify, but most of the vices that adorn mankind."

"He flatters me, Miss Campbell, the villain! I have been reading Jonathan Edwards lately, and find that the devil is a most handsome, clever, and fascinating dog."

"Is he?" said Miss Campbell; "then would there were more than one; I read Calvin a few years ago, but it seemed to me God and the devil were so mixed up in theology, that I never could tell which was which, so I gave up the study. How do you like Boston, Mr. Van Courtland?"

"Extremely," answered Van; "though the manners of the ladies here may not, at first blush, seem so cordial as those in New York, yet there is a ——" Wentworth did not stop to hear the rest of Van's sentence, but courteously walked off to speak to Mrs. Morris.

"What a delightful ball you are giving to-night!" he said to his hostess.

"You are very good to think so, Mr. Saulsbury; but I shall not allow you to remain idle; I wish to present you to my niece, Miss White; she is very pretty and clever."

"What a terrible day it has been, Mr. Saulsbury!" said Miss White; "my ears were nearly frozen this morning; is it not strange that when one part of the ear freezes, the whole grows cold? I heard of you at Newport last summer; how delightful it is there! so much life and gaiety; so much pleasanter than Nahant! How lovely this air is! This floor is splendid to dance on; it spoils one for dancing at private houses. How do you like Miss Campbell's dress? Does she not dance well? Do you know the gentleman she is with? he is very handsome and romantic looking. Women never think of a man's appearance, they only look at his character. Ah, Mr. Saulsbury, you are so satirical; I don't believe one word you say; how familiar this Trab, Trab, gallop is; they dance waltzes almost altogether now. There is Miss Leigh talking to Mr. Rakeman; I wonder if it will turn out an engagement? How can a blonde like Miss Black, wear such a shade of purple? All women dislike flattery, but they like appreciation. What a classical nose Mrs. Brown has, and so white; they say she powders; how can persons say such horrid things about each other?" "I beg your pardon!" entreats the proprietor of a clumsy foot which has walked through Miss White's dress. "Certainly," returns the young lady, with a look of gratitude (that perfection of breeding). "Mr. Saulsbury, I must beg you to escort me to the dressing room."

Wentworth led his shattered convoy to the harbor into which she put for repairs, and then steered his way to Miss Leigh, to whom he was engaged for the next waltz.

Miss Leigh was a type of a class of New England girls whose innocence, beauty, and earnestness surprise you wherever you meet them, at a ball or a funeral, at a farce or a tragedy. They are bright, well read, and of a purity unsullied by a thought of evil; had they a sense of humor and a mixture of passion in their nature, they would be perfect.

"I am glad to see you," said Miss Leigh, as Wentworth bowed to her. "We were talking about the Worcester races; I hope the stories they told of the students there are not true," she added, turning to Rakeman, who was standing at her right.

"Not at all, I assure you," replied Rakeman. "A Methodist camp-meeting could not have been more quiet; the excesses the townies may have committed, of course I do not try to excuse."

"I am so glad to hear it; I always said it was so. Remember you are engaged to me for the next waltz after this."

"I shall forget everything before that," returned Rakeman, kindly leaving the field to Wentworth.

"What a capital fellow Rakeman is," said Wentworth, as his friend disappeared in the waves of crinoline.

"I like to hear you say so," said Miss Leigh, blushing, for like all Southerners Rakeman was a favorite with the fair sex. "There is something *spirituelle* about his face, I think."

"I don't know so much about these delicate shades of character," replied Wentworth. "I know Rakeman would think nothing of risking his life for a friend, or sharing his last crust with him;" and our hero told Miss Leigh the story of his creeping over the ice two years before, to which she listened with great interest.

"I like you, for liking your friends so well," she said warmly, when he had ended. "I knew I was right; a woman's instinct never deceives her: when that Mr. Sweatrame speaks to me, it sends a shudder through me: he seems to pride himself on being dissipated; he talks lightly of married women flirting."

"That, Miss Leigh, should argue him a very innocent fellow. A Joseph likes to affect the air of a Lovelace; your real Don Juan always wears the look of a lamb. Have you been skating to-day?"

"Yes, all the afternoon. I don't know which I enjoy most, skating or dancing, both are so full of grace; I should like to waltz all night."

"It is delightful, Miss Leigh, to find a girl who enjoys such things; most of your sex love nothing but hard study."

"How dare you give a wrong turn to every thing I say? I have known men bright enough to appreciate women, and men wicked enough to laugh at them, but never any one except you who did both; it must come from your reading Thackeray."

"Do you not like Thackeray?" asked Wentworth.

"No, I admire him, but I do not like him; I never rise from one of his books without feeling less respect for myself and for human nature; that is a good test, I think, don't you? and then Thackeray never seems to be very deep."

"Which do women like best, deep men or men superficially clever?"

"They like deep men, of course, infinitely better. I prefer Kingsley to Thackeray; his characters are so manly, and strong, and dashing; but they don't wholly satisfy me. I respect men who study and think, more than men who are merely hardy and venturesome; it is splendid to combine the two. I wish I were a man and could go out into the world."

"You should give lectures on Woman's Rights, Miss Leigh."

"There is nothing I dislike so much as strong minded women: yet I think that what they say has a great deal of truth in it. I do not see why women should not do any work for which nature has fitted them, nor how they can tell for what they are fitted until they try; and if they work, I don't see why they should not get fair pay. But I never like to talk about politics with men; they are never in earnest; they always treat women as half goddesses, and half fools."

"Heaven is my witness," said Wentworth, "that I have not the slightest objection in the world, to anybody's working except myself. I should think you philanthropical young ladies would take a peculiar pleasure in balls, from their contrast to your ragged schools, and poor women. It were almost worth while to be good to enjoy the variety; it must be so entertaining to see the same human nature in its different dresses!"

"I think I like the poor better than the rich: there is so much more reality in their life; I have often regretted that I was not born in the lower classes," said Miss Leigh, who would have died of a soiled collar.

"Hush! Hush!" said Wentworth, laughing. "Such sentiments will produce a new French Revolution: though your head, Miss Leigh, would look well anywhere, I think it looks better where it is than it would on the end of a pike!"

The grand march of Norma now sounded a truce to further warfare, and both armies flocked to their great physician, the supper.

The brave bucks gathered up their shattered frames; the ladies their broken fans, torn dresses, and wounded reputations. I have always liked this last metaphor, but truth compels me to confess that it is here somewhat forced, since in Boston there is little or no scandal; society is made up of Josephs and Penelopes, and personalities rarely rise above the dignity of gossip.

Wentworth found a seat in the supper-room for Miss Leigh, who was inwardly complaining that her waltz with Rakeman had been cut off, and then rushed forth into space and from it wrested two chairs, which he brought back into the hall for the German. Round these he knotted his handkerchief lest some fiend in human shape should steal them away in his absence; and then returned to the supper-room and soothed the ethereal appetite of his partner with birds, ices, cakes, and the thousand and one delicacies of the table.

Among many faults in his intercourse with the gentler sex, our hero had one redeeming trait, he fed them well. Pretty youths whose aim in life it is to captivate the fair, remember this habit to imitate it. Nothing covers more sins, or discovers more virtues in their eyes, than this recognition of the fact, that though coming from a higher, they are yet dwellers in this human sphere. I once knew a man who lost a blooming girl and half a million of dollars by neglect of this simple rule.

"If a man," so reasoned the pretty casuist with the daring logic of her sex, "will not take the trouble to offer the object of his affections enough food, when it is lying before him, he will at the slightest pinch leave his wife and children to starve to death." At this horrible thought, Beauty and her fortune vanished forever from the eyes of her broken-hearted lover.

Supper ended, the dancers took their seats, and the German began to weave its mystic figures of beauty. Oh ye mothers, who wish your sons to sleep of nights, guard their eyes from the sight of this peace-destroying dance! Grace is beauty, armed and in the field, and her weapons are dipt in a poison that drives tranquillity and peace far from the couch of youth.

Miss Campbell, as she melted from one form of enchantment to another, seemed from some hidden fountain to rain love and beauty around her.

There are two classes of noble natures; the one, from an ideal without itself works out the actual: the other, from the actual shapes for itself an ideal; the latter climb slowly to the heavens, but the former seem to spring from the very bosom of God.

Miss Campbell's left hand rested lightly as a rose on Wentworth's shoulder, and her other, held in his own, thrilled his whole frame with fire.

"I never saw you so full of life," he whispered, as his

eyes hung upon every movement of the graceful girl. A shadow flitted over Miss Campbell's face.

"It is strange," she said half to herself; "when saddest one often appears most happy: to forget our grief, we throw ourselves into what is without us, into our ideals, with a spirit that deceives every one but ourselves: sorrow thus becomes the mother of the highest art, which is always objective— What am I saying!" she added with a forced laugh, observing the surprised look of the boy. "Do not let us go back to our seats yet: there is Mr. Pitt walking towards them; I cannot breathe in that vacuum; if he speaks to me I shall die."

"I thought, Miss Campbell, that Mr. Pitt was great favorite with ladies."

"Far more than that," she replied, "he is a parlor Samson; with a jaw of an ass he has slain thousands: I don't see how he does it; they die, I suppose, like kittens in an air-pump."

"Your figures," said Wentworth with a look of humor; seem a little mixed; but they are both very good."

"I can't think," mused Miss Campbell, "why Mr. Pitt should devote himself with so much earnestness to being a fool."

"Perhaps he has a divine gift for it, and thinks it would be impious not to obey his genius."

"Very likely, and yet," she added, softening, "I have a sort of kindly parental feeling for him, for I have recreated him three separate times. When he was introduced to me last winter, he could only be said to live by a bold metaphor: I gave him an idea that kept him alive for three months: when the vital power of that was exhausted he came to me for a second, and a third; but I am tired of it, and think I shall let him die, or compromise with death by marriage. There, he has gone to speak to Miss Leigh who hates him; let us sit down; I am almost tired. Will you not fan me—not yourself I don't mean, you monster. See what a strict surveillance Miss Otis keeps over me," and Miss Campbell glanced towards the sister of her *fiancée*, who was seated a short distance from them.

"Do you not know her, Mr. Saulsbury? She is well worth your study; she is the model of a great many of our most fashionable ladies here; I have tried her on every subject in the world, and the only one that interests her is the genealogy of about a hundred of what she calls old Boston families. She can tell you to a man whom Mrs. Green, Grey, Brown, or White did marry, whom they did not marry, whom they could have married, whom they should have married; the dresses that won the victory; the children, rattles, measles, prospects; really it frightens me even to think how much she knows. She looks down with infinite contempt on any one who has not mastered this branch of learning, and has a very slight opinion of any one who knows anything in addition to it, as a person who has scattered his powers."

"Who is that gentleman with whom she is talking?" asked Wentworth.

"That is Mr. Hapsburgh; he is one of our greatest poets; he is the mouthpiece of a set of men here, who think because they know enough to eat with a fork, and not to drink out of a finger bowl, that they form the proudest aristocracy in the world. This prejudice carries him so far that, though nothing if not witty, he has never allowed a *parvenu* jest to appear in all his writings."

"I suppose," said Wentworth, "that any true Christian gentleman would rather be suspected of parricide than of drinking out of a finger bowl."

"I forgot," answered Miss Campbell, "that you were a poet; I remember some charming verses you once sent me," she added, lowering her voice. "I know them by heart. I wonder why every Yankee does not become a poet, since a poet of all men practises the highest economy. A common person when he is betrayed, insulted, or wounded squanders all his grief without getting anything in return. A poet is no such spendthrift; a friend's treason, a broken heart, a cruel wrong, all these things he knows have their market value. 'I will puff them well,' he says to himself, 'and barter them for a coat, or a hair brush,' of which he often has need. After all, I am not so sure that I would not prefer you to be a lawyer; I love that profession; they are all so charitable; a thief, a lawyer looks upon as a practical disciple of Fourier; a murderer as an over-zealous follower of Malthus. Whatever you are, however, I want all my friends to be distinguished."

"Do not fever yourself, Miss Campbell, about my future career," replied Wentworth, charmed with the girl's raillery. "I am resolved to become a philosopher; last night I heard one of our greatest thinkers lecture, and that determined me."

"What was the lecture about?" asked Miss Campbell.

"The subject was the plus of growth. Do not you wish to hear the exordium? It was very striking, and I remember every word of it. ''Twas remarked,' he began; ''twas remarked by Plato or Thoreau, I forget which, but the remark is worthy of either, that vagueness is the first element of clearness, and that all growth must be upwards, downwards, or in some other direction. Take the end of a horse's tail between your teeth; draw back a few steps; the horse kicks; the kick is fatal; spring upon his haunches, and you are safe. 'Tis thus with truth: pluck the wild rose; but God made the thorn: pluck the thorn also. This is the whole duty of man, to pull the tail from the tad-pole, to break the chrysalis for the butterfly, to give the wings of Pegasus to the hack. Every soul wears the pinions of an angel if it will but unfurl them. Why do we not soar? Why are our eyes under the soles of our feet? The heavens are above us; we have made them. The least of us is a Shakespeare, the least of us is a god; nay, the least of us has created Shakespeares, the least of us has created gods.'"

"Those two words, 'Our Father,'" said Miss Campbell, with a seriousness that forgot time and place, "not *apropos* of what you were saying, I don't mean, but of nothing, are worth all the philosophies and creeds that ever were written." A shade passed over the girl's face; her spirits seemed to droop and her gaiety to give way, as she thought of the part she was soon to act.

"How the goddess of respectability beams upon us here!" she said a little later, with bitterness. "And what a cruel purpose she carries under her smile; she dips her pen in the blood of the weak to write her laws; I don't know which I respect least, the vices or the virtues of her subjects."

"Van," said Wentworth, surprised, but always ready to follow the vein of any one's conversation, "Van says that next to sinning themselves, the greatest pleasure people have is to detect and abuse sin in others; that in the latter case it is the thought of the sin that gives them pleasure; the abuse is merely a cloak to hide their impertinence for meddling in others' concerns, though they prefer to call it virtue."

"I hate Society and her cruel laws," said Miss Campbell, with earnestness.

"There is Mr. Pitt bringing you your fifth bouquet," exclaimed Wentworth.

"The angel!" cried our heroine, with enthusiasm, and her spirits rose at the graceful tribute, which always touches a woman's heart at the altar, in the ball room, or, I doubt not, in the coffin.

The night danced on more slowly; the spectators began to dwindle. Pippins retreated with his four *mots* in good order; the more venerable bucks had already retired to heal the torture of the boot and the other mortifications of the flesh, which fashion inflicts upon her votaries; even the heroic brood of pelicans upon the sofas grew weary; a mother's love, strongest and holiest of passions, alone propped up their falling eyelids. Miss Campbell had never achieved a greater success; in the flower figure she had received seven bouquets, which was three more than any other girl in the room, and gained her no little envy and admiration. Girls prize these distinctions as highly as knights their garters, and perhaps as justly. At four the ball broke up."

"Miss Campbell has flirted shamefully to-night," whispered Miss Otis to her brother, as he was leading her to Mrs. Morris.

"I must request you," replied the latter, who was a thorough gentleman; "never again to make any disparaging remark about Miss Campbell; it is insulting to me, and only makes me feel less respect for you."

"Your carriage is ready," he said a few minutes later, to his *fiancée*, and walked down before her in silence.

"Good night, Nell," he said, gently but with a touch of reproach in his voice, as he seated her in her carriage, and then, holding her hand a moment, stooped down to kiss it.

Miss Campbell drew back her hand. "I have been requested to give you this," she said, with a voice that tried to be calm, but was choking with emotion, and she handed him a letter; Mr. Otis took the letter mechanically, shut the door, and the coachman drove away.

"That he should dare accuse me of flirting!" said Miss Campbell to herself, as she in vain tried to check her sobbing. Reaching her home, she threw herself upon her bed and there lay through the weary hours, her long hair falling over her throbbing breast. Now that she had forever separated herself from her lover, she felt how much she had really cared for him, and half regretted the act into which her pride had hurried her.

In his distant chamber her lover sat gazing at the letter, and the two rings it contained. The letter was short, and stated that Miss Campbell had heard of his conduct, and that of course their engagement must be considered at an end; that she owed it to the love she had once borne him never to disclose the cause. The poor fellow read the letter over and over again with fresh pain; he then took one of the rings, on which were the words, "Céleste, from J. E. O.," and with a curse at the treachery of his mistress, opened the window and threw the ring into the street; he again returned to his seat, kissed the cruel words of the woman he truly loved, and again arose, pacing up and down the room in bitter grief.

Wentworth, however, had mounted his tilbury with Van and Rakeman, and warmed his way over the cold bridge with songs and jests, and was now fast asleep with pleasant music ringing in his ears, unconscious of the tears and sighs that were raining and breathing in breezy Boston.

But shapely Céleste, lovely cause of so great evils, that very evening, untired by her morning's acting, had been taking with ravishment the applauding eyes of a crowded audience in a neighboring theatre, and showering grace and beauty around her, had gathered the bouquets thrown at her feet. Thus turns the great grindstone of the world, and grinds of some the axes, but the noses of others.

CHAPTER XX.

"Intervenerant quidam amici, propter quos major fumus fieret: . . . . Varius nobis sermo fuit, ut in convivio, nullam rem usque ad exitum adducens, sed aliunde alio transiliens."

TRUTH is a slippery baggage," said Hayward, who, with other friends, was in Wentworth's room early in the evening of the "Seniors' benefit," at the Mush and Milk Club; "She can only be held by the three members of a syllogism, as an eel by the three fingers of a fish-wife."

"We know not what we know, nor of that fact are we conscious," said the gentle Desdemona, who was lying in a window-seat and displayed a very pretty foot and ankle. As she spoke, Desdemona threw her Hamilton's Metaphysics into a corner of the room and lighted a fresh cigar. "Iago," she then remarked, taking from her bosom a spotted handkerchief of great size, "though to be sure something of a rascal, was what we should now-a-days call a very smart man."

Our friends, as the studies of the year had led them, had, in the interim between their college gossip, been dissolving the universe into a dew; metaphysics and logic were their blow-pipe and test-tube: they had doubted matter; they had doubted mind; strangest of doubts, they had doubted their own identity! Happy skeptics! They had no creditors—sad but sure cure of this infirmity.

"These metaphysicians," said Wentworth, who had been arguing against his friends, and who always maintained a bigoted belief in his own existence at least—"these metaphysicians sharpen their ideas down until they reduce them, and not the universe, to nothing. They don't seem to me to be much wiser than common folks. Even in definitions we often meet with as nice differences among the ignorant as among the learned. Servants, in naming doors, draw as fine distinctions as the German professors with their subject and object. If a house has two front and two back doors, they style them the front-front door, the front-back door, the back-front door, and the back-back door."

"I never felt so encouraged since I came to college," said Bowyer, whose bulk lay stretched out upon a sofa, wreathed in peaceful smoke, "as when I learnt that the highest studies were nothing more than mental gymnastics. I am sure that in that case I must be a greater proficient in them than any of our shadowy professors," and the "oar" doubled up an arm, whose mere relaxation would have placed half the College Faculty *hors-de-combat.*

"I think that theory of Hamilton is false," rejoined Wentworth. "The belief that the search after truth, not truth itself, is the object of life, is suicidal; no one searches with any heart after that which he does not much care to find; no one cares to find what he does not think much worth the finding. Truth is in itself a good, not an *ignis fatuus* to lead us dancing over bogs and quagmires, to enlarge our muscles. God, from the centre of the universe, rays out his physical, intellectual, and moral laws ; our aim is to place ourselves at that centre, and as far as our finite powers permit, to see all things as the calm eye of God sees them ; to know and embody the highest truth, is the one aim worthy of an immortal soul."

"This is a dog-day of a conversation," said Desdemona, who was no other than Van, tripping to a chair, where lay what looked like a baby wrapped up in a blanket, but proved to be a lump of ice, which she placed in a towel, and pounded into small pieces prophetic of cobblers.

"There goes Sweatrame to the Mush and Milk rooms," said Rakeman, who was lying on the window seat, opposite Van's, and whose face wore a look of melancholy. "Do you remember, Van, Freshman year, when Dummer and Sweatrame used to go on 'benders' together? Wine always attacked Sweatrame's knees, but spared his head, while Dummer's legs were firm long after his head was gone; when both were drunk, together they formed one sober man. After a spree, Sweatrame always mounted on Dummer's shoulders and steered him safely home. They had thus all the advantages of being drunk and sober at the same time. How those good old times come back to us!" he added, musingly. "Don't you recollect Robin, when you were a Freshman, how you used to wait in Boston for the twelve o'clock car? I have known you to stand on the sidewalk two or three hours for no other purpose ; you thought it was so 'nuttish' to say, 'I came out in the last car last night.'"

"I don't recollect anything of the kind," replied Robin, rather ruffled; "I remember the first day we came to college your running to prayers at the first bell; a dozen Sophomores got up early to watch you."

"It was that rascally Brandreth," said Rakeman. "He told me to be sure to be in the Chapel before the first bell was over; I thought I was late."

"Holloa, boys!" cried Van, "it is half past seven; I must be off; the play begins at eight," and Desdemona gathered up her skirts, threw the stump of her cigar into the grate, clapped Rakeman a virtuous box on the ear, that nearly beheaded him, and fled from his embraces pursued by Hayward.

"Emmett," said Wentworth, after Van had gone, "Emmett told me the other day of his attempt to cast his vote against us at the Class Elections. 'When the meeting came off I was lying,' he said, 'in my house in fragrant Brighton, prostrate from the attack of a fever and two physicians. One of them was just making his diagnosis; 'When I place my finger thus, you feel a severe pain—what? no pain! that is in itself a dangerous symptom.' Suddenly Cade burst into the room. 'Zounds, Emmett!' he cried out to me, 'how have you the leisure to be sick in such a justling time! We need but one vote to overthrow the Mushes; one more vote and the class-poet is ours. Sickness! Death! These are names. Virtue! Religion! Freedom! These are realities! If you must die, die in a blaze of glory voting against the Mushes!' with these words Cade hurried me into his tilbury; the steed felt that he was bearing the fortunes of the anti-Mushes; he shot over the road: the Flying Childers was but a snail to him. In a few minutes, borne on Cade's shoulder, wrapped in a blanket, I burst into the Institute. It was too late; the voting was over; the poet of the Mushes was making his speech of acceptance. It was a brave effort, though, and nearly cost me my life.'"

"How can you speak to such scrubs?—when they told such lies about us, too," said Robin. "They said I tried to bribe a man with an oyster stew to vote for the Mushes; I would not demean myself by bowing to them."

"These social distinctions are matter for tailors, not for scholars," rejoined Wentworth. "We ought to have a professor here to lecture ou the naked man"——Wentworth was interrupted by Rakeman, who fetched a deep sigh.

His friends, who knew its cause, said nothing for some moments.

"Will you not take something to eat?" Robin at length gently entreated him. "It will do you good."

Rakeman glanced at the oily olives, the strenuous crackers, the restless cheese, and the golden sherry ranged upon the table, but shook his head.

"I did not make a good impression on Miss Leigh last night, I'm sure of it," he muttered, and unloosed another sigh.

"Tut: tut; man!" said Wentworth, "you Southerners always succeed with women; you have that reckless, careless manner that throws them off their guard, and lays open their hearts to your thrusts, before they know it."

Rakeman only shook his head; despondency deepened on his face; love was fast bringing his wild spirit to slavery. Yet he would not yield without a struggle; he had learnt from Western trappers to fight fire with fire; he summoned against the flame of love, the gentle but powerful ally, tobacco. He drew from his pocket a huge red clay pipe; scarce twice six chosen Freshmen, such Freshmen as Harvard now produces, could have sustained it upon their shoulders. This Rakeman filled with Herculean perique and with heroical puffs strove to smoke Dan Cupid from the hole in his heart, in which he had burrowed. He threw himself back into the window-seat: his eyes sought the ceiling; he smoked and sighed, and sighed and smoked in sadness; his pipe glowed like a volcano; Empedocles might have sought immortality down its fiery crater.

"I have been through it, myself: I know what it is," said the warbler feelingly.

"It is the suspense, the suspense, that is killing me," groaned Rakeman, "If I only knew, what I dare not ask."

"I condole with you, with all my heart," murmured Robin, "'Tis terrible! When the fit was on me, I tasted nothing for three hours. Can I not do anything for you? Shall I not sing to you?"

"Do! Do! Robin," sighed Rakeman.

"Shall I sing that sweet song,

'Come away, come away, Death,
And in sad cypres let me be laid'"

"Yes, yes."

"Shall I sing it as if I meant it?"

The poor victim bowed his head. The songster pressed the sufferer's hand, and poured forth his softest notes into his ear.

"What is the world but an empty pipe, when love does not fill it?" said Rakeman, knocking the ashes from the bowl as Robin ended. "My heart feels lighter."

"You are growing very spooney," said Wentworth; "the play at the Mush and Milk must have begun," and he left his friends and walked to the society's rooms, whither they soon followed him.

"I congratulate you on your success, to-night, Van," said Wentworth to his chum, after their return from the plays and supper at the Club. "You are our American Siddons! Your neck is the fairest sight; and that sweet smile you wore, when Othello made at you with the poker; 'twas ravishing; you would make a very dangerous woman."

"I saw Mr. Otis out here, to-night," said Van; "I wonder what made Miss Campbell throw him over; every one, I hear, blames her for it."

"I don't know, I'm sure," replied Wentworth. "It has made her very sad and unhappy: as I know nothing about her reasons, I don't form any opinion on the subject."

"I wouldn't give a fig for the opinions of society about it," said Van; "a thousand blind persons can't see any farther than one. Why don't you go in and win her?"

"I am afraid to ask her," said Wentworth, "I feel that the happiness of my life depends on her answer."

"Nonsense!" replied Van, "don't have such a feeling. If you lose the girl, it will probably be because you love her too much; a woman never loves a man who makes himself cheap: she wants some one to look up to, some one to command her, some one, as she grows older, to abuse her. Women in their hearts admire a Bluebeard or a Henry VIII. more than a Bayard. Still, perhaps it is better to combine the two methods: let them feel that at any moment you may off with their heads, but that meanwhile you will treat them with all gentleness."

"With such a counsellor in the cabinet, who could fail in the field," said Wentworth, good humoredly.

CHAPTER XXI.

"Ad restim res redit mihi quidem planissume."

**"Ergo cum tenuem fuero mutatus in umbram
Candidaque ossa super nigra favilla teget,
Ante meum veniat longos incompta capillos
Et fleat ante meum mæsta Næera rogum."**

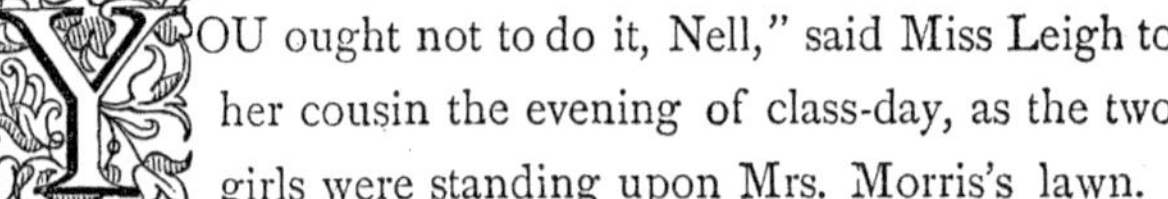

OU ought not to do it, Nell," said Miss Leigh to her cousin the evening of class-day, as the two girls were standing upon Mrs. Morris's lawn.

"Women, Amy," replied Miss Campbell, "are born to flirt as the sparks fly upward. Don't look so serious; there is no danger, and if it should happen it would not do him much harm," she added in jest; "it would be a sort of vaccination to keep the real disease from being too violent.'

"That is the very reason it is so wrong, Nell," said Miss Leigh lowering her voice; "it takes from a man the power of ever after enjoying the noblest passion."

"Have you turned physician, Miss Campbell?" asked Wentworth, who had caught her words as he came forward to speak to his friends. "How many hast thou killed to-day?"

"Some fourteen, a trifle, a trifle," answered Miss Campbell. "Tell me, Mr. Saulsbury, who were the characters that Mr. Gowan sketched in your class oration?"

"The rowing man was Bowyer, the fast man Sweatrame, the scholar Hayward, and the singing man Ayres; I can't guess the others."

The conversation was here interrupted by one Mrs. Field, who appears for the first and last time upon this stage.

"I wish to ask you, Miss Campbell, if you will excuse the question," she said, drawing the girl aside, "why you broke off your engagement with Mr. Otis?"

The roses fell from Miss Campbell's cheeks; her eyes like marigolds shot forth jets of flame.

"My dear madam," she replied in her sweetest voice, "Mr. Otis had ceased to amuse me."

Mrs. Field turned away and always afterwards spoke of our heroine as the most heartless of women.

Shortly after this inquiring lady had retired, Rakeman came up and carried off Miss Leigh to the President's Reception.

"I am glad you do not want to go to the Reception," said Wentworth, as the other guests followed Rakeman. "It is pleasanter here than suffering the *peine forte et dure*," and he ran into the house and brought out a seat.

"Thank you very much," said Miss Campbell, "I am tired from going to the spreads and dances. How pretty the lanterns look through the trees! they seem like fireflies in the hair of a Southern beauty. Do you not feel sad at leaving so pleasant a place? Yet it must be glorious to go out into the world and fight for its prizes. A woman has no career open to her except that of a martyr; I could have stabbed that woman for what she said to me; Hawthorne says that there is nothing tragic in America to write about; but lift the veil that covers society, how many women do you see dying from the poison that lurks in their social life? Women of high aims, what sympathy do they meet from the world? They are abandoned to the censure and malice of prudes and rakes. The souls of such women 'starve in ice!' They cannot tell what it is that makes them wretched; they cannot point out any single word, or act, or wrong, but their disease is none the less fatal. The air! you cannot see, nor taste, nor touch it, but it holds your life and death in its power." She checked herself in the bitter strain Mrs. Field's insolent question had provoked.

"How romantic everything looks to-night," she said, looking around her.

"You look like Circe," said Wentworth, thinking of her, not of her words, and his eye wandered over her dress, which was of the color in which the fields set their flowers, and the sea clothes its gems.

"Have I transformed you? I will disenchant you," she said pleasantly, and sprinkled a few drops of cologne over the boy. "If the Father of the Universe originally made you a goose,"—"Bird," said Wentworth, "don't be so concrete. It is more artistic but not half so flattering."

"You have destroyed the charm," said the girl with a shake of her head; "I fear you will always remain what you are. How well the college songs sound here in the distance. You ought to be with your friends and not flattering me at their expense. They are singing Fair Harvard, what a charming song it is.

'Believe me if all those endearing young charms.'

I wish we had Cousin Amy here; we would make her sing

for us; what a sweet voice she has! She is one of the few women I know who are true friends to other women. It is rare to find an honorable woman, I think, don't you? You would, if you knew them better. If I were a man I should fall in love with her; she is so true and good. Why do you laugh? I do not like you for that. She is not like most good persons; their goodness shows itself in condemning their fellows without a trial; it is but the accomplice of bolder evil which gives it the cue."

The girl's lips quivered; she was thinking of the unjust things that had been said of her.

"I did not laugh unkindly," said Wentworth. "It cuts me to hear you talk so wildly. The world is very beautiful, and human nature grand and noble; and you, Miss Campbell"——

"I did not mean to wound you," said the girl, quickly, "I spoke hastily; I beg your pardon. Will you not call me Nell? Miss Campbell seems so distant. You promised me a long time ago to be my friend; you have broken your promise, but will you not mend it? mother says friendship is impossible between men and women; but I do not see why. I want friends whom I can trust; I feel so alone of late. You are different from the rest; you are so loyal a friend, I hear. Promise me to be my friend, will you not?" The boy tried to speak, but his tongue was chained. Suddenly his life passed from his keeping; he lived and breathed only in the beautiful woman before him.

"Friend!" he cried, his passion at length finding words,

"friend! You are my life, my soul!" He caught her hand to cover it with kisses.

"Miss Campbell's snowy skin stained with scarlet; then, as when the foam breaks over a bed of coral, she turned as suddenly white.

"What have I done?" she cried, as the boy sank at her feet. It cannot be; I did not think you loved me; I thought you were cold and—and like a friend, Mr. Saulsbury. Wentworth, do forgive me! I did not mean to deceive you; do not think so unkindly of me." Miss Campbell poured forth her words with passionate earnestness.

"I love you!" said Wentworth, with the vacant look of one who sees the hope of his life, just as he had grasped it, vanish.

"There is some one coming," said Miss Campbell, hastily; "forget what you have felt. You have done me a great honor; I shall always remember it. You will still think kindly of me, though not as before, do promise me!" Miss Campbell reached out her hand; Wentworth took it, mechanically, and with the same look turned and walked away.

Through the long hours of the night, now slow, now fast, the boy walked on. The flowers which a few hours before had blossomed bright around him, were withered and dead; the music of the summer breezes had changed into a wail; the world, which love had filled with life, had become a tomb. At length the boy's steps brought him back again to the college. As he passed his club-rooms he caught snatches of the songs of some late revellers; their merriment seemed to him a mockery, but a wild desire seized him to drown his memory; he turned to enter the door, but his pride checked him. "It is cowardly not to face the enemy," he muttered to himself, and kept on his way to his rooms.

There he threw himself upon the bed, and tried to fall asleep. Suddenly he sprang up wildly; the words of Miss Campbell to her cousin, were traced in fire before his eyes.

"It would not do him much harm; it would keep the real disease from being too violent."

"She must have made one love her for her amusement," he cried fiercely, and sank down in despair.

It is not the loss of a woman he loves, but the loss of respect for her, that most deeply sears the heart of a man of honor.

CHAPTER XXII.

"Tabuit in calido vulnere mucro tener."

THE next day and for many days afterward, Wentworth was subject to fits of passion, followed by long hours of listlessness. The departure of his friends excited in him no feelings of regret. A few days after Class Day, he received letters from Bowyer and Ayres, stating that they had gone into business in New York. A week later came one of a different tenor from Rakeman, announcing his engagement to Miss Leigh. The same day he received an invitation from his cousin to visit Newport: the postscript added, what Wentworth well knew before, that his old flame, Miss Campbell, was staying with Mrs. Morris.

Van, who had remained in Cambridge after most of his class had gone, had guessed his friend's trouble, but had been silent about it. The day before he went to New York, however, whence he was soon to sail for Europe, the two friends sat late into the night, talking over their college-days. As the hours wore on, they grew confidential, and Van at length spoke to Wentworth about what he knew lay nearest his friend's heart.

"Promise me," he said, "promise me, Wentworth, that you will not let your disappointment drive you into dissipation. If our love for a woman makes us base, we learn in a short time to hate both her and ourselves. The suffering that comes from the loss of what we love, is a pleasure compared with that which springs from remorse.

"We rakes," he added with a bitter laugh, "make the best preachers when we read the real lessons of our lives. Truth is found in the dregs of the cup of pleasure, as often as in the temple, only it is found there dead, for us. The next best thing to being good ourselves, though," a look of noble generosity brightened on the boy's face, "is to aid others to be good."

"Van! Van!" cried Wentworth, "your unselfishness makes me forget myself. Don't talk so wildly; you are not going to abandon yourself to waste and decay; you are generous and ambitious and full of talents. Because you find some sins in your past life—because you find some traitors in your camp, you do not think of surrender; hang them up in sight of the army, and fight on all the more bravely. Promise me, Van, in the battle of life, into which we are entering, you will be true to yourself: I shall thank you more for that example, than for all your words, however kind."

"I will try," said Van humbly.

"We will both try," said his friend, grasping him by the hand.

A happy smile played over Van's face that evening; the sneer disappeared from his lips; the innocence of his boy hood shone in hls iooks and spoke in his words; Wentworth had never loved his friend so well.

The next morning they parted with many assurances of affection. When Wentworth returned to his rooms alone, the passion he had thought half conquered, again broke out. An easy way to forget anything, philosophy teaches, is to throw our minds into something else. The knowledge of relatives is one, and the direct attempt to banish an object from our thoughts, only chains it there the more closely. The only difficulty about this rule lies in its practice. Wentworth opened his books and tried to work on his Commencement part, but without success. Each word that spoke of beauty or grace summoned before his eyes by a fatal magic, the vision of the woman he loved.

"I wonder," he thought, "if the dimples on her hand look as pretty as ever. Does she still wear that coral sphinx on her neck? What a sweet smile she has! Is she playing with her cousins? How little children love her! Each word she speaks to them seems a caress. Who is enjoying her smiles now? Curse my fate! I will not waste my life in this maudlin way. That she should dare so to play with the souls of men! I will see her once more; I will tell her I no longer love her, that I—— but why do I fret? Happiness! happiness! a thorn, a tooth, a woman can destroy it! Knowledge! Growth! Strength! There is something noble in these. I will see her once more and end it."

With this determination our hero took the cars for Newport.

What is the use of these last interviews of disappointed aspirants? Are they truces under which the defeated party carries off his wounded sentiments? Are they funeral ceremonies at which love is decently interred? They differ from the latter in one point at least. Truth, whom death strikes dumb, here has a voice potential; she breaks through the veils of convention, opens her ill-favored mouth, and saws the air with her bony hand. Pretty maidens, who count with pleasure each new scalp added to your girdles, beware of these last meetings; they are devices of the enemy; they are tricks to rob you of your spoils. When you have once refused a man, never see him alone; he has nothing further to lose; you have nothing more to win.

Wentworth, on reaching Newport, called upon Miss Campbell, and invited her to walk. They passed along the path by the rocks, over which a year ago they had often climbed together. Miss Campbell, as they went on, was struck with the change in her companion's appearance, which the last few weeks had made. Wentworth had grown from a boy into a man. His struggle to master his passion had given him strength and self-command; his face looked earnest and proud; his manner wore a grace and ease which were far from unattractive. After a short walk they reached a natural seat in the rocks, where Wentworth the summer before had passed many a pleasant hour reading to Miss Campbell.

She now complained of being tired, and seating herself in the familiar seat, looked at the cloth of gold which the setting sun was spreading over the ocean. At their feet the waves were rolling in grandly, and dashing their foam high up against the rocks. A few rods from the shore, a jagged pyramidal rock rose above the water's level. Each wave, as it rolled inland, hung over the peak of the rock, broke, and flowed down in a thousand streamlets. A small rainbow at the same moment rose above the rock's summit, hovered over it, and disappeared.

"How exquisite!" said Miss Campbell, pointing out the rainbow to Wentworth. "It is the soul rising from the body's death-bed."

Wentworth's eyes glanced at the rainbow and returned to feed, against his will, upon the lustrous beauty of the woman before him. His thoughts, despite his struggles, became captive to its spell. She was seated with her face half turned from him. Her rich dark hair flowed back in waves from her forehead. The roses of the setting sun could not vie with her cheeks. Her fair neck and breast breathed forth a power that brought Nature enchanted to her feet. Half Cleopatra, half Madonna, the passion and purity of earth and heaven mingled in her beauty. Her form carved in colorless marble would have commanded worship; instinct with glowing life, one touch of her hand seemed to have power to call back the dead to love.

"She seems the embodiment of love and truth," thought Wentworth. "How can she be so false?"

"You are very beautiful," he said, aloud, careless of offence; the words came so naturally from his heart that they scarcely seemed amiss.

"I wonder," thought Miss Campbell, "why I did not love him. He is handsome, clever, and full of ardor! Shall I ever meet another whom I shall like better? If he had not been so violent. A man should try to make a woman love him, and not merely to show his love for her. I suppose I shall repent when it is too late."

"I once loved you," said Wentworth, breaking from the spell of the girl's beauty. Miss Campbell gave a start of surprise. "I once loved you, but I did not come to tell you that. Loved you!" he cried, his passion mastering him; "I would have given my life to your service without return! Would that I might have gathered its years into a moment of devotion to you, and then died. How much wiser, having climbed to the height of life to throw oneself headlong, than to creep slowly down to death."

Wentworth checked himself by a great effort: Miss Campbell could not help feeling a thrill of admiration for him as he uttered his wild words.

"I talk like an actor," he continued, contemptuously. "I did not come to tell you these things—I should not have minded it in another, but you, who held the key of my destiny! that you should so use your power! that you should sacrifice my life to flatter your vanity!—that you should so degrade what is noblest in the human soul! that you should use to feed the paltriest of vices the fuel that should burn at the very altar of God! Enough of this!—I came to tell you that I no longer care for you: that if you would win even the friendship of a man of honor, you must first gain his respect."

Miss Campbell, as Wentworth poured out these reproaches, tried to speak, but her words failed her. She reached out her hand to him imploringly, but he did not heed it. As he uttered his last cruel words she pressed her hand to her heart and uttered a cry of pain.

"You are unjust, you are ungenerous," she said, speaking at length by a great effort. "I never meant to deceive you; I could not do a thing so contemptible. It was lonely; I wanted you to be my friend. If I wronged you, I can but humbly beg you to pardon me." The proud girl burst into tears, and buried her face in her hands.

The sight of her grief, recalled Wentworth to his senses.

"Forgive me!" he cried, passionately. "I knew not what I said. My love for you has made me beside myself. It was my wounded vanity that spoke. It is my misfortune, not your fault, that you did not love me. Tell me that you forgive me. Though I love you more than all the world besides, I will never see you again."

"Never again; Wentworth?" The girl raised her head; a smile broke through her tears; her lips quivered with tenderness.

"Darling! I will never leave you!" cried her happy lover, and caught her half reluctant in his arms, and set love's sweet seal upon his vow.

A diviner beauty shone from the girl's fair face; a tenderer light beamed from her sunny eyes.

"Dearest!" she whispered,—the magic of her voice unlocked the gates of sense, filled the air with visions of beauty, and called over the laughing waves the music of heavenly choirs—"Dearest, tell me again that you love me." She sank upon her lover's breast transfigured.

"Dearest!" she again whispered, "will you love me always as now?"

"Always, darling, always! Would that now were forever! Nay, love, I would give my hope of immortal life to win this moment of delight!"

"Hush! hush!" the girl clung closer to her lover. "Not such love, but that you will always be noble and true and—and will love no one else so well."

"Eheu fugaces."

THE END.

A List of the Publications

OF

G. P. PUTNAM & SON,

661 Broadway, New York

ABBOT. MEXICO AND THE UNITED STATES. Their Mutual Relations and Common Interests. With Portraits on Steel of Juarez and Romero. By Gorham D. Abbot, LL.D. 8vo, cloth, $3.50.

"This volume deserves the careful study of all true patriots. It has been prepared with great care, from the most authentic sources; and it probably furnishes the materials for a better understanding of the real character and aims of modern Romanism than any other volume extant."—*Congregationalist.*

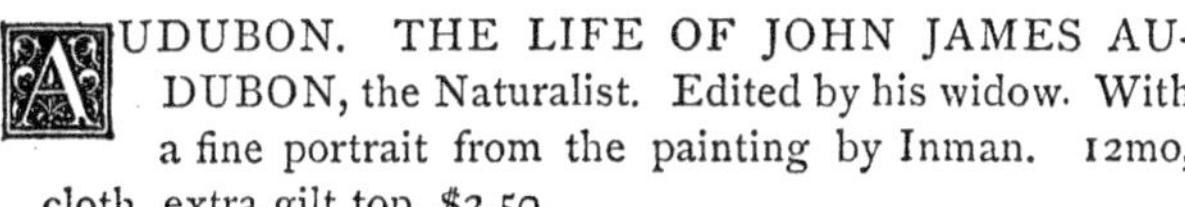

AUDUBON. THE LIFE OF JOHN JAMES AUDUBON, the Naturalist. Edited by his widow. With a fine portrait from the painting by Inman. 12mo, cloth, extra gilt top, $2.50.

"It is a grand story of a grand life; more instructive than a sermon, more romantic than a romance."—*Harper's Magazine.*

BASCOM. PRINCIPLES OF PSYCHOLOGY. By John Bascom, Professor in Williams College. 12mo, pp. 350, $1.75.

"All success to the students of physical science: but each of its fields may have its triumphs, and the secrets of mind remain as unapproachable as hitherto. With philosophy and not without it, under its own laws and not under the laws of a lower realm, must be found those clues of success, those principles of investigation, which can alone place this highest form of knowledge in its true position. The following treatise is at least a patient effort to make a contribution to this, amid all failures, chief department of thought."—*Extract from Preface.*

LACKWELL. STUDIES IN GENERAL SCIENCE. By Antoinette Brown Blackwell. 12mo (uniform with Child's "Benedicite"). Cloth extra, $2.25.

"The writer evinces admirable gifts both as a student and thinker. She brings a sincere and earnest mind to the investigation of truth."—*N. Y. Tribune.*

"The idea of the work is an excellent one, and it is ably developed."—*Boston Transcript.*

BLINDPITS—A Novel. [Reprinted by special arrangement with the Edinburgh publishers.] 1 vol. 12mo, $1.75.

*** A delightful story, which everybody will like.

"The book indicates more than ordinary genius, and we recommend it unreservedly."—*Buffalo Courier.*

OLTE (Amely). MADAME de STAEL; A Historical Novel: translated from the German by Theo. Johnson. 16mo, cloth extra, $1.50.

[*Putnam's European Library.*]

"One of the best historical novels which has appeared for a long time."—*Illust. Zeitung.*

"Worthy of its great subject."—*Familien-Journal.*

"Every chapter brings the reader in contact with eminent personages, and entertains him in the most agreeable and profitable manner."—*Europa.*

"This is one of those valuable novels that combine historical and biographical information with amusement."—*Cincinnati Chronicle.*

RACE. THE NEW WEST; or, California in 1867 and '68. By Charles L. Brace, Author of the "Races of the Old World," "Home-Life in Germany," "Hungary in 1851," etc. 12mo, cloth, $1.75.

"We recommend it as the most readable and comprehensive book published on the general theme of California."—*N. Y. Times.*

RYANT. LETTERS OF A TRAVELLER. By Wm. Cullen Bryant. New edition. 12mo, cloth.

—— LETTERS FROM THE EAST. Notes of a Visit to Egypt and Palestine. 12mo, cloth, $1.50.

—— The Same. ILLUSTRATED EDITION. With fine engravings on steel. 12mo, cloth extra, $3.

AVÉ. THE CAVÉ METHOD OF LEARNING TO DRAW FROM MEMORY. By Madame E. Cavé. From 4th Parisian edition. 12mo, cloth, $1.

⁎ This is the *only method of drawing which really teaches anything.* In publishing the remarkable treatise, in which she unfolds, with surpassing interest, the results of her observations upon the teaching of drawing, and the ingenious methods she applies, Madame Cavé . . . . renders invaluable service to all who have marked out for themselves a career of Art."—*Extract from a long review in the Revue des Deux Mondes,* written by Delacroix.

"It is interesting and valuable."—D. HUNTINGTON, *Prest. Nat. Acad.*

"Should be used by every teacher of Drawing in America."—*City Item, Phila.*

"We wish that Madame Cavé had published this work half a century ago, that we might have been instructed in this enviable accomplishment."—*Harper's Mag.*

CAVÉ. THE CAVÉ METHOD OF TEACHING COLOR. 12mo, cloth, $1.

⁎ This work was referred, by the French Minister of Public Instruction, to a commission of ten eminent artists and officials, whose report, written by M. Delacroix, was unanimously adopted, endorsing and approving the work. The Minister, thereupon, by a decree, authorized the use of it in the French Normal schools.

G. P. PUTNAM & SON have also just received from Paris specimens of the MATERIALS used in this method, which they can supply to order. I. The GAUZES (framed) are now ready. Price $1 each. With discount to teachers. II. The Stand for the gauze. Price $1.50. III. MÉTHODE CAVÉ, *pour apprendre à dessiner* juste et de mémoire d'après les principes d'Albert Durer et de Leonardo da Vinci. Approved by the Minister of Public Instruction, and by Messrs. Delacroix, H. Vernet, etc. In 8 series, folio, paper covers. Price $2.25 each.

N.B.—The Crayons, Paper, and other articles mentioned in the Cavé Method may be obtained of any dealer in Artist's Materials. Samples of the French Articles may be seen at 661 Broadway.

HADBOURNE. NATURAL THEOLOGY; or, Nature and the Bible from the same Author. Lectures delivered before the Lowell Institute, Boston. By P. A. Chadbourne, A.M., M.D., President of University of Wisconsin. 12mo, cloth, $2. Student's edition, $1.75.

"This is a valuable contribution to current literature, and will be found adapted to the use of the class-room in college, and to the investigations of private students." —*Richmond Christian Adv.*

"The warm, fresh breath of pure and fervent religion pervades these eloquent pages."—*Am. Baptist.*

"Prof. Chadbourne's book is among the few metaphysical ones now published, which, once taken up, cannot be laid aside unread. It is written in a perspicuous, animated style, combining depth of thought and grace of diction, with a total absence of ambitious display."—*Washington National Republic.*

"In diction, method, and spirit, the volume is attractive and distinctive to a rare degree."—*Boston Traveller.*

CHILD'S BENEDICITE; or, Illustration of the Power, Wisdom, and Goodness of God, as manifested in His Works. By G. Chaplin Child, M.D. From the London edition of John Murray. With an Introductory Note by Henry G. Weston, D.D., of New York. 1 vol. 12mo. Elegantly printed on tinted paper, cloth extra, bevelled, $2; mor. ext., $4.50.

CHIEF CONTENTS.

Introduction.	Winter and Summer.	Wells.
The Heavens.	Nights and Days.	Seas and Floods.
The Sun and Moon.	Light and Darkness.	The Winds.
The Planets.	Lightning and Clouds.	Fire and Heat.
The Stars.	Showers and Dew.	Frost and Snow, etc.

"The most admirable popular treatise of natural theology. It is no extravagance to say that we have never read a more charming book, or one which we can recommend more confidently to our readers with the assurance that it will aid them, as none that we know of can do, to

'Look through Nature up to Nature's God.'

Every clergyman would do well particularly to study this book. For the rest, the handsome volume is delightful in appearance, and is one of the most creditable specimens of American book-making that has come from the Riverside Press."—*Round Table, N. Y.*, June 1.

CLARKE. PORTIA, and other Tales of Shakespeare's Heroines. By Mrs. Cowden Clarke, author of the Concordance to Shakespeare. With engravings. 12mo, cloth extra, $2.50; gilt edges, $3.

*** An attractive book, especially for girls.

COOPER. RURAL HOURS. By a Lady. (Miss Susan Fenimore Cooper.) New Edition, with a new Introductory Chapter. 1 vol. 12mo, $2.50.

"One of the most interesting volumes of the day, displaying powers of mind of a high order."—Mrs. HALE'S *Woman's Record*.

"An admirable portraiture of American out-door life, just as it is."—*Prof. Hart.*

"A very pleasant book—the result of the combined effort of good sense and good feeling, an observing mind, and a real, honest, unaffected appreciation of the countless minor beauties that Nature exhibits to her assiduous lovers."—*N. Y. Albion.*

CRAVEN (Mme. Aug.). ANNE SEVERIN: A Story translated from the French. 16mo, $1.50.

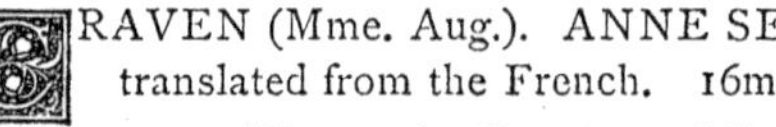

[*Putnam's European Library.*]

*** "The Sister's Story," by the same author, has been warmly and generally eulogized as a book of remarkably pure and elevated character.

"By her great success, Mrs. Craven has larger power for good than perhaps any other writer in France."—*Pall Mall Gazette.*

AVIS. A STRANDED SHIP. A Story of Sea and Shore. By L. Clarke Davis. 16mo, cloth, 80 cts.; paper, 50 cts.

"It is told with exceeding grace, and portrays the lives of two unhappy men with remarkable skill and insight into human nature."—*Phila. City Item.*

DENISON. ASTRONOMY WITHOUT MATHEMATICS. By Edmund Beckett Denison, LL.D., Q.C., F.R.A.S. From the 4th London edition. Edited, with corrections and notes, by Pliny E. Chase, A.M. 12mo, cloth, $1.75.

E VERE. WONDERS OF THE DEEP. By M. Schele de Vere, Professor of Modern Languages in the University of Virginia. 12mo, cloth, $1.75.

Chief Contents.

Pearls.	Oysters.
Corals.	Light-house Stories, etc.
Facts and Tables.	Odd Fish.
Mercury.	&c., &c.

INGELSTEDT (Franz). THE AMAZON. Translated from the German by J. M. Hart. 16mo, cloth extra, $1.50.

[*Putnam's European Library.*]

"Full of scintillations of wit, . . . sparkles throughout with vivacity and fanciful humor."—*Leipsic Blätter.*

"Unquestionably the most charming novel that has appeared for some time."—"*Ueber Land und Meer,*" *Stuttgart.*

EGLESTON (Geo. W.). THE SEARCH AFTER TRUTH. Addressed to Young Men. Dedicated to the Young Men's Christian Associations. 16mo, cloth, $1.25.

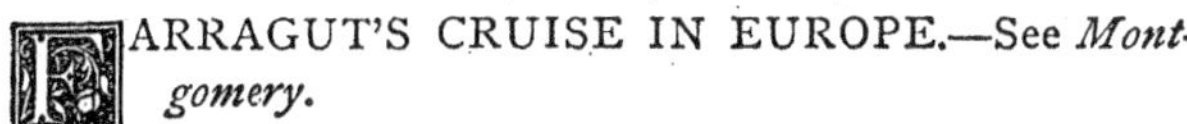

FARRAGUT'S CRUISE IN EUROPE.—See *Montgomery.*

FAY. A NEW SYSTEM OF GEOGRAPHY. By Hon. Theo. S. Fay. With finely executed Maps. For Families and for Students. 12mo, with Atlas, quarto. Cloth extra, $4.25. School edition, $3.75. [See separate Circular.]

*** An introductory work for young classes is in preparation.

These volumes have been prepared with the greatest care, and have cost several years of labor, under the suggestions and supervisions of Humboldt, Ritter, and the most eminent Geographers and Astronomers of Europe. They are on a new plan, and the maps and illustrations are admirably executed at large expense.

OFFICE OF THE CLERK OF THE BOARD OF EDUCATION,
Cor. of Grand and Elm Sts.

New York, March 9th, 1869.

GEORGE P. PUTNAM, ESQ. :

Dear Sir :—"Fay's Geography for Schools" has been added to the list of books furnished to the schools under the control of the Board of Education.

Yours, &c.,
THOS. BOESE,
Clerk of Board of Education.

*** It is used in Vassar College by about one hundred pupils.

"The Great Outline of Geography can neither be dispensed with nor superseded."—HENRY B. TAPPAN, *late President of the Michigan University.*

"It makes Geography almost a new science."—*Henry W. Bellows, D.D.*

"Comprehensive and complete."—*N. Y. Nation.*

"It gives life to what seemed before a dead science."

"The book improves upon acquaintance. My classes are much interested, and *teaching is a pleasure.*"—E. A. GIBBONS, *Harvard Rooms, N. Y.*

FAY. A new System of Astronomy. By Hon. Theo. S. Fay. Richly illustrated. For Families and for Students. 12mo, with Atlas, quarto. (*In press.*)

FAY. NORMAN LESLIE. A New York Story. By Hon. Theo. S. Fay. Price $1.75.

"It affords a faithful picture of old New York, and it is a readable and meritorious work."—*N. Y. Citizen.*

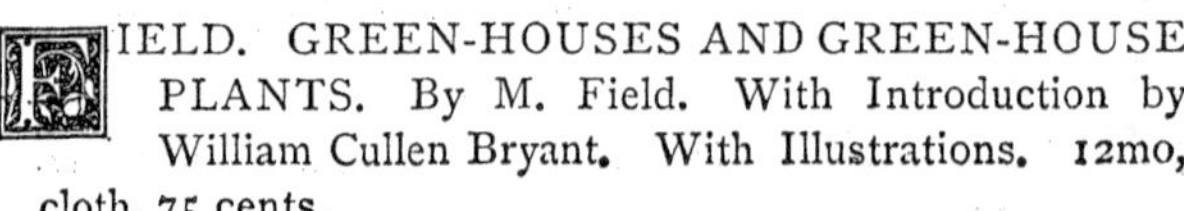

FIELD. GREEN-HOUSES AND GREEN-HOUSE PLANTS. By M. Field. With Introduction by William Cullen Bryant. With Illustrations. 12mo, cloth, 75 cents.

www.ingramcontent.com/pod-product-compliance
Lightning Source LLC
LaVergne TN
LVHW020224110826
845151LV00003B/820